INTO BATTLE

The clarion call of the bugle sped over the dragoons. Every man stiffened in the saddle.

"Charge! Charge! Charge!" The cry of the lieutenants rang out to their troopers. The Americans pulled their weapons and sped towards the mass of Mexican cavalrymen.

Chilton's heart beat faster and he felt the powerful muscles of his horse, knotting and stretching between his legs. In each hand he carried an iron pistol. He felt no fear, only the primal instinct of a man in battle.

A large lancer bore directly down on Clinton. The lieutenant raised his right-hand pistol and shot the man through the heart. He holstered the empty gun and slid his saber from its scabbard. Chilton dodged the thrusting point of a lance and cut off the enemy's hand wielding it. He fired into the face of the second Lancer, then pivoted his horse to view the danger to his men.

In the fight, they had become separated from the other units. The Lancers were trying to surround them. They had to break out of the trap or they would all be killed.

"Back! Back!" Chilton bellowed to his men.

Other Books by F.M. Parker

THE FAR BATTLEGROUND
THE SHADOW MAN
A SCORE TO SETTLE
WINTER WOMAN
THE SEEKERS
DISTANT THUNDER

Published by Pinnacle Books

BLOOD DEBT

F. M. Parker

Pinnacle Books
Kensington Publishing Corp.
http://www.pinnaclebooks.com

PINNACLE BOOKS are published by

Kensington Publishing Corp.
850 Third Avenue
New York, NY 10022

Copyright © 1988 by F. M. Parker
Originally published as *The Far Battleground*

Pinnacle and the P logo Reg. U.S. Pat. & TM Off.

First Pinnacle Printing: March, 2000
10 9 8 7 6 5 4 3 2 1

Printed in the United States of America

We are in a strange situation—a conquering army on a hill overlooking an enemy's capital, which is perfectly at our mercy, yet not permitted to enter it, and compelled to submit to all manner of insults from its corrupt inhabitants.

—From the diary of Ephraim Kirby Smith, Captain, U.S. Army, dated August 29, 1847, at Tacubaya, Mexico. Wounded in battle on September 8, Captain Smith died September 11, 1847.

Soon, too soon, come faithful warriors to their rest.

—Author Unknown

To D.A. Hoffer.
Sorry you never had a chance to read it.

Upon the rocks, five hundred feet below the rim of one crater, a yellow rime of pure, elemental sulfur precipitated from the deadly vapors.

The volcanic mountains dammed the courses of several rivers. A bolson, a deep depression some five thousand square miles in length, was formed, into which the rivers poured. The streams died there in five lakes and an immense area of swampland.

Far north of the bolson, a continental glacier came to life. It stole away thousands of cubic miles of water from the oceans. The ice accumulated to more than a mile thick and flowed south for many hundreds of miles. In the lower latitudes, ice fields were birthed on the tops of the tall mountains, filling all the high valleys.

The woolly mammoth, the saber-toothed tiger, the giant bison, and many other species of animals of the broad plains, fled before the irresistible advance of the ice monster. They migrated south, traveling just below the hanging walls of ice of the mountain glaciers.

A new animal, small compared to the woolly mammoth and the saber-toothed tiger, came upon the western border of the northern continent. The man, with his woman and sturdy children in tow, trekked south along the coast. With his flint-tipped spears and his courage, the man was a deadly hunter and a formidable opponent even to the largest of beasts.

In three hundred generations, nine thousand years, the man had ranged a very long distance and reached the deep intermontane bolson of the five lakes.

On the slopes of the smoking mountain above the bolson, the nine hunters of the clan of man halted in the edge of the coniferous forest beneath the hanging glacier. Quietly they squatted around a pile of dung dropped by a mammoth. Steam

Prologue

The two continents were enormous plates of granitic rock seventy miles thick rafting upon the hot basalt core of the planet. For one hundred and sixty million years, the mighty continents had struggled to tear themselves apart. Tortured and stretched by tremendous rending forces, they reached nearly from pole to pole. Only a long, narrow neck of land still held the warring continents together.

A tall mountain range eighteen hundred miles long ran north-south upon the broad back of the northern continent. Many rivers poured from the mountain highlands in rock-devouring violence down the steep escarpment, to plunge their endless floods into the salty brine of the waiting oceans.

Over the aeons, the powerful tension continued to build between the continents. In one section of the narrow neck, the strength of the rock was breached and a fault split the crustal plates, creating a rupture down to the hot bowels of the earth.

Along the zone of weakness, lava boiled upward thrusting apart the rock holding it entombed. The glowing, red-hot lava exploded onto the surface, spreading across the land, cooling and hardening. The molten mass erupted again and again from the deep cauldrons. Tall mountains grew, reaching three, four miles into the sky.

The violent explosion ceased. But the mountains only rested. Within their craters, poisonous sulfur fumes brewed endlessly.

still rose in tiny gray tendrils from the brown pile. A rank odor was sour in the nostrils of the men. The leader gave a hand signal, and the men slipped, silent as spirits, along the spoor of the large animal.

The mammoth lifted his massive head, and the long trunk snaked out to suck at the cold, moist air. The scent of the alien creature that trailed him was stronger now. The shaggy beast shook his sharp ivory tusk. He trumpeted shrilly. His angry challenge bounced and echoed ferociously among the large boles of the pines.

At the cry of the mammoth, the band of men broke into a swift-footed run. They spread out when they came into sight of the animal. The leader drew back his arm and flung his stone-tipped spear.

The mammoth screamed at the sharp punch of the weapon. He whirled and lunged away. The men raced behind, howling wild, excited calls of encouragement to each other.

The beast hurled himself across a broad mass of rock and gravel washed out from the glacier, and onward down the mountainside to a jumble of fallen trees. There in the tangle of downed and rotting timber, the nimble-footed men overtook the mammoth. Thirty, a hundred times, the men stabbed the animal with their spears. And slew it.

Man had made his first kill on the mountain. The land would know his savage presence for the next ten millennia.

The mammoth, the saber-toothed tiger, and the giant bison would survive but two thousand years more. Over the passing ages, man would forget the big beasts had ever existed.

The man developed a grand civilization, a far-flung empire, and a powerful religion, with human sacrifices. All control of the vast domain was centered at a city of a quarter million citizens lying beside the five lakes in the wide bolson. It was a nation of proud people, rich with gold, silver, and jewels.

Until the white men came from the ocean and climbed the

mountains. Twice the white men came—warring. Both times they conquered the brown men, killed them by the thousands, and stole their gold, silver, and jewels.

One

The Mexican Lancers left their place of concealment in the cypress woods on the flank of the hill, El Peñor. Trotting their horses, the red-uniformed cavalrymen came down into the deeply worn and rutted El Camino Real, The King's Highway, which connected Mexico City with Vera Cruz. The captain of the Lancers shouted a command, and his men formed into a single rank, stretching six hundred feet north from the base of the hill to an anchor point on the edge of a deep arroyo.

The captain reined his mount about and stared south along the ancient, centuries-old road. A plume of brown dust was swiftly approaching. The dark shapes of many riders on galloping horses were framed against the moving dust. He heard the mutter of the iron-shod hooves of the horses on the hard, dry ground.

These damnable Americans had invaded his land. They had won all five battles in the north on the Rio Grande, even Buena Vista, though General Santa Anna had declared that a victory for himself. But under what circumstances does a victorious army desert the battlefield secretly in the dark of a moonless night?

Flush with conquest, the Americans had come in an armada of ships and captured Vera Cruz. Brashly they marched inland, beating aside every attempt by the Mexicans to stop them at

Cerro Gordo, Jalapa, Puebla, and many other battlefields. Now, two hundred and sixty miles deep in the heart of the country, they lay panting at the walls of Mexico City. The captain had begun to think God was a Yankee.

Lieutenant Thomas Cavillin halted his troop of thirty Texas Rangers, and they sat their weary, sweat-streaked mounts under the huge yellow sun. The men pulled their neckerchiefs up over nose and mouth as the dust the horses had stomped into the air washed over them in a dense, gritty pall. It drifted away, and several of the Rangers hawked to clear their throats and spat on the ground.

"I count two officers and about a hundred Lancers," said Cavillin, surveying the line of Mexican cavalrymen blocking the road three hundred yards ahead. He wiped at the sweat trickling down through the stubble of his red beard and flicked a droplet from the tip of his nose.

"That's near my count, too, Lieutenant," said Sergeant Granger, who sat his mount nearby.

Cavillin leaned his rawboned body toward his enemies as he speculated upon his next move. He lifted his head and sniffed at the slow wind flowing over him in hot, slippery waves, as if he could smell the intentions of the Mexicans on it.

The Rangers were part of a regiment of five hundred men sent by Texas to join the war against the Mexicans. They were hardened, staunch veterans, having fought in all the battles with General Zachary Taylor in the north on the Rio Grande. Then they had sailed from Brazos Santiago, south across the Gulf of Mexico, and helped General Scott capture Vera Cruz and fight inland to Mexico City.

Neither Cavillin nor his men owned uniforms. They were clad in a hodgepodge of leather boots, flannel shirts, cotton trousers, and caps or hats. All were armed with short-barreled carbines, bowie knives, and a pair of Paterson Colts, .36-caliber and holding five shots.

"Sergeant, those fellows seem intent on preventing us from reaching General Scott at Tacubaya." Cavillin watched one of the Mexican officers in his tall, black, shako hat begin to ride along the rank of his men and talk to them, his arms gesturing for emphasis to his battle speech.

Cavillin pivoted his horse to scrutinize the terrain in all directions, searching for more enemy soldiers. There was nothing except the brushy hills, lying empty and smoldering in the heat.

Cavillin raised his voice and spoke to his men. "Our orders are to avoid a fight if we possibly can. General Scott wanted us to scout back along the road to Aytola and then return. But I see no way to get past these Mexicans, unless we take to the hills and try to outrun them." His patrol had ridden hard for two days with only one six-hour camp made in the middle of the night. Fatigue showed in the strained faces of the men and the drooping heads of the jaded horses. Even Cavillin's magnificent black mount stood without movement, taking advantage of the brief moment of rest.

"My cayuse is too wore out to run over that steep country," said Sergeant Granger, sweeping a hand up at the rugged hills, covered with brush and trees.

"So is mine," said a second Ranger. The other men called out a chorus of agreement.

Lieutenant Cavillin glanced again at the Mexican cavalrymen drawn up in battle formation. Their red uniforms were dazzlingly bright in the sunshine. Bright flashes of silver flared and died as rays of the sun caught the sharp points of their ten-foot lances. Cavillin had met the long lances in combat and knew them to be wicked weapons, once the guns were empty and hand-to-hand fighting remained.

The enemy officers had ridden to a position slightly forward of their troopers. Their black hats with the waving plumes made them conspicuous among the white-hatted rank and file. The two men were foolish, Cavillin knew. They would be easily identified targets for the sharpshooting Texans.

Cavillin faced his Rangers. "I wouldn't want to be chased like a coward into headquarters by a bunch of Mexicans, even if they did outnumber us more than three to one. We'll kill a few of them and punch a hole through their line. Then see if they want further fight.

"We'll spread out to match their entire length and move forward at a trot. No faster than that. We want time to use our guns before we get within reach of those lances."

"Amen to that," interjected Granger.

Cavillin continued. "At thirty yards, fire your rifles. Pull revolvers and veer in to close ranks and ride knee-to-knee with each other, and the sergeant and me. Kill the officers in the black hats first, if you can get a shot at them. Empty as many saddles in the center of the line as you can, and open a hole for us to ride through."

"Lieutenant, they're ready to move on us," said Granger, looking past Cavillin at the enemy cavalrymen.

Cavillin called his last order. "Take positions at twenty-foot intervals. Move out!"

The Rangers touched the flanks of their mounts with spurs and lunged away. A thin line formed quickly. Carbines were jerked from scabbards and held ready to fire.

Cavillin cast one last look both ways to check his men, then to the front at the solid rank of Lancers. A knot tightened in his stomach. There was always this moment, the few short seconds before the charge and the crash of the first shot. After that, the battle consumed all thought and strength. And death was a thing that happened always to someone else.

All preparations were as ready as they would ever be. It was time to kill.

"Ho!" Cavillin called in a loud voice. "Forward at a trot. Carbines ready to fire."

Shrill, piercing yells erupted from the Lancers when they saw the Americans moving. They lashed their mounts into a run. The Rangers maintained their steady advance. The distance between the opposing sides shortened swiftly.

Cavillin fired his carbine at the Lancer's captain. The man recoiled at the strike of the bullet but did not fall.

The crash of the Rangers' rifles rippled along the line. A score of Mexican riders were slammed from the backs of their mounts. Four horses went down in a jumble of kicking, thrashing legs.

Answering shots blazed from the rifles and pistols of the racing Lancers. Cavillin heard the round balls of lead tearing past with a deadly, whirring noise. Several of the Lancers had him identified as the officer and were concentrating their shots on him.

A quick, crashing sound of lead cutting into flesh came from close on Cavillin's left. It was followed instantly by a guttural gasp of pain. One of his men was hit. It was dangerous to be near an officer in battle.

Hastily the Rangers rammed the single-shot carbines into scabbards and snatched revolvers from holsters. The rapid stutter of the firing Colts rose to an earsplitting din.

The Mexican captain was rushing directly at Cavillin. Their eyes were locked on each other. Cavillin brought the barrel of his revolver to bear on the center of the man's chest and fired.

The captain flung both his arms up, pointing his pistol at the sky. An expression of great surprise swept his face. He fell backward from the saddle, rolling and tumbling onto the ground.

Cavillin swung the revolver and killed a Lancer who was aiming a big pistol at him.

The concentrated fire of the Rangers' revolvers scythed away the center of the Mexican rank. Horses and men fell screaming. A score of red-uniformed riders dropped their weapons and, wounded, clung to their mounts. Frightened, riderless horses veered steeply away from the tumult. The screams of combat and the cries of the dying were drowned by the exploding guns and the thunder of hooves.

A hundred-foot breach blossomed in the line of red-clad Mexicans. The Rangers dashed through, twisting in the saddle to shoot at the backs of the Lancers.

The Americans yanked their excited mounts to a halt. They shouted a high-pitched, triumphant yell. The charge was over, and they had broken the ranks of their foe. And they were still alive. They laughed at each other, then sobered and began to look for friends, to see if they, too, had won safely through the hail of bullets.

"Well done! Well done!" shouted Cavillin. "Form up and reload rifles and pistols. Get set for another charge."

The Rangers pulled their powder flasks and started to pour black powder into the chambers of the cylinders of their revolvers. Round lead balls were pressed down upon the powder with the ramming levers. Number 9 firing caps were slid onto nipples. As they speedily worked, the Rangers made a new line facing the Lancers.

Cavillin breathed the bitter powder smoke and watched the Mexicans milling about and looking across the two hundred yards separating them from the Rangers. One of the officers was still alive, but he had to be held in the saddle by his sergeant. The sergeant began to call out orders. A few men gathered around him, the others paying him no attention.

Cavillin shifted his attention to the battleground. Two of his men came running up on foot.

"Madsen's out there and badly hurt, Lieutenant," one of the men shouted, pointing back at the bodies of horses and corpses of men scattered over the ground. "We need somebody to catch us some horses to ride. Ours got killed."

"Right," replied Cavillin.

The agonized moans of the wounded and suffering stumbled

across the land from the battle zone. A Lancer struggled to his feet and gazed around with a dazed, befuddled stare. He started toward El Peñor but tripped over a corpse and fell. Awkwardly he again gained his feet and this time limped in the direction of the Mexican line. Another Lancer sat up and started to beckon and yell plaintively to his comrades.

"Sergeant, take a man and get Madsen," ordered the lieutenant. "We have time before the Mexicans get organized."

Granger nodded and spoke to the man nearest him. "Wilson, come on." They rode away.

"Kent, Towson, catch two of those mounts," Cavillin directed two Rangers, and pointed at a group of riderless horses wandering away from the smell of death on the battlefield.

"How many of you are wounded?" Cavillin asked the remaining men.

"I've got a leg wound that's bleeding badly," said a small man. "I could use some help in stopping the blood."

"Chambers, help Pitt with a tourniquet."

"Took a ball in the arm, Lieutenant," said a young man named Tillston. He was tightly gripping his upper arm. Blood oozed steadily between his fingers.

"I'll help you with a bandage and make a sling for that arm," said a large black-haired man.

"Thanks, Felmers," said Tillston.

"Anybody else hurt?" questioned the lieutenant.

No one responded.

"All right. Get ready to ride."

Kent and Towson galloped in, leading an extra mount each. "All are Mex animals, Lieutenant, but they're good ones," said Kent.

"Mount up, you fellows," Cavillin said to the men on foot. "Stand ready. Let's see what the Mexicans are going to do."

The sergeant of the Lancers and three other men had separated from the remainder of their company and were riding quietly toward the two Rangers who were bent over their wounded comrade. The Mexicans held rifles ready across the saddles in front of them. Granger and Wilson, lifting the unconscious Madsen upon a horse, did not see or hear the approaching Lancers.

Cavillin called out to his men nearby. "Hold your positions here unless the whole bunch of Mexicans charges. Then come to help us."

He whirled and shouted out at the top of his voice. "Granger, watch out!"

Cavillin spurred his mount into a streaking run. He did not want to order a full charge by all his men. That could start the battle again.

Sergeant Granger released his hold on Madsen and spun around when he heard the warning call. Wilson caught the wounded man and began to lower him to the ground.

The Lancers had also heard Cavillin's shout, and they saw him bounding forward. They raised their whips and struck their mounts savagely, driving them at the top of their speed. They jerked muskets to their cheeks and sighted at the two Americans.

Granger swiftly drew both revolvers. He lifted his right-hand weapon and extended the hammered iron barrel to point at the Mexican in the lead. Shoot the lead man of a charge, let his followers see him die. Sometimes that threw off the others' aim, or broke the charge.

The revolver crashed and bucked in Granger's hand. The Lancer sergeant fell from his saddle. Granger leapt to the left and rotated the gun to aim at the next man.

Wilson hurriedly placed Madsen on the ground. He sprang erect, pulling his revolver. Two of the Lancers fired at him. A wind seemed to whip the front of Wilson's shirt. He was flung crashing backward.

Granger settled a second Mexican in the sights of his gun.

He squeezed the trigger. At the spout of smoke, the cavalryman dropped his rifle and slid from the saddle.

A third horseman had swapped his empty rifle for a pistol. He was leaning over the neck of his mount and pointing the gun at Granger.

The sergeant hurled himself to the side.

The Lancer missed his swiftly moving target. He instantly unlimbered his lance.

Granger thought himself dead, for the remaining two Mexicans were within three horse jumps of him. One was bringing a pistol to bear. The second had his long lance gripped tightly and angling down to pierce the Ranger.

The Mexican with the gun jerked as a mighty force struck him. He reeled, tried to catch himself, failed, and toppled from the back of his horse.

Granger heard the explosion of a Paterson Colt. Then a horse, coming from the direction of his own line, slid to a stop with its front hooves pressing against his body.

Directly over his head the Colt roared again, and the cavalryman with the lance pitched to the ground.

Granger looked up. Cavillin was staring at him, with that wild, wicked twist to his face that he always had in combat. A wonderful face to see when foes are about to kill you.

Granger sprang to his feet. "Thanks, Lieutenant, you saved my ass." He kicked at the fallen Mexicans at his feet. "Another four of Santa Anna's bastards dead. That's good."

The lieutenant sucked in a large breath of air, and his face softened as he looked at the motionless, silent bodies of the five Lancers. He knew his men's hatred for General Santa Anna, the butcher of the Alamo, Goliad and other battles in Texas. The passing of the years since 1836 had not weakened those terrible memories. That was why five hundred Rangers were here with General Scott to whip the Mexicans.

"The Sergeant and his three men were brave," he said.

"Their deaths may rally the rest of the Lancers for another charge. Let's get back to our men."

He swung down. "Wilson was hard hit. Is he dead?"

The sergeant knelt beside Wilson and examined him. "I'm afraid so, Lieutenant. Shot right through the center."

"Help me put him and Madsen on their horses," said Cavillin.

They lifted the limp form of Wilson across the back of his horse and lashed it securely. Holding Madsen in the saddle, they hurriedly returned to the line of waiting Rangers.

Cavillin listened to the voices of the Mexicans rising and falling in angry discussion. They were demoralized by the sudden death of their group, killed by the rapid-firing revolvers of the Rangers. Their single-shot pistols and the lances had been no match for the new weapon. Cavillin knew that with the officers and sergeant dead or badly wounded, the Lancers would start no action until a new leader emerged and pulled together the disorganized cavalryman.

"Do we go at them again, Lieutenant?" asked Granger. "While they're licking their wounds, we can give them one more taste of Mr. Colt."

"I believe you're right, Sergeant. They don't want any more of us, and we could rout them. But my orders from General Scott still stand: Return to headquarters as soon as possible. Send the wounded men on along the road. Tell a man to go and help Madsen stay in the saddle. We'll catch up to them soon."

"Yes, sir."

The Mexican Lancers became silent, and they turned to watch the Rangers. Cavillin counted a handful of seconds that slid past. The men in the red uniforms did not advance or retreat.

Cavillin spoke to his men. "They've lost a lot of men, and the fight has gone out of them. They only want their dead. Let's leave. Ride only at a walk. If they follow past the battle area, we'll turn back on them. Then it will be to the finish. Now move out."

The lieutenant looked back once. The Mexicans had come forward and dismounted among the corpses of their comrades.

Two

Cavillin guided his small cavalcade of Rangers along the El Camino Real toward General Scott's command post at Tacubaya. It was the same road Cortés had led his band of soldiers over more than three hundred years ago. And like Cortés, Scott had cut his army off from their supply base on the coast. Cavillin wondered if Scott would be as fortunate as the Spaniard and capture the grand capital city.

Cavillin mopped at his face with his neckerchief and scanned the area. No birds flew, and no insects were kicked up by the passage of the horses. All living things were pressed to the earth by the heat, so heavy that it felt like liquid gravity. He glanced behind to see how his wounded men were holding up.

Two of Madsen's comrades rode by his side and held him in the saddle. The bullet had torn a hole through his lungs, and he was bleeding from the mouth. He would most likely die. Tillston and Pitt rode unaided, their bandages soaked with blood. As Cavillin looked, Pitt's pain-filled eyes caught his. The man's haggard face twisted into a crooked grin. Cavillin nodded encouragement at him. During the first sixteen months of the war, the Rangers and Cavillin had fought eight battles together. He looked back to the front.

The Rangers crested a range of hills, and Tacubaya, with its whitewashed stone and adobe buildings, came into view ahead.

The town had once been the home of two thousand people. They had all fled into Mexico City as the Americans had drawn close.

Many of the weary Americans had taken possession of the deserted houses and set up camp within them. Some men who could not find space inside the structures, pitched tents in the courtyards and patios. Most of the soldiers had to spread out, onto the surrounding hills where their soiled, worn tents created hundreds of dingy, gray splotches on the rolling, green meadows.

As the Rangers entered Tacubaya, soldiers gathered quickly in the street. They reluctantly gave way to let the riders pass. "How many Mexicans at Aytola? Did you get farther than that?" an infantry corporal asked as he paced beside Cavillin.

Cavillin did not reply or slow. He would report only to General Scott that Aytola was now garrisoned by approximately a thousand enemy soldiers. The Mexicans had closed in behind the American army as it advanced northwest toward Mexico City. No ammunition or other provisions would be coming from the supply depot at the American-controlled port city of Vera Cruz. Mexico City must be taken with the armaments still usable after the long campaign to fight inland.

Cavillin continued directly north across town and up the rise to the Catholic Church, La Piedad. He noted movement in the belfry of the church and saw Lieutenant Matthew Chilton of the Dragoons and Phillip Steptoe of the 47th Artillery watching him. The young officers raised their hands in greeting.

Tom returned the salute. Though the two were regular army officers from West Point, while Cavillin was a volunteer with but a smattering of education, they were of the same age and had formed a close alliance. "Wait there for me," called Tom. "I'm taking my wounded to the hospital and then I'm going to report to General Scott."

"We'll be here," Chilton called back.

Cavillin called a halt at the open door of the chapel and

climbed down from his horse. The army surgeons had appropriated the church and several of the nearby buildings and converted them into a hospital. There were more than a thousand sick and wounded men being cared for within the ten buildings.

Cavillin smelled the odor of medicine and rotting flesh. The surgeons, with their sharp steel scalpels and saws, were quick to amputate the seriously mangled limbs of the soldiers to prevent the infection and gangrene that almost invariably occurred. Still, sometimes the infection became uncontrollable and the wound gangrenous, and the flesh turned putrid and stinking. Those men died.

"Sergeant, help the wounded men down," directed Cavillin. "I'll get the surgeons ready." He walked hurriedly to the doorway and shouted loudly inside. "Wounded men out here. I need two stretchers. Hurry it!"

Four medical orderlies carrying a pair of stretchers came trotting from the chapel. Tom stepped aside to let them pass and then went into the building.

All the pews had been removed, and now, on the wooden floor beneath the high, arching dome of the chapel, lay scores of wounded men on cots or blanket pallets. The stink that had been evident outside now smote Cavillin like a solid force.

A man, lying a few paces away, saw Cavillin and motioned for him to come closer. He struggled to sit up, pushing with his arms, pushing mightily, for he had no legs below mid-thigh to counterbalance the weight of his upper body. His eyes were hot and piercing, and they never left Cavillin.

"Laudanum, damn you!" the man cried in a tortured voice. "Surgeon, hear me. Give me laudanum. I'm not getting my share. Oh God! My legs hurt. You say they are gone, but you are wrong. They hurt to the very tip of my toes."

Cavillin circled around the man, feeling repulsed by him and sensing a deep shame that he was. The poor bastard was just an unlucky soldier.

"Major Campbell," Cavillin called out as he recognized the senior surgeon at the far end of the chapel. Swiftly he moved down one of the aisles separating the rows of wounded men.

"Major, I have three men who've been shot. One is quite seriously wounded in the chest. They're being brought in now."

"Take them straight to the operating room." Campbell pointed off to the side at a large room with several wooden tables visible through a wide door. "I'll get another doctor to help and be with you in a minute."

"Right. Thanks, Doctor." Cavillin returned to the front door and directed the stretcher bearers and Tillston, who walked behind, to the surgery. Tom remained until Campbell and a second doctor arrived and began to examine the men. Then silently he left.

Sergeant Granger stood alone in the street. "I dismissed the men, Lieutenant. I didn't know how long you would be in the hospital, and the men were plenty tuckered out."

"You did right, Granger. You're dismissed also. Please take care of my horse. I must report to General Scott."

"Certainly, Lieutenant. I'll take good care of the big devil." Granger kicked his mount near Cavillin's, picked up the reins from where they dragged on the ground, and towed the horse after him.

Cavillin hurried off along the street with long strides. He halted at the entrance of a long stone building fronting the main street. Two command guards stood alert with rifles. Over the door hung a sing that read: ALCALDE DE TACUBAYA, Mayor of Tacubaya. Tom passed the sentries and entered.

Tom sweated as he climbed the steep stone steps leading up to the top landing of La Piedad. He came out of the stairwell and halted in the shade near Chilton and Steptoe. Lifting his hat, he wiped his wet forehead with his shirt sleeve.

"You look like you've had a long ride," said Chilton. "I'm sorry some of your men were wounded. Where did it happen?"

"The Mexicans tried to stop us at the foot of El Peñor. They must've spotted us earlier, going along the road toward the coast. Figuring we were a scouting party, they waited until we returned. About a hundred of them with two officers."

"I saw no prisoners with you," said Matt.

"My Texans don't take prisoners." Tom's eyes were as flat and as emotionless as still water.

"I suppose we are cut off from Vera Cruz and the coast," Steptoe said.

"I estimate a regiment of about a thousand soldiers at Aytola," replied Cavillin. "We captured one of Santa Anna's messengers coming from Puebla. A large force of Mexicans has our two thousand men at Puebla under siege. From what we could learn, the fighting has gone on for several days now. What has Santa Anna done here while I have been gone?"

"The Mex general has continued to bring up reinforcements and throw up defending walls," replied Chilton. "Here, see for yourself." He handed his spyglass to Cavillin.

"Thanks," said Tom. He raised the brass tube to his eye and began to study the terrain and the man-made structures through the magnified field of the glass.

The tall structure of La Piedad resided on the highest elevation of Tacubaya. From the church's high belfry, Cavillin could see not only the fortified hill of Chapultepec, meaning Grasshopper Hill, and its walled castle, but also the Mexican powder magazine, Casa Mata. A large part of the Mexican city inside its thick walls could be seen. The increased number of cannon emplacements on Chapultepec and at the city walls was readily visible.

"The city is one damn, giant fortress," said Steptoe. "There's cannon in every possible place that they can be installed, and thousands of soldiers to repel any attack." He lowered his telescope and angrily slapped it closed in his hand with a sharp snap.

Cavillin methodically continued to range his spyglass to examine the city of two hundred thousand inhabitants. The splendid city lay on a flat plain some thirty miles wide, a land surface that had once been the bed of a long vanished lake. One tiny remnant of that ancient body of water remained, Lake Texcoco. Steep green mountains surround the broad basin on all sides. Between the base of the slopes and the city, thousands of acres of fields of many sizes grew corn, squash, cotton, sweet potatoes, beans, sugarcane, citrus fruits, and a score of other crops.

The walled city was a formidable objective for any army to capture. Marshes encircled the city, and access was possible only by eight causeways, narrow, raised roadways flanked by canals filled with water. Each causeway ended in a massive *garita,* a large paved space at the base of a strong stone building, where in peaceful times taxes were collected by Mexican officials on goods entering the city. Now the *garitas* bristled with cannon, laid to rake each road with shot.

The American army had fought its way to Tacubaya on the hills above the ancient center of the Montezuma Empire two weeks earlier. Every day since then, except for the past three spent on patrol, Tom had surveyed the city.

In the evenings he searched out the civilian American teamsters who hauled supplies from the city to Scott's army, and questioned them as to what they had seen. The teamsters confirmed that more cannon were being placed, and more soldiers assembled to defend the city.

"The armistice is over," Chilton told Cavillin. "Scott finally sent Santa Anna a notice that because of violations of its provisions, the armistice would end at noon today. We will attack soon, perhaps tomorrow, or the next day for sure."

"It was a mistake for General Scott to make an agreement with General Santa Anna," Steptoe said. "Sure, it had a stipulation that allowed us to purchase food from the Mexican merchants, but there was to be no improvement in position or fortifications on either side. Scott has required us to honor his word. Santa Anna has used every day of the two-week period to collect his scattered army and add more cannon. If Scott would have allowed reconnaissance, he would know the extent of it."

"We had the Mexicans beaten," said Chilton. "Now we have all our fighting and dying to do over again."

Cavillin had pondered that same thought many times since Scott had halted the swiftly advancing Americans at the village of Tacubaya. There was much muttering and grumbling from the soldiers throughout the army. They complained that they had come to whip the Mexicans and not to talk with them. Tom knew the Texans had made the long, difficult campaign and fought the many battles to kill so many Mexicans that they would never again invade Texas.

Several officers, both in the regular and volunteer forces, had strongly objected to the terms of the armistice. They urged Scott to move his forces into commanding position, and especially to occupy Castle Chapultepec, which, with its cannon and soldiers, threatened the southern and western approaches to the city.

Scott refused every request, stating he wanted to leave the Mexican Republic something on which to rest her pride and to recover her temper. Cavillin thought those were strange words, coming from the general of an invading army.

He lowered his spyglass and spoke to his two friends. "To the east, the hill, El Peñor, with its heavy fortifications, guards the paths to the city. Lake Texcoco blocks any advance from the northeast. We'll have to attack from the south or west along one of the causeways leading to Garita de San Some or Garita de Belen."

Steptoe evaluated the narrow, raised roadways with his artilleryman's eye. "I agree. That would force us to pass under the cannon of Castle Chapultepec at a range of three hundred yards or less. They'll blow us to hell."

"Chapultepec will have to be taken first," replied Tom. The two-hundred-foot-high volcanic hill rose abruptly to loom over the plain a mile north of them. A strong stone castle, the resort of the long dead Aztec princes, and later used by the viceroys of Spain, capped the hill. A huge retaining wall with a broad terrace was entrenched with dozens of cannon. Scaling ladders would be required to mount the twelve-foot-high walls. Directly into the muzzles of the muskets of thousands of Santa Anna's most experienced troops.

"Santa Anna killed hundreds of Americans in the war to free Texas," said Tom. "He will kill thousands of us when we try to take Mexico City away from him. How do you feel your luck is running?" He looked at the two regular army officers.

"It has been good so far." Chilton showed his teeth in a cold smile. "Maybe I should resign my commission and go back north before the battle."

"You would never do that," said Steptoe. "The cavalry is your life. You, like me, will stick around to see how this war finally ends."

A bugle sounded from the direction of Scott's command post. The three lieutenants turned to gaze in that direction. "Officers' call to assembly," said Chilton. "General Scott is finally ready to attack."

"The meeting will come to order," said General Scott. Silence fell instantly upon the roomful of officers. All turned toward the general.

Cavillin pressed his back against the wall and observed the gathering. The space was large, with a high ceiling. It appeared to have once been some sort of a courtroom, for there was a raised, padded seat with a low, polished, wooden partition separating it from the remainder of the area. Scott and three of his

aides, Sam Grant, P. G. T. Beauregard, and Robert Lee, all
engineers, were at the center of the room around a wide table
covered with maps and drawings.

All the generals, Twiggs, Quitman, Shields, Pillow, Cad-
walader, Pierce, and Worth had taken positions up front, near
Scott. The junior officers, from colonels to lieutenants, were
gathered in groups by unit, behind their generals.

Scott swept the room with his greenish eyes. Many of his
young officers were graduates of the new military school of
West Point, located on the Hudson River. They were dressed
in clean, neat uniforms, even after so many months of combat.
The older officers were also well groomed. The Texas Rangers
wore unmatched, ragtag clothing.

The men from Texas were an undisciplined lot and difficult
to control. Their savagery and deadliness to the Mexicans were
unrivaled by any other unit of the army. But they were damn
fine fighting men.

"Gentlemen, the armistice has been ended since noon," the
general said. "We're back at war with the Mexicans. We are
in a hostile country, greatly outnumbered, cut off from our
supply base, and encumbered by more than a thousand sick
and wounded men. Retreat is out of the question. We must
capture Mexico City or perish in the attempt. We will not perish. We will take the city."

The officers stomped their booted feet loudly on the floor
in approval. "Here! Here!" bellowed the white-haired, old war-
horse, General Twiggs, of the infantry.

The general smiled broadly, rotating around to see all the
officers. "I see that pleases you, but to conquer General Santa
Anna will be most difficult. Our information leads us to estimate his force at eighteen thousand men. We have but eight
thousand effective troops after allowing for our sick and
wounded. Further, our enemy is in a very strong position. He
is behind the thick walls of the city, on the fortified hills of

Chapultepec, and in the strong stone buildings of Casa Mata and Molino del Rey."

Scott hesitated for a second. "Before we advance on Mexico City, we have another objective to accomplish. It is but a limited one. We have heard from several sources that Santa Anna has been collecting church bells in the city and sending them to a foundry in the Molino del Rey, the King's Mill, to be recast into cannon. Also, there has been considerable movement of the general's best troops to those buildings. I believe that confirms what we've heard."

The smiles of the officers vanished, and their faces grew troubled.

"Sir. If I may speak . . ." said General Pierce.

"Yes, certainly. Please do," said Scott.

"Well, sir, we really do not have positive proof of cannon being made there. Santa Anna is a wily fellow and may have deliberately started the rumor to mislead us. Further, Molino del Rey is well fortified, and there may be as many as nine thousand of his veteran troops protecting it. To take it could be quite costly."

"Let's hear other views," said Scott. His normally ruddy complexion had become more dark at Pierce's disagreement with the plan.

Other generals spoke, and the argument went back and forth between those in favor of the attack on the mill and those believing that they should bypass it and march directly upon the city. The opinions appeared to be about evenly divided.

Cavillin had listened to the discussion. He felt confident that any assault on the Molino del Rey would be a foolish mistake.

"You, Lieutenant Cavillin, I see you shaking your head like a horse with a fly in its ear. What do you have to say on the subject?" Scott's voice was sharp.

Cavillin stiffened as Scott's eyes fastened upon him like the twin barrels of a shotgun. Tom had not realized he had been shaking his head. However, he did have something to say. He moved forward two steps to a more open spot.

"Sir, I have observed Molino del Rey many times in the past two weeks. I have never seen enough smoke or heat coming from the chimneys to indicate there was a fire hot enough to melt iron. Further, any cannon they should pour in the next day or so could not be assembled into a usable weapon in time to be used against us in our attack on the city—that is, if we move promptly to take that action. I agree with those who say to bypass the mill."

"And leave nine thousand enemy troops at our rear to hit us when and how they please? Lieutenant, that is not a wise maneuver."

"Sir, if they should come out of their fortifications, we could then turn—"

"That's enough discussion, Lieutenant. We'll take the foundry and destroy the cannon molds and any machinery used for making weapons. Also, we'll continue our attack and take the powder magazine of Casa Mata. General Worth will have command of the operation."

Cavillin held his face emotionless at Scott's abrupt interruption. He glanced at Chilton and saw his friend nod his head once in agreement.

"The meeting is dissolved," said Scott. "The general-grade officers present here will remain for the development of the battle plan. Also, my aides will stay. The rest of you will be briefed at six o'clock this evening. Keep yourselves available."

As Cavillin moved with the other junior officers toward the door, he looked at the general. Scott's steely gaze was upon him fully, then shifted away.

Well, hell, thought Cavillin, *you asked for my opinion.*

Three

"Damnation, why ain't there a moon tonight?" The man's curse came drifting along the street and in the open window.

Cavillin lay awake on his cot, listening to the sounds of the rumbling wheels and tramping feet of horses and men. The artillery and infantry were moving out of their encampment toward their assigned battle positions in front of the Molino del Rey. The noise was so loud, the Mexicans surely must have heard it. In any event, they would see the unaccustomed lighting of the American camp and know an attack was coming that day.

Without making a light, Cavillin dressed and buckled on his brace of revolvers and bowie knife. He walked from his sleeping room out into the large central space of the Tacubaya residence he shared with Major Hays and Captain Ripley.

The major's door was open, and he was dressing in the light of a flickering candle. There was light showing around the edges of the poorly fitting door of the captain's rooms, and Tom heard him moving around.

Tom stepped outside and stood waiting in the darkness. Overhead, the sky was clear and full of a million stars. Shadowy groups of men glided through the murk, the only sound the muffled thump of their boots on the ground.

Hays and Ripley came from the door and halted near Tom for a moment as they glanced about. Without speaking, the

three men moved along the street. A block later, they entered
the officers' mess hall.

Thirty or so officers sat at long wooden tables drinking coffee and eating. They talked in low, hushed voices.

The three Rangers filed past the mess orderlies behind the
serving table and filled plates with fried eggs, sliced fruit, and
biscuits. Carrying mugs of coffee, they found seats at the end
of the room.

"There's the Cavalry," said Hays, nodding at the entrance.

Cavillin turned to look. Major Sumner and his three lieutenants, Chilton, Crocker and Appleby, had entered and were
ordering coffee from one of the mess orderlies. The dragoons
drank the black beverage while leaning against the wall near
the door.

"It appears they don't want any conversation," said Ripley.

Cavillin caught Chilton's eye for a second. Then the dragoon
lieutenant concentrated on his coffee mug.

"This could be a damn rough day for them," Hays said.
"They're few in number, and our scouts report that there are
three or four regiments of Mexican Lancers on the hills to the
west."

"We should've been allowed to help them," Ripley said.

Cavillin felt his throat tighten. He cursed silently in his head.
Scott had given the Rangers no part in the battle that would
start with the arrival of daylight. Tom knew Hays and Ripley
were aware they had been excluded because of his outspoken
comments about the attack on the Molino del Rey. Yet his two
superiors had not condemned Tom.

The coffee was hot and bitter, and Chilton drank it down
to the dregs. As he tilted the cup for the last drop, he glanced
at Cavillin.

The Ranger's freckled face was strained and drawn. Matt
felt sorry for him. Never had the Rangers missed being in the

thick of the fighting. The general should not be so vindictive as to refuse to allow them to join the assault upon the Molino del Rey and Casa Mata. Other officers had recommended against the attack, and still Scott was permitting them to participate.

The Rangers would not long endure such treatment. One day they would ride off for Texas. Their fighting skills would be sorely missed.

"Let's see to our men," said Major Sumner.

Chilton followed the other cavalry offices from the mess. They went south across the town and approached the rows of the dragoons' lighted tents.

Matt veered away from the other two men and quickened his pace toward the double rows of tent lights that marked the location of his company of troopers. Major Sumner had landed at Vera Cruz with a regiment of three hundred cavalrymen. In the long, continuing battle inland to Mexico City, their numbers had been whittled away until only two hundred and seventy remained. Sumner had divided them into three companies of ninety men, each headed by one of his lieutenants. Chilton commanded the 3rd Company.

Sergeant Stoffer of the dragoons paced between the two rows of tents pitched to face each other across a space of twenty feet. The flaps of the tents were untied and tossed back over the ridgepoles. Lanterns shone out from the openings to light the aisleway. He glanced into each tent as he passed. Every one was empty; the men had finished preparing their equipment and weapons for the battle and now were at the remuda, saddling mounts. Good. All was on schedule.

At the edge of the darkness, Stoffer halted and looked out into the impenetrable gloom of the moonless night. The lieutenant will arrive soon, he thought.

Chilton regarded his sergeant. The man appeared to be staring straight at him, but it was impossible for him to see Chilton in the dark. Yet Chilton often seemed to be able to sense eyes upon him, especially an officer's.

The lieutenant chuckled soundlessly. Above all things, he appreciated his men. They were all good troopers. And they were his to lead and protect. He walked out into the light.

" 'Morning, Lieutenant," said Stoffer, and saluted.

Chilton touched the brim of his hat. "Good morning to you, Sergeant." The man was a thirty-five-year-old veteran cavalryman, ten years older than Chilton. The lieutenant believed Stoffer felt at ease with him, perhaps might actually like him.

"The men are saddling up now," said Stoffer. "Everything will be ready for assembly at four o'clock."

"Fine. Let us get our horses."

"I have them staked out just off there, Lieutenant." The sergeant pointed out into the Stygian gloom. "Do you want a lantern to see by?"

"No," answered Chilton. An officer should be able to find his horse and saddle it in the darkness. All the troopers could; Sergeant Stoffer had seen to that part of their training.

"Colonel, I think we should go and watch the battle," Cavillin said. "Scott surely can't find fault with that."

Colonel Hays shifted his view to his junior officer. Cavillin was a fine fighting man, but perhaps too brave to live through the remainder of the war. Hays was surprised Tom had survived this long. "What would you do if you saw some of the Americans being beaten?" Hays questioned.

Cavillin did not respond, staring back noncommittally. The seconds dragged by.

Captain Ripley stirred, his chair creaking in the awkward silence. He saw the colonel's anger building because of Cavillin's slowness to reply.

"Colonel, I also would like to observe how the battle goes

today," Ripley said to fill the taut emptiness between the two men. "We could hold back on the hill above our forces and out of the battle zone."

Hays let his gaze drift away from Cavillin, releasing him from the need to answer. Tom did not want to make a statement and then have to abide with it. The colonel let his attention wander over the nearly two score officers eating in the mess hall. They, like the Rangers, had been given no assignment by Scott for the assault.

"Very well. We will observe. Cavillin, take two hundred Rangers and ride to the western end of the American lines. Ripley, you go to the opposite side with two hundred men. I'll ride with the remaining eighty or so and take a location in the center, near and above the command post. Make no move to assist any American. Let the reserves Scott has stationed for that purpose do the rescuing if some unit is in danger of being overwhelmed. Scott would surely court-martial you if you enter the fight without orders.

"Still, arm your men for full combat. If our attack fails, the Mexican forces may break out of their defenses and try to overrun all our positions. Let's move fast. It'll soon be daylight."

In the gray darkness, Cavillin and Granger rode down from Tacubaya and across the slant of the hill. His company of Rangers straggled after him in a long, broken line. He had not formed the men into ranks because he was concerned that General Scott might mistake the military formation as an intent to join the battle and order the Rangers back to barracks.

The dawn began to unfurl its pale light across the cloudless sky. Lava mountains took shape coming out of hiding and rearing up in steep, craggy peaks. The black night shadows in the valley bottoms started to shrink and die away.

Cavillin stopped on the rounded dome of a rocky hill and

pulled his telescope from a saddlebag. He stretched the brass tube and raised it.

The command post for the day's battle was a small cluster of canvas tents, wagons, and horses on a rise of land somewhat less than a mile north and slightly below him. General Worth, a longtime friend of General Scott, was the officer in charge.

A thousand yards in front of Worth, the grim walls of the great stone Molino del Rey became distinct in the growing light. Many windows opened out to the front toward the Americans. A stone parapet two feet high rose above the roofline. Excellent protection for riflemen. Other stone buildings flanked the mill on the west. The narrow passageways between them were barricaded. In total, the mill's several structures, linked with walls and courtyards, stretched for five hundred yards.

Beyond the Molino del Rey was a large grove of cypress trees extending to the base of Chapultepec Hill. The entire park was surrounded by a high stone wall four feet thick. An entryway through the walls was protected by a sandbag barricade. A roadway that wound up the precipitous flank of Chapultepec was fortified with dirt trenches and cannon.

Chapultepec Castle, a massive stone structure of two stories, capped the hill. Many cannon were positioned on its huge, flat retaining walls. The guns could be aimed to support the full length of Molino.

The principal assault column of five hundred men, led by Colonel George Wright, was in a low swale between the command post and the Molino. All the men were volunteers selected from the various infantry units. Their assignment was to capture a field battery of cannon the Mexicans had entrenched in front of the fortified walls of the Molino and near the center of its length. Tom knew that many of the men of the initial charge would die. The cash bonuses and promotions promised to obtain volunteers would mean nothing to dead men. Life had little value in war. It was merely a commodity traded for land area or the high ground.

On the far right end of the American line was Garland's brigade of infantrymen, supported by two six-pound guns. In the dim light Cavillin saw a large knot of horsemen above Garland. That would be Ripley and his Rangers. Nearer to Tom, but still half a mile away, were two twenty-four-pound cannon supported by a battalion under Captain Kirby Smith.

"Let's take a look at the rest of the battle forces from beyond that high land," said Cavillin, gesturing at a long, sharp-crested ridge running to the northwest and blocking the view. "I want to see what the dragoons are facing."

The iron-shod hooves of the Rangers' mounts clattered over the rocky slant of the hill. Huffing and snorting, the horses scrambled up to the top of the hill.

Cavillin dismounted from the heaving horse. He raised his spyglass and slowly worked it to the west.

The strong stone citadel of Casa Mata, seven hundred yards directly north of Cavillin, anchored the right flank of the Mexicans. More than a score of batteries of cannon had been placed in strongly constructed redoubts in the sloping outer earthworks. A regiment of soldiers ringed the square structure. The Mexicans did not want to lose their powder magazine.

Facing the Casa Mata was a full brigade of American infantry under Colonel McIntosh. A battery of "flying artillery" was on the left side of the massed troops.

Tom's attention lingered on those beautiful guns. Of all the artillery, he liked these swift, maneuverable cannon best of all. They had graceful barrels, four feet long with a range of fifteen hundred yards, capable of hurling a six-pound iron ball almost three inches in diameter, or a powder-packed exploding shell, or a deadly hail of round bullets. The barrels rested on a caisson slung low between two large wheels. The caisson was attached to a two-wheeled limber, a vehicle that carried ammunition and was drawn by a fast and well-trained team of six horses. Part of the gun crew rode the horses, while the rest clung to the caisson.

A battery of four guns operated as a unit. As the horses stopped, the men dropped off the caisson, unlimbered it, broke out rams, swabs, powder, and shot. An officer laid the gun for direction and elevation, while men rammed home the powder and ball. After the gun fired, the men could relay it, swab its smoking barrel, and ram home another charge in ten seconds. The swift, murderous firepower had saved Cavillin's company of Rangers several times from experiencing heavy casualties.

Tom lowered his telescope and collapsed it in his hand. Scott had said this battle was to be a limited operation, yet three thousand four hundred soldiers were committed. That was nearly half of the whole American army.

Cavillin spoke to Granger. "The Mexicans are in a damn strong position. The cannon of Chapultepec can cover the eastern segment of the battlefield. The guns of Casa Mata, the western sections. Molino del Rey makes a continuous breastworks covering the entire front. The line is about a mile long, and I see no weak point."

"Those cannon on Casa Mata are the ones that'll do our fellows the most harm," said the sergeant. "They're looking right down their muzzles."

"It'd be good if we could take the powder magazine, for we need the powder," said Cavillin.

"Many men will die doing it," said Granger.

"Come on, let's move," Cavillin said, pulling himself astride. "I want to be at a spot closer to Chilton and the dragoons." He touched his black horse with spurs and led off along the ridge top.

Major Sumner and his regiment of dragoons sat their mounts on a low hill three quarters of a mile to the southwest of the Molino del Rey. The officers and troopers stared intently into the darkness to the west. For several minutes the sounds of movement of a large body of horses and the distant, muted voices of men had reached them from the opposite side of a dry ravine.

The troopers waited nervously for the morning dusk to brighten. Now and then there was a whisper from one of the men. It was a weak sound that drifted away and quickly died in the rocks and brush.

"God Almighty!" a trooper ejaculated in a fervent voice. "Look! Look! Don't you see them?"

On a sloping hillside a quarter of a mile away, company after company of red-coated Mexican cavalrymen, drawn up in battle formation, barely could be made out. A storm surf of anger roared from their ranks when they saw the Americans.

"There must be thousands of them," exclaimed a trooper. "There's no way in hell we can hold that many Lancers from attacking the artillery and the infantry."

"Silence in the ranks," snapped Sumner. "I'll tell you what we can and cannot do."

Sumner lowered his voice and spoke to his lieutenants. "I estimate about four thousand. They won't be committed all at once. Not until they determine what our plan of attack is and how the Mexican defense holds out. We have a little time. Lieutenant Chilton, position your company fifty yards north. Appleby, stay where you are. Crocker, go fifty yards south. All of you stand by for my command. We'll respond in a manner to stop their advance. Bugler, stay close beside me."

Chilton reined his horse and rode to the head of his column of troopers. He called his orders. In half a minute they were all in place.

"Lieutenant, we are outnumbered ten or twelve to one," said Sergeant Stoffer, pulling his mount close on Matt's right side. "This is the tightest spot we've ever been in."

"Captain Duncan and Steptoe, with their 'flying artillery,' are just over there a ways." Matt pointed to the east. The rays of the sun were being reflected down from the heavens, and the bronze of the cannon barrels glistened like dull gold.

"They can see the Mexicans threatening us and will support us with their fire. That will make the difference that will pull us through."

"We are close to the limit of the range of those guns," said Stoffer. "Their shots could fall short and hit us. Or they could get so busy helping the infantry that they forget about us." The sergeant fell silent.

The *whump* of one of the twenty-four-pound, smooth-bore cannon jarred the air. All the dragoons turned in that direction, saw the smoke, and then quickly looked at the mill.

A gaping fissure appeared in the front wall of the center of the Molino as the solid iron ball landed. A section of the roof above collapsed, tumbling men and weapons into the void. Mexicans were dead. The battle had begun.

The big guns continued to work, two shots per minute, shaking the land. A cloud of gunpowder smoke formed and hung over the battery.

Twelve rounds boomed out, and then the guns became silent. Much too soon, thought Chilton. The defenses could not yet have been much weakened. He jerked his spyglass to his eye. Half a mile away, the five hundred men of the main assaulting party were dashing toward the Mexican artillery. Their presence on the field had halted the firing of the huge cannon. Why hadn't the men waited for the big gun to knock the buildings to rubble and kill the Mexicans with cannonballs?

The charging infantrymen began to fall. A few men and then many. The sound of the Mexican cannon firing grape and canister reached Chilton. He could see the column thinning, leaving behind a ground covered with blue-clad bodies.

The furious cannonading was slaughtering the Americans by the dozens, by the scores. *Wright, damn you, you advanced too early.*

Despite the deadly hail of cannonballs and the musket fire

from the walls and roof of the Molino, the Americans drove the Mexicans from their cannon. But Mexican troops kept shooting from the parapets and windows, and Wright's column faltered and broke. Some of the men whirled around to the rear and ran in terror.

Mexicans surged out of the Molino and swarmed over the last of the Americans at the battery. Chilton saw the Mexican infantrymen shooting into the Americans left lying on the ground.

"They're executing the wounded," Matt told Stoffer.

A mass of American infantrymen that had been stationed near the American twenty-four-pounder started to swiftly move toward the Molino.

Chilton relayed to Stoffer. "Kirby Smith's battalion is counterattacking."

The two regiments of men rushed down the slope of the hill and swept over the Mexican battery. One regiment continued onward, swerving right to go around the end of the Molino. The second, taking heavy musket fire, halted, then regrouped and stormed the central walls of the Molino.

"Lieutenant, there goes McIntosh's brigade toward Casa Mata," Stoffer called.

Chilton pivoted to look in that direction. He lowered his telescope. The distance was short, and he could see clearly without the glass.

A large force of American infantrymen was running toward the square stone fortress. When they were a hundred yards away, the Mexicans opened fire. The lethal torrent of shot rained steadily upon the advancing troops, cutting a dreadful swath of death through the column.

"They are falling by whole platoons," cried Stoffer.

For a few brief moments, the rapidly thinning remnants pushed on to reach the slope of the parapet of the outer works of Casa Mata. Then the command shattered and, in disorder, ran.

"Oh, damn! Damn!" yelled one of the troopers in the ranks behind Chilton. The lieutenant did not reprimand the man for talking in rank.

"Cavalry charging!" Major Sumner's shout cut through the boom of cannon and the rattle of musket fire.

"Hold your ranks. Prepare to follow me."

The wide body of Mexican Lancers poured down the incline of the hill in a bright red tide. The leading edge plunged into the ravine, like a ripple of clots of blood, and surged up onto the flat land with the dragoons.

A shiver shook Chilton, as if a feather had been drawn along his spine. He felt a premonition that he would never leave the battlefield alive, a strange emotion for a man who had fought eight battles and many skirmishes in the past year and a half and had never been nicked.

Suddenly wide holes began to blossom in the ranks of the advancing Mexican Lancers. Horses and men were blown down in broad patches. Chilton heard the lovely sound of canister loaded with scores of musket balls packed in sulfur whizzing by. Duncan's flying artillery was firing over the heads of the dragoons and pounding the Mexican cavalry.

Matt cast a quick look at Duncan's battery. Two of the four cannon were firing on Casa Mata, trying to help an American counterattack there. The remaining two guns were supporting the dragoons. It would require many more guns than that to save Matt's troopers.

The leading ranks of the Lancers raced their steeds out of the impact zone of the flying artillery and charged at the dragoons. A thousand Lancer carbines began to fire at the Americans.

Four

The clarion call of the bugle sped over the dragoons. Every man stiffened in the saddle.

"Charge! Charge! Charge!" The cry of the lieutenants rang out to their troopers. The band of Americans pulled their weapons and sped toward the mass of Mexican cavalrymen.

Chilton's heart beat with great pulses of blood. His senses opened wide. He felt the powerful muscles of his horse, knotting and stretching between his legs. The air became a wind, cool upon his cheeks.

In each hand he carried an iron pistol, light as a feather. His men were beside him, left and right, the hoof falls of their running horses a close, comforting rumble. He felt no fear, only the primal instinct of a man in battle pumping strength into his arms and legs.

The dragoons began to fire their guns. The Mexicans returned the fire, dense as a hailstorm.

A large Lancer bore directly down on Chilton. The lieutenant raised his right-hand pistol and easily, so easily, shot the man through the heart. Matt holstered the empty gun and slid the saber from its scabbard.

He dodged the thrusting point of a lance and, as the Mexican came within reach, cut the man's hand off at the wrist. The Mexican lifted his arm and looked at the stub, now spouting a red geyser. A horrified expression blanched his face. Then the man's horse carried him past Chilton and out of sight.

A second enemy with a lance spurred at Chilton. He rolled to the side, lifted his left-hand pistol, and fired it into the man's face from a distance of less than four feet. A bullet hole rimmed with burned powder appeared in the man's forehead. The face lost its look of hate and took on the ugly mask of death.

Matt holstered the pistol. For a brief moment he was free of foes. He pivoted his horse to view the danger to his men.

His company had cut a deep swath into the body of the Mexican cavalry. In the fight, they had become separated from Crocker's and Appleby's units. Worse yet, Lancers were trying to close a ring around Chilton and his men. If the Mexicans should succeed in making the circle, there would be no escape for the dragoons.

"Back! Back!" roared Chilton. They had to break out of the trap. He looked for his men to insure that they had heard his command. Stoffer and a trooper named Kirrine were surrounded by ten or so Lancers. Before Chilton could move to help, Kirrine was gutted by a lance driven hard from the side. He was lifted from his saddle by the force of the brutal weapon and slung to the ground.

Stoffer screamed like a madman, raised his sword high, and jumped his horse straight at the Mexican who had killed Kirrine. Their steeds slammed together. Stoffer slashed down with his long blade, slicing at the man's face. The cut went deep, exposing the white bone of the skull for an instant before the blood flooded out.

The sergeant flailed left and right, and he spurred savagely. His horse crashed through the circle of Lancers, and he was free.

Chilton bellowed at the top of his voice and motioned for his men to center on him. He saw only fifty or so. Where were all the others?

The troopers rallied around the lieutenant like filings to a magnet. He whipped his horse's rump with the flat of his sword. He plunged his men back the way they had come, fending off the lances and cutting with his saber.

A Mexican rider drove at Chilton, gripping his long lance and bracing it under his arm. Matt swung himself to lean far left and twisted to present the narrowest possible target for the sharp iron point. It skittered across his ribs, burning like a flame.

The Mexican shifted his sight from Chilton, selected another dragoon farther along and in line, and continued his drive. Chilton reached out as far as he could with his sword, trying to cut the Mexican as he passed. The distance was too far.

Matt rotated to watch behind and saw the lance drive into the center of one of his men's chests. The impaled trooper flopped from the saddle.

Hard pressed from all sides, the saber-swinging dragoons cut clear. But the reprieve lasted but a moment. A Mexican captain, yelling orders, drew a hundred Lancers around him, and they hurled themselves upon the battered band of dragoons.

Chilton formed his men in a tightly clustered knot, the horses facing outward. The crush of Mexicans slammed into them. Swords and lances cut and stabbed and struck lethal blows. The wild clamof or red- and blue-clad men in a fight to the death rose to a mind-shattering din.

Smothered by the sheer numbers of the enemy, the dragoons were losing.

The air filled with the crash of large-caliber pistols. The Mexican Lancers surrounding Chilton and his men began to fall from the backs of their horses. A large section of their ring melted away. The captain took a shot through the neck, becoming a limp hulk that pitched sideways.

Chilton recognized the crack of the .36-caliber revolvers of the Texas Rangers. He heard the men's shrill, keening battle cry. Then Cavillin, on his big, black horse, was by his side.

The Ranger, a big revolver in each hand, his thumbs cocking the single-action guns, fired again and again. Without seeming to aim, he hit a target every time.

Cavillin flung a fast glance at Chilton. The Ranger's red hair flared like flame in the sunlight, and his large blue eyes were hard and smoky. He grinned a wild, reckless grin.

The Mexicans retreated in a full rout, spurring and lashing their horses and casting frightened looks behind them. Matt watched them jump their mounts down into the ravine and scramble up the far side.

He turned to examine the Rangers that had come to support him in the fight. He estimated two hundred men. With the firepower of their five-shot revolvers, they were equal to a thousand dragoons and their single-shot pistols. The army must soon equip all of its cavalry with this fine repeating weapon.

A cannonball sailed by a hundred feet in the air. Chilton heard the whizzing passage and then knew the Rangers had not beaten the Lancers by themselves. Duncan's artillery had continued to fire left and right of the battle zone, and beyond it, to prevent the advance of additional Mexican cavalry to the conflict. Now the "flying artillery" was striking the Mexicans with shot as they fled.

Matt surveyed the carnage that had occurred in a few seconds of battle. Bodies lay thickly on the ground, crumpled in awkward, grotesque forms.

He lifted his view to count his men that still lived. It was a heart-rending number; nearly half of his company was missing.

Nearby, south of him, Appleby and Crocker were assembling their men. They had taken heavy losses also, but not so badly as Chilton.

A bomb from the mortars at Casa Mata arched down in a steep angle, struck the ground, and rolled a few feet. The slow-burning fuse sent its hot flame into the canister, touched the powder, exploded. Round lead musket balls and fragments of the iron casing scythed outward, cutting men down with the murderous metal, shredding horse flesh and human flesh simultaneously.

A second ball, a third, fourth, each ripping into hundreds of metal pieces, sent death in all directions.

Chilton shouted for his men to ride. He savagely spurred his horse. He heard more shouting, and men riding close behind him.

Chilton sped clear of the falling steel balls and flying slivers of lead and iron. He dragged his mount to a halt and whirled around.

All the dragoons and Rangers that could ride were out of danger. Except for one. Cavillin sat astride his black horse in the impact area of the cannonballs.

The big horse was spinning slowly around. Cavillin was raking the black's ribs harshly with the sharp rowels of his spurs and trying to rein it in the direction his comrades had gone, trying to bring the faithful animal to safety with him.

The horse was oblivious to the commands and the pain of the spurs. It continued its wheeling turn, following the dictates of a brain pierced and damaged by shrapnel.

Then the brain quivered within the ruptured skull and died. The horse fell, throwing its rider.

A cannonball exploded near Cavillin, flinging a dead horse into the air. The shrapnel missed Cavillin, spraying over his head as he lay stunned on the ground. He clambered upward to stand, dazed, in the smoke.

Matt drove his horse in a flat-out run toward Cavillin, through the pall of yellow sulfurous smoke that hung like a poisonous vapor. His lungs burned with the bitter acid fumes, and his eyes were almost blind. He screamed ahead at Cavillin.

The Ranger's stunned mind cleared, and he saw the form of the horse and rider bearing directly down on him in the haze. He reached out and caught Matt's outstretched arm. Cavillin ran two steps beside Matt, then vaulted upward, adding momentum to the wrenching jerk the horse had applied to him. He swung onto the horse's rump behind Matt.

Chilton spurred. Cavillin gripped the horse with his legs. The stalwart beast bunched its legs beneath it and lunged away, carrying the two men.

In the strong redoubt of the Casa Mata, the artilleryman again bent to sight the black, iron barrel of his long-range killing gun. He poked the touch hole with the slow match. The cannon roared and recoiled, bounding backward.

The round iron cannonball rotated one time as it arched through the heavens. The burning fuse was perfectly timed. The shell detonated as it touched the earth between the front legs of Chilton's running horse.

The flash was an impossibly bright red color intermixed with the brilliant yellow of burning sulfur. Chilton saw it all. And he felt the rending, tearing of the horse's body. Its neck and head became bloody, tattered things.

A tremendous concussive wind of hundreds of miles per hour slammed Chilton, lifting him from the saddle, sailing him high into the air.

Iron and lead shrapnel flew with the wind. Many of the sharp pieces were stopped by the horse's body. Still, horrible, puncturing wounds speared Matt in numerous places. One of the angular iron fragments stabbed to the very core of him.

The pain faded; his mind, unable to withstand the agony, had turned off the tortured nerve endings.

Chilton rotated slowly in the air, ever so slowly. The slice of time seemed to last and last. He saw the battlefield and all the dead and wounded beneath the burning mist of gunpowder. Then, as he turned farther, he was looking up at the high, blue dome of the sky. So magnificently clear and blue. So beautiful and clean. Then Cavillin came into the edge of his view. The

Ranger was rising from the ground where he had been flung by the explosion.

I was correct, after all, thought Chilton. *I will not leave this battlefield alive.* Darkness caught him like a thunderclap.

Cavillin saw Chilton's spinning body strike the ground. He dashed to the crumpled form. He scooped his friend up in his arms.

Tom ran, his legs pumping in frantic haste. A cannonball landed to his right and detonated in a bright orange flash. Miraculously no shrapnel hit them.

His lungs sucked at the air. The veins in his throat swelled to thick blue cords as he strained every muscle to carry his mate at a faster pace.

"Wait! Stop!" exclaimed the surgeon, his ear pressed tightly to Chilton's chest. "His heart is fluttering and ready to stop."

Dr. Campbell halted the movement of the long metal probe and held it motionlessly, deep within Matt's chest. The shrapnel had entered the body just below the rib cage and angled steeply upward. The fragment lay against the heart, perhaps even embedded in its muscular wall. Each time Campbell endeavored to grip the piece of metal with the jaws of the probe, the sharp sliver pricked the heart, and its beat faltered, nearly ceasing. Until now, the heart had always steadied and returned to its strong contraction when Campbell ceased his probing.

"Well? Talk to me," Campbell's tense voice snapped at the second surgeon.

"Only an irregular flicker, a most weak pulse." Sweat leaked from the second surgeon's brow and dropped onto Matt's chest.

The two medical orderlies, their hands slippery with perspiration, continued to hold Matt pressed firmly to the operating table. Tightly drawn leather straps on Matt's arms, legs, and across his forehead aided the men.

"Yes. There it is," said the second surgeon. "I hear it. Go ahead and try again."

Campbell eased the open prongs of the probe slightly forward. The grit of metal on metal could be felt plainly. He squeezed the handles harder to open the jaws more widely. He caught the piece of shrapnel and began to withdraw it.

"Oh, stop! The heart has quit. There is no pulse. Not even a quiver."

"I have a grip on the metal piece. I'm bringing it out." There was nothing to be gained by halting now. "Listen for the beat," ordered Campbell.

The second surgeon continued to press his ear to Matt's chest. "No sound or pulse."

Campbell completely extracted the probe. Between its jaws was a bloody sliver of iron. He dropped all on the table and lunged forward. "Get out of the way," he shouted.

Campbell shoved an orderly and the surgeon aside. He raised a clenched fist and struck downward onto the ribs over the heart. He paused and hammered down again. "Beat! Beat!" he cried. "Live, damn you."

Campbell bent his head and put his ear to Matt's chest. "Weak. Very weak. But it does beat. The young man is very hardy."

He turned to look across the room at Cavillin, standing in the doorway. "The lieutenant has almost died several times. In fact, he should already be dead with a wound such as that. I fear that if I probe again to search for more shrapnel, he will surely die."

"Do you think he has other pieces in him near his heart?" Cavillin asked.

"I have no way of knowing for sure."

"If there are more, can he live with it?"

"Not if the heart should rub against a sharp metal edge. Very soon, even if the outside wound heals over, the metal could do enough damage to stop the heart permanently. Then, on the other hand, scar tissue may form around the shrapnel and protect the heart. I simply do not know what the outcome will be."

"Will he heal otherwise?"

"He has dozens of less serious injuries. They would normally heal without complications. The heart wound is in the hands of God and Chilton's own young strength. But now we must close the wound and finish with him, for there are hundreds of men coming off the battlefield that need our help."

"Where will you put him to rest while he recovers?"

"I don't really know. All the space and beds we have are filled."

Cavillin looked out the window of the operating room at a line of twenty or so houses stretching along the crest of the hill. They were well built, with large windows, obviously the rich man's section of town. He knew the houses had been constructed in that particular location to take advantage of the prevailing winds rising up and concentrated into cooling breezes over the hills.

Tom said to Campbell, "I would like for him to be placed in that house with the big windows on the point of the hill. The one with the tree. The cool breezes blow most often there. They should make him more comfortable and maybe heal more quickly. Would that be too far for you to look after him properly?"

"Before we are finished with the wounded of this battle, patients will be further away than that, and we shall still give the best care that is possible."

"Then I will go and set up a bed for Matt."

"You may have some trouble in doing that. The Missouri Mounted Riflemen live in that house and many others around it. I have already asked them to vacate and give their rooms to the wounded. They refused, telling me to have the Kentucky Volunteers on the other side of the church move. I am afraid I'll have to go to General Scott and ask him to prepare an order and send men to force the Missourians to go somewhere else."

"We can't wait for that," said Tom. He owed his life to the bleeding man on the operating table. He could still feel the shudder and jerk of Matt's body as the concussion of the exploding bomb had slammed him and the shrapnel sliced into his flesh. Tom had been flung backward to the ground but not wounded, protected by Matt's body. Now he would do whatever was required to help Matt live and heal.

"You are a major and the army's chief surgeon," Tom said. "If you write an order based on your rank, I'll enforce it."

"That would most likely be beyond my authority. But this is war, and we need space for many wounded, and right now."

Campbell moved to a desk and began to write. He finished and handed the single-page document to Cavillin. "The order is quite simple, merely stating that twenty houses along the hilltop road are needed for the care of the wounded. That all officers of the regular army or volunteers are directed to enforce the removal of any and all occupants of those structures at the earliest possible hour."

Cavillin folded the paper and shoved it into his pocket.

Campbell saw the face of the Ranger lieutenant harden with determination. "Try not to shoot anyone. The last thing I need is another patient," Campbell said.

"How soon before Matt will need the bed?" asked Tom.

"About twenty minutes. We must clean the wound and then close it."

"Have the orderlies bring him to that house. It will be vacant by the time they get there." Cavillin stalked from the operating room.

Five

"What in the hell are you doing in here?" growled a square-built, muscular man coming into the room where Tom was rolling up the blankets from a bed. "Get your hands off my gear."

"Sure," said Tom, straightening. "I'd like it better if you did it. And your partner's too." He pointed at the second bed. "Move his belongings out of here too."

The man shouted out the door. "Hey, Oscar. Come in here. There's a Texan fooling with our stuff. He says he wants us to move out."

A large, bearded man stomped inside and looked at Tom. "What's eating on you, redhead? We was here first and aim to stay. Now get out before you get hurt."

"The hospital needs more room for the wounded that're coming off the battlefield," Tom replied.

"Well, none of our folk took part in the fight and got themselves hurt, so I reckon we don't have to give up our choice location. Take them that's got shot down where the Kentuckians are camped."

Tom shook his head in the negative. "These houses on the ridge of the hill are the best ones because of the breeze that blows here. Surely you'd help the fellow that's taken a ball or some shrapnel and needs a cool bed to lay in while he heals?"

Neither of the mounted riflemen moved. They stared truculently at Tom. "I have an order here from the chief surgeon to clear all these houses right away." Tom removed the directive from his pocket and unfolded it. He offered it to the first man who stood closest. The man did not take the paper. He glared at Tom. "That kind of order should come through our colonel."

"There is no time for that. The injured will start coming in a few minutes. One of them is a friend of mine and badly hurt. He will require the best if he is to live."

"To hell with all that. We're not moving. We like the cool air too."

Tom repocketed the paper. "Then I'll move your things myself," he growled low in his chest. He bent to take hold of the blanket on the bed.

"Damn you." The first man snarled. "I told you to leave my gear alone. Now get out of here." He leapt forward and reached out to catch hold of Tom's arm.

Cavillin spun aside, then stepped strongly back at a right angle to the charging man to stiff-arm him, ramming him into the wall.

Oscar swiftly moved his hand to rest on the pistol in his belt.

"Don't do anything foolish with that," warned Tom. His hands hung poised over his revolvers. The rims of his nostrils were ice-white, and his eyes burned with a controlled fury. Damn the callous, bastard Missourians.

Tom's voice was like metal striking metal as he spoke. "I mean to have this room. One way or the other."

The first man pushed away from the wall, his face twisted with hate. "One call and I can have fifty Missourians here."

"And I can get two hundred Texas Rangers with a whistle. But right now there's just you two and me."

The time for talk was ended. Tom's hands dipped down and came up with his two revolvers. He cocked them as he drew.

"These Colts can blast both of you out the door. Now, do

I put my wounded friend in a bed given gladly, or do I put him in a dead man's bed?"

With hard stares the two Missourians measured the Texas Ranger. They smelled no fear in the redheaded man; there was only the quiet readiness to kill, or to die, if it came to that.

Oscar's fingers twitched on the butt of his pistol. Quickly he let his hand fall from the weapon, to hang by his side. A glassy sheen covered his eyes. He had doubt as to who might live through a gunfight if it came to that.

"Come on, Oscar," said the first man. "That surgeon officer has given his order. General Scott and our colonel will honor it. If we should kill this Texan while he has that order, we might hang. We may as well move our duffels now."

Oscar glowered at Tom. "You drew guns on me. I won't forget that. We will meet again."

"Maybe so, but only in the dark. If I ever have to pull my guns again, you will die," said Cavillin.

The men snatched their blankets from the beds, picked up their remaining possessions, and stomped out.

Matt swam upward from the pool of hot, liquid black. He could see light far above. Maybe this time he could reach it. But he was so terribly weak.

He struggled. He felt sweat running down his forehead and collecting in stinging pools in the sockets of his eyes. Yet with all his effort he gained only a little toward the beacon that beckoned so tantalizingly. He felt extremely sad, for there seemed to be some important reason why he should gain the light. And he truly was closer this time than ever before.

He ceased his attempt, totally exhausted. Immediately he began to sink back into the inky depths. The light grew dim, then winked out abruptly. Maybe the next time he would reach the surface and know the significance of the light. If there *was* a next time.

The pure, sweet air filled Matt's lungs. His mind became crystal clear. He sensed the presence of his body and knew he still survived. He drank in the intoxication of that knowledge.

He must have more of the delicious air. He breathed again, deeply. A sharp pain shot through his chest, and his heart cramped and fluttered.

Matt held his breathing shallow, his ribs barely expanding. The agony gradually lessened. Ah! He could live with the pain at that level.

His eyelids parted a crack. Glorious, golden sunlight streamed in through an open window, struck the white bed sheet that covered him, and, in shimmering waves, reflected onto the whitewashed walls of the room. Matt watched the play of light. God! So beautiful.

He tried to raise his hand. It was impossibly heavy, like a cannonball was tied to it, holding it down. Finally it came trembling into view and he examined it, marveling that the land of the dead had not taken him.

Matt lowered his arm, all the strength wrung out of him. "Anybody here?" he croaked. "Can anybody hear me?" His voice was broken and strained, like that of a very old man.

He rolled his head and peered around. The room was empty. A rocking chair sat near the door. Matt wondered who had rested there and held vigil over him. If the battle was over, that person would probably be Phil Steptoe.

How long had he lain here? Hours? Days? Was the battle ended? He was not in a Mexican prison, so the Americans must not be defeated yet.

Well, he could wait. Someone would come again. He let the blackness wash over him.

* * *

A rocking chair creaked rhythmically on a gritty floor. The sound had slowly penetrated Matt's slumbering mind. He came fully awake and looked around.

A redheaded man sat with his back to Matt. His booted feet were braced on the windowsill, and he rocked himself backward and forward. He gazed steadily out the window.

"Tom, tell me what you see out there," Matt said.

Cavillin let his feet fall to the floor with a thump. He quickly stood and turned.

His mouth spread in a great smile. "What is out there can wait. What I see here is a friend who is alive. And one who saved my life when the cannonballs were falling. Welcome back, Matt, from wherever you have been."

Chilton smiled back at the Ranger. "It is more painful here than where I have been. My chest hurts horribly. What happened?"

"You took several pieces of shrapnel. Some in the chest. The surgeon, Campbell, can tell you more about it when he comes around. Is there anything I can get you?"

"It feels like I haven't had a drink in days. So some water to wet this dry throat would be just right."

"You name it and I'll get it." Cavillin made to leave.

"Tell Steptoe to come see me. I want to thank you and him for saving my troopers from all getting killed. They would all have been killed without the help of your pistols and Steptoe's cannon."

Cavillin halted and faced Matt. His eyes filled with sorrow. "Phil is dead. A bomb from a Mexican mortar hit his gun. Killed him and all his crew instantly."

"Damn it!" exclaimed Matt.

He looked out the window for a long time and watched the sky. The sunlight still beamed down, but it had lost its beauty.

"How many of my men were hurt?" he finally asked.

"I spoke to your Sergeant Stoffer. He told me thirty-six men were killed and thirty-two wounded, some badly."

Sixty-eight men dead or injured out of a force of ninety. A sickening loss. "I'm glad Stoffer made it," Matt said.

"He was wounded. He'll limp for the rest of his days."

"That's too bad. He is a fine sergeant. What did they find at Molino? Was there a foundry there?"

"We were correct about the mill. They found nothing except an old cannon mold that had not been used for years. Santa Anna tricked Scott again."

"All that killing and dying for nothing. How many men did we lose?"

"It has been three days since the battle, and men are still dying from their wounds. But the last count was seven hundred and eighty men killed or injured. That's twenty-five percent of those that fought. The 5th Infantry lost thirty-eight percent of their men. A horrible waste. A few more victories like this and we will not have an army.

"Scott is a damn poor commander. He does not learn from other battles. He captured Vera Cruz with almost no loss of life, but now this blunder."

"You said the fighting had been over for three days. You mean, just for Molino?"

"Yes. Scott and his generals are now preparing the battle plan for the attack on Mexico City." Tom moved to the door. "I'll get your water. We can talk more later. I'll bring Dr. Campbell back with me if I can find him."

Cavillin left with a long stride. Matt turned to the window again. A few brief minutes of battle and more than a third of his dragoons were dead. That amounted to fifteen hundred years of future with family and friends destroyed. He had been the officer. He had felt death riding his shoulder like an expectant predator. Self-centered, he had thought death was for him. Could he have somehow known otherwise and saved his men?

Chilton lay for a long time and brooded upon that question. Somehow he must try to pay his men for the bad leadership of their officers. But how could one discharge a debt to dead men?

Six

Wade Ussing removed a golden statue from a coat pocket and placed it on the table in front of Captain Tarpon, master of the clipper ship, *Wind Seeker*. Wade leaned back in his chair and watched the face of the captain in the lampshine.

Tarpon's eyes narrowed covetously. The whiskers around his mouth bristled as he compressed his lips and silently evaluated the statue.

The lamp hanging from the ceiling swung on its chain as the docked ship rolled to a wave, sweeping across the harbor of Vera Cruz. Rays of light glinted off the four-inch figure of the woman with a swollen stomach and large, round breasts. As the beams of the lamp moved over the statue, her lips seemed to smile, and first one sculptured eye, and then the other, winked as it filled with black shadow.

"She is a woman of passion and fertility," said Ussing. "She is very old, made by the ancient Aztecs. Man's concept of woman has never changed."

"Lovely little bitch," said the captain. He reached out and touched the cold, hard metal of her stomach with a finger. He shut his eyes to hide a cunning thought. Ussing was a sharp man and dangerous to plot against.

"She's very valuable," said Wade. "I have many other objects of gold and silver." He brought a golden panther from a pocket, held it in his hand a moment, enjoying the weight and smoothness of the figurine, then set it on the table beside the woman. Once a man has touched gold, he is never the same thereafter, mused Wade.

"In fact, I have half a ton of valuable things cast in gold and silver that I want to sell. Are you interested?"

"Half a ton!" exclaimed Tarpon. He jerked his view up from the statues to look at Ussing. "Have you robbed every rich Mexican in Vera Cruz?"

"I rob nobody, for I am not a thief. I only buy what is brought to me. In war, many precious items become lost. American soldiers and Mexicans who want to trade those things for money seek me out."

The price you pay for those things is like stealing, thought Tarpon. "Are all the objects you have statues such as these?" questioned the captain.

"No. Most are things of silver."

"I don't have enough money to buy what you offer, even if it is mostly silver. Unless you allow me to sell the items in New Orleans and then pay you later on my return trip to Vera Cruz."

"I can't do that," Ussing said. No man should be tempted with a fortune in precious metals. "How much cash do you have?"

"I received a fair price for the cargo I brought to Vera Cruz. Still, I have only about fifteen thousand dollars, for I just finished purchasing cargo to fill my hold for the return trip north."

"Fifteen thousand is only a small fraction of what my merchandise is worth."

Tarpon shrugged. "Then we can't trade."

Ussing pondered the situation. Tarpon was sole owner of the *Wind Seeker*. It was a fine ship, relatively new and fast. There was sufficient trade for many such ships. "I have a plan that can make us both rich. Come see my goods and listen to what I have to say. I think there's a way we can make a deal."

Tarpon combed his beard with his fingers as he thoughtfully studied the large, black-haired man sitting across the table from him. He knew Ussing's way. A whoremaster and dealer of stolen goods and contraband. A tough man who drove a hard bargain.

"I'll look at your goods," said the captain. "Then we'll talk some more."

The clipper ship suddenly rose and rolled port, then starboard. The lamp pendulumed, throwing flickering shadows on the bulkhead. Tarpon caught the swinging globe and stopped the crazy dance of the shadows on the bulkhead.

The ship heaved upward more violently as a stronger wave swept in under its keel. The mooring line snapped taut, jerking the vessel against the pier. The *Wind Seeker* vibrated, and the mast and rigging creaked and groaned under the hard blow.

The captain sprang up and went out on deck. Wade picked up the statues and followed to stand beside Tarpon.

A coarse-voiced man bellowed an order. "Starboard watch, on deck!"

Running feet sounded, and a knot of men assembled swiftly amidship under the light of a coal-oil lantern.

The coarse voice shouted again. "Fasten a line bow and stern and lead them to the next pier. Hurry it! Then stand by for my order to take up slack."

"The mate will have lines rigged to hold the ship off the dock," Tarpon said. He motioned at the stars, glittering like pinpricks in the black-velvet bowl of the night sky. "Clear as a bell and only a slow breeze blowing toward the land. But we have a moderate sea running. Must be one hell of a storm out in the gulf to send its waves across Campeche Bay and into this protected harbor."

Ussing's eyes jumped the miles to the eastern horizon. Not one cloud was visible.

Tarpon spoke. "When can I see your cargo?"

"My place. Eleven o'clock."

"Good. I want to sail at daybreak. The storm could be heading in this direction, and I want to leave and be in the open sea before it reaches here. How about the soldiers patrolling the waterfront?"

"I'll see that there are no sentries between eleven-thirty and midnight. You can load without fear of getting caught by the army provost."

"You'll have some way of hauling the cargo to the ship?"

"Yes. A light wagon." Ussing turned away and walked across the deck.

Wade was pleased to have discovered Tarpon and his clipper ship in Vera Cruz. He had conducted business with the captain in New Orleans. The man had to be watched carefully. However, he was an excellent sailor and skilled at smuggling contraband.

Wade went down the gangway and walked along the piers past a dozen docked merchantmen, a mixture of tall-masted ships and squat steamers. Beyond the docks, the darkness of Campeche Bay was broken by dim lights of Navy warships and merchantmen at anchor. The scattered points of glowing yellow swung in short arcs as the vessels pitched to the ocean swell.

Bobbing lights moved on the water as several small boats were rowed toward the beach. Off-duty sailors and marines were heading for a night of liberty in the cantinas and brothels, those that had not been destroyed by the cannonading of the city. Nothing would be denied them in this conquered place.

The most outlying sprinkle of lights on the bay marked the location of Fort San Juan de Ulua, constructed by the Spanish two centuries earlier on a coral reef one thousand yards offshore. American soldiers and navy gunners now controlled that might fortress.

For many weeks past, merchant ships had come, hurrying

southwest from New Orleans with cargo holds packed full of weapons, ammunition, hospital supplies, uniforms, and the myriad types of provisions needed by the army in its conquest of Mexico. However, El Camino Real was closed by guerrilla attacks of the Mexican army, and no supplies were moving inland to Scott. All the warehouses in Vera Cruz were full, and more than two hundred ships lay at anchor, unable to unload.

General Scott had left a garrison of two thousand soldiers behind to hold Vera Cruz. He had also fortified and intended to hold Puebla, one hundred and thirty miles away in the mountains. The Mexicans had now held Puebla under siege for more than a month. Rumors flew that Scott and his army would never be able to fight their way back to the coast. Wade felt confident that the fighting ability of Scott's army was badly underestimated.

Two soldiers with rifles on their shoulders paced toward him through the murkiness of the waterfront. Wade stopped as the sentries drew close. One of the men spoke to his companion and continued on alone.

" 'Evening, Mr. Ussing," the soldier said.

"Good evening to you, Corporal Taylor."

"Something I can do for you, sir?"

"What we spoke of yesterday. Is it possible to do that?"

"Yes, sir. I talked to my friend, and he's willing. We can be gone from the docks. Is the time still eleven-thirty to midnight?"

"Excellent. I am glad you could do me this favor. Yes, you have the time right." Ussing brought a packet of paper money from a pocket and handed it to the sentry. "Divide this with your comrade. As a bonus to you, Corporal, after you go off duty, go to the side door of my business and ask for Emily. I think she would be glad to see you."

"Thank you, Mr. Ussing. You have pretty women."

"Good. Then everything's arranged."

Wade reached out in a swift movement and grabbed the man's hand, which held the money. He squeezed, feeling the bone, muscle, and paper crunching. The corporal winced under the crushing grip.

"Do not fail me," Ussing hissed. Without waiting for a response, he pivoted and walked off.

Corporal Taylor gingerly opened his aching hand and watched the black-suited man disappear into the night. Taylor knew he had been warned on pain of death. Ussing made no idle threats.

Ussing unlocked the iron gate of the large private house he had rented upon his arrival in Vera Cruz three months earlier. The house had been a rich Mexican's home. All the furnishings still remained. The rental price had been so low as to be robbery, but the owner had readily accepted the amount, for the house was within two blocks of the docks, and the warehouses full of army supplies, a zone forbidden to Mexicans by the American army for security reasons. The house was ideal for Wade's purposes.

He proceeded through a walkway flanked by head-high stone walls and entered a broad, totally enclosed patio. In the light of a lantern, his man, Luis Gonzalez, sat at a table with a second man.

"Hello, Gonzalez," Wade said to the Spaniard.

"Wade, this hombre wants to talk to you."

The second man stood up. He was a skeleton, mere skin stretched over long bones. His face was sharp angles with sunken cheeks, all framed with black hair. A stiff, bushy mustache fanned out from beneath a long, drooping nose. His eyes were set deeply in black holes under the ridges of his brows. A revolver was in a holster on his side. He held his hand near the butt of the weapon.

"Translate for me, Gonzalez," directed Ussing.

"Yes, sir. I will. Do you remember him? He's one of Berdugo's gunmen. The fat thief that has always brought trifles to sell."

"Yes. I remember Berdugo. He's been testing us. And I remember this handsome fellow. Tell him to start talking, for I have much to do tonight."

Gonzalez spoke quickly to the Skeleton. The man extracted something from his pocket and held it out under the light. Three gems, each flashing in its own distinctive brilliant color, red or blue or green, lay on the leathery palm of his hand.

"Do you recognize rubies and sapphires and emeralds?" asked the man.

Ussing picked the three jewels up and carefully examined them close to the light.

"Señor Berdugo has many such stones. These are the three smallest. What do you think of the quality?"

Wade handed the jewels back to the man. "Why come to me with these stones? Why didn't Berdugo come himself if he wishes to trade?"

The Skeleton stared stonily at Ussing. Then his mouth opened wide and cavernous, and he laughed without sound. "You should know the answer to that."

Ussing's anger rushed hot in his veins. He wanted to pull his revolver and shoot the ugly bastard. "I do not know what you mean. Now, quickly, what do you want of me?"

"Come with me and see many lovely jewels. Berdugo believes you will want to buy these valuable objects."

"Tell Berdugo to come here," said Ussing.

"Berdugo is an important man in Vera Cruz. He is cautious and has lived and prospered for many years. If you are a man to be trusted, then you must go to him and show your good intentions."

The only important men in this city are Americans, thought Wade. However, in all his buying of stolen objects, the truly great treasures he knew existed in Mexico had eluded him.

Now the opportunity may have arrived. It was dangerous, but he could not hold back and refuse to investigate what Berdugo offered.

"Where's Berdugo and his jewels?" Wade asked.

"Ten blocks along the street that runs beside your business and away from the restricted waterfront." the long, thin arm of the man pointed. "There's a two-story warehouse that your cannon has struck. One end is blown away. Berdugo is there. He waits on you. Bring many American dollars for you will want to purchase all that he will show you."

"I'll bring pesos."

"Berdugo says he will only accept American dollars, for the money of the victorious army has the most value."

"I'll be there in an hour." Ussing did not like to be dictated to. Berdugo was playing a hard hand. But there were still wild cards in the deck.

"Bring only your interpreter." The Skeleton turned and stalked away on the stone-floored walkway. The iron gate creaked open and then clanked shut.

"Gonzalez, what do you think of Berdugo's offer?"

"It's bound to be a trap. He's heard that some of our visitors disappear, and now he wants to turn the trick on us. He will show jewels, and you your money. Then the Skeleton and other gunmen will kill you. Your American dollars will become theirs. Berdugo will become a bigger man among his friends."

"I think you're exactly right."

"Then we do not go."

"Oh, we'll go. Except we'll take their things of value. And we'll also take their lives, which have no value. How many of them do you think there will be?"

Gonzalez considered the question but did not answer. Wade did his own calculating. He estimated a minimum of four men. Knowing the Mexican penchant for always wanting to outnumber Americans in a fight, Ussing added one more to his number. What trick could he use to kill five armed thieves and take their fortune?

"We have preparations to make," said Ussing. "Let's get to it."

"I hope you have a good plan, or we'll soon be dead men."

Seven

Sophia wiped her hot forehead with a handkerchief and leaned against the hard wooden sash of the open window. She felt lightheaded and weak. Her knees trembled. But the spell of illness should soon pass. It always had before.

She must think of other things and forget her sickness. She looked out from her second-floor window across the flat rooftops of the nearby buildings to the waterfront and the several ships tied up beside the piers. She breathed the sea breeze, carrying the damp smell of salt water and the multitude of odors from the docks and warehouses jammed full of army war supplies. Now and then she saw shadowy forms of men moving on the docks and the decks of the ships, and heard the sailors faintly calling to one another.

She watched the lights of the ships at anchor on the dark water of Campeche Bay and wondered which one was the warship *Massachusetts*, Commodore Conner's flagship. The commodore had come ashore and visited the other women and Sophia. He had sat in the parlor and drank rum and talked with the women. He had been cordial to them and smiled often but left after only half an hour. Wade Ussing had been jovial and very pleasant to the women for the remainder of the day.

The visit of the senior naval officer in Vera Cruz had put a stamp of approval on Ussing's business. Now the officers of the army garrison, and those of the navy and merchant ships, came openly and frequently.

The music of a piano playing a lively tune drifted up from the lower floor. A woman laughed gaily, a sign that guests had arrived. Sophia must go down.

She took one last deep breath of the cool sea breeze. As the air expelled, a convulsion shook her. There was a rending and tearing in the center of her chest. The breath in her lungs became tortured and scalding. She started to cough, harsh, ripping explosions of air that bent her forward in pain.

She pressed a handkerchief tightly to her mouth to stifle the agonizing sound. The racking cough went on for what seemed an interminable time.

Finally she controlled the paroxysms of coughing and leaned limply on the wall. The white of the handkerchief was frothed with fresh red blood, more than had ever occurred before in such an attack. She tasted the blood, musty and copperish in her mouth.

The large discharge of blood frightened her. One day she would hemorrhage and drown in her own blood. The fear swelled within her, and she grappled with the slippery thing, fought it with every ounce of her strength.

Chilled yet hot, she subdued the horrible beast of terror and shoved it, squirming and kicking, into a far, deep recess of her mind. If her body was weak, then her mind must be strong, or she would surely find death. That must be delayed as long as possible. She must have time to accumulate more money and return to New Orleans. She did not want to die in this foreign land.

Ussing entered the house and proceeded to the front. At a small alcove just off the parlor, he stopped and spoke to a large, powerfully built man. "Jungling, the women will not need your protection for a time. I have something more important for you to do."

The two men talked for a moment, then Jungling left the house. Wade walked into the large, richly furnished parlor and ranged his sight over the three young blond women and a pair of army lieutenants. Emily played skillfully on a piano, and Helen was mixing drinks at a table full of decanters containing a wide variety of whiskey, rum, and liqueurs. Martha sat on a giant, overstuffed divan with the lieutenants. They laughed and talked together.

Wade stepped close to Helen. "Where's Sophia?" he asked.

"I saw her earlier, Wade. She looked ill. She shouldn't work tonight. The three of us can handle the business."

"I didn't bring her from New Orleans to loaf in Mexico," Ussing said in a surly tone. He pivoted and crossed the room to climb the stairs to the second floor.

Sophia heard Ussing's hard step coming along the hallway. He shoved the door open without knocking.

"The show has started, Sophia. Are you going down to play your part?" questioned Ussing in a sharp voice.

"Yes, Wade," replied Sophia, and she closed her hand around the bloody handkerchief. Her sight clashed with Ussing's. He was a violent man, but she was not afraid. A greater danger than him threatened her.

"Don't try to order me around. We both have the same goal and have agreed on how to reach it. I'll carry out my part." She started to move forward.

Ussing blocked her passage and gazed into the strikingly beautiful face. He recalled their journey to this distant land of Mexico. The reports of General Scott's victories in battles with the Mexican army had reached New Orleans in May. That news had birthed in Wade thoughts of the great wealth that a strong man could take from a conquered land.

He had sold his saloon on the waterfront. He let all his whores go, for he wanted a special quality in the women he would take to Mexico. For days afterward he had searched through New Orleans to find the most beautiful of women, fair and blond, to take to a land of dark-skinned men. Women who would undertake a great adventure and brave a long passage on the ocean to a warring country to make a fortune. Sophia was the most lovely of all he had found, the centerpiece of his collection.

She was thin yet womanly—rounded, and most appealing. However, Ussing recognized symptoms that greatly concerned him. Sophia's cheeks were flushed, her eyes unnaturally luminous, her breathing shallow. She had consumption, a malady the military doctors called tuberculosis. The disease was far advanced, and with its almost constant elevated temperature, it gave the victim a false appearance of good health, until the person grew too weak to walk.

Sophia was very important to Wade's scheme and could not soon be replaced. He must reap the greatest profit in the shortest possible time.

The women were but a front, though a very lucrative one, for his true endeavor. For centuries men had torn gold and jewels from the mountains of Mexico. Ussing meant to accumulate a great horde of that treasure.

He moved from in front of Sophia. She strode purposefully past him.

Ussing and Gonzalez made their way among the shattered hulks of homes, factories, and office buildings. The streets were mostly cleared of the rubble blasted from the buildings by cannonballs and mortar bombs. There was no light except for the occasional rectangle of pale yellow from the windows of the less damaged houses, occupied by a Mexican family or an American officer who had set up a residence for a mistress.

The two men halted in deep blackness and let a squad of four soldiers on patrol, enforcing the military law and the curfew, pass by on the opposite side of the street. Ussing did not want to waste time explaining his presence there at that hour.

Beside them, a building with two walls blown away sagged over the street. It swayed and groaned with a warning of imminent collapse as a puff of wind pressed upon it. Wade glanced up at the remnant of the structure.

Vera Cruz was a town in shambles, when once it had been the major port city of the Mexican nation. The famous King's Highway began here and led through the mountains to Mexico City and onward, hundreds of miles, to Santa Fe and Taos. Now no traffic moved in or out of the city except by the American charter ships or naval vessels.

The Mexican army had defended the city with four thousand soldiers. The ocean side of the town was protected by a massive granite seawall and the might fort of San Juan de Ulua. The fort had one hundred and thirty-five cannon, including heavy ten-inchers.

The remaining two sides of the triangular city were protected by fifteen-foot stone walls. Nine redoubts had been constructed into the walls at spaced intervals. One hundred cannon had fortified these strong points.

The Americans came ashore on the ninth of March. By March twelfth, they had laid a seven-mile siege line around the city. In addition to the cannon and mortars of the army, they had brought three of the navy's most powerful cannon, capable of hurling thirty-two pounds of solid shot against the enemy's walls. Two hundred sailors and soldiers dragged each of the three-ton cannon three miles through deep sand and across boggy sloughs.

On March twenty-second, the Americans began firing on Vera Cruz. The rain of cannonballs and bombs fell continuously day and night. One battery commander told Ussing that he had fired six hundred ten-inch shells into the town in thirty-six hours.

The Mexicans returned the bombardment only during the

daytime. They did little damage to the entrenched American forces.

After four days of destruction and death, the city surrendered. Scott now had a port of entry and a base for the landing of reinforcements, equipment, and supplies.

The general ejected all the Mexican population from the waterfront. He wanted his own men there to guard and hold the harbor. But also to billet them on the shore, open to the sea breeze, hoping to protect them and prevent them from catching the dreaded *vomito,* coastal fever.

Ussing had established his business near the beach to catch the sea breeze but also to be in the center of the residences of the soldiers and near the men on the ships.

The sounds of the soldier's footfalls faded away. "Let's go," Wade said to Gonzalez. They continued inland across the devastated town.

Wade and Gonzalez walked along the side of the stone-and-wood warehouse building with its gaping cannonball holes. An open door showed a dim glow of light ahead. They entered warily.

Four men stood near a table upon which sat a large navy hurricane lamp. Though the wick was turned up high, it cast but a small pool of light in the yawning hollow of the warehouse.

"Welcome, Señor Ussing," said Berdugo. "We have been waiting for you."

Gonzalez translated for Ussing.

"Well, we're here," Ussing said. He approached and stopped by the table.

Gonzalez restated the words in the language of the thief.

The Skeleton caught Ussing's eyes upon him and stretched his lips across snaggleteeth in a gruesome smile. The other two men were tense and nervous. All were armed with pistols.

There's another man somewhere out there in the dark, thought Wade. But he would do nothing until Berdugo gave a signal. That would happen when Wade showed his money.

"Let's get down to business," said Ussing. "What have you stolen that you now want to sell?"

"You have brought yankee dollars?" Berdugo's eyes glittered. *Madre de Dios,* how he hated these gringo dogs. He had once been the biggest thief in Vera Cruz. Now he must barter with this American invader.

"First the merchandise must be shown, then comes the money."

"Very well." Berdugo slid a hand inside the front of his shirt and extracted a leather pouch. He placed it on the table before Ussing. "These are very valuable," said the thief.

Wade picked up the pouch and bounced the bulk of it in his palm. He loosened the tie at the neck of the container and poured a mound of rubies, sapphires, and emeralds onto the top of the table. The jewels glistened and sparkled in a hundred rays of red, blue, and green, each a brilliant, perfect spear of color that saturated the capacity of the eye to enjoy beauty.

"Ah! *Muy magnifico,*" Gonzalez whispered in wonder.

Wade took a magnifying glass from a pocket and systematically examined every fifth gem. He looked into the center of the jewels, searching for impurities—bubbles, inclusions, or fractures. Every stone was without flaw.

"They are very beautiful and should bring a fortune in your United States," said Berdugo. "Now show me your Yankee dollars and let us determine how many of my treasures you can afford."

"Certainly." Ussing climbed to his feet.

A rifle crashed in the dark recesses of the warehouse, the shock waves reverberating the walls. The lamp exploded, glass and coal oil spraying in all directions. Total darkness engulfed the men.

Wade scooped up the jewels with one sweep of his hand.

He jumped to the side. A lance of flame stabbed out where he had been a moment before.

Ussing drew his pistol. That shot would have come from the Skeleton. Ussing shot high and to the right of the origin of the flash. A body struck the floor with a thump.

Ussing moved swiftly. Others shots exploded, burning the blackness with hot streaks of incandescence. Gonzalez and Berdugo's men were firing.

Wade selected a gun flash, judging it to be from Berdugo's position, and fired where the man would be standing. Instantly Wade pivoted away and dropped to his knees. He heard a man gasping in mortal injury in the direction he had shot.

Stooping low, Ussing silently slipped off in the dense murk.

Ussing sat at his desk and fondled the jewels, some as large as the end of his thumb. He selected the largest and most precisely cut and polished of each kind and put it in his pocket.

He raised his hand to listen as a clank of metal came from the gate of the patio. Gonzalez and Jungling had stayed behind. They were good fighters and would insure that none of Berdugo's men followed. Still, unexpected events sometimes happened. Wade stepped out of the lamplight and put his hand on his pistol.

Jungling came in with long, quiet strides. The Spaniard kept pace with a lithe, sliding step. They both began to smile.

"Berdugo and the Skeleton and all the other men that were with him are dead," said Gonzalez. "One was still alive when we lit another light, but he died quickly."

"I caught one man in the dark before you got to the warehouse," added Jungling. "Put a knife between his ribs. Boss, your plan worked exactly as you said it would."

"A very simple strategy is enough when those who execute it are the very best," responded Ussing. He gestured at the jewels on the table. "Take your pick, one of each kind. It is a bonus for a job well done."

Jungling's big hands eagerly spread the gems, and he and Gonzalez began to evaluate the treasure trove. Wade watched the two. Always pay your men well and promise them much more, until the time comes when they are expendable. The men were grinning broadly as they pocketed their choice of three gems each.

"Ussing, open up," a man called out. The iron gate began to rattle vigorously.

Wade raked the jewels from the table and put them into a pocket. He spoke to Jungling. "That's Captain Tarpon. Go let him in."

"Sure, Wade." The big man left.

Tarpon and his two ship's officers entered ahead of Jungling. "Well, Ussing, we've come to see all that gold and silver you were bragging about," the captain said.

"I was telling the simple truth," Wade replied. "All of you follow me. We'll need witnesses to what we're about to do."

He guided them along the hallway to a heavy plank door reinforced with iron straps. He inserted a key and twisted it in the strong lock. The door swung open. He struck a lucifer and touched the wick of a lamp that was fastened to the wall.

The lamp's beams fell upon a crowded array of silver statues, goblets, plates, crucifixes, urns, and many other shapes and forms. In the center of the brightly shining silver, dully glowing golden objects covered three square yards of floor.

"By God, Ussing," muttered Tarpon in a reverent voice. "You didn't stretch your tale one inch. Now I know how the pirates must feel when they capture a treasure ship."

"All of this has been collected in three months," said Wade. "The war is young and should continue for several more months. Imagine how much more we can take from this town! However, there is danger in allowing this wealth to remain in Mexico. The Mexicans may capture Vera Cruz, but that's highly unlikely. More to worry about is the American army finding out about this and laying claim. It must be removed from the country very soon. Tarpon, this gold and silver should be taken to New Orleans and sold. There's a large and rich market in that town."

"I agree," said Tarpon. "There would be no trouble disposing of this for good American dollars. And the customs officials would never be the wiser."

The captain glanced at Ussing with a questioning expression. "My whole ship is not worth this amount of precious metal. In fact, you could buy three clippers with it."

"That is just what I want you to do. I will turn all this wealth over to you for one-half interest in the *Wind Seeker* and half ownership in the next two ships you buy. You are skilled in ships and the ocean. You may have a free hand in making the purchases."

Wade moved close to Tarpon. "By working with me, you can become very rich. On the other hand, if I ever find you cheating me of even one cent, I'll kill you." His voice was taut with malice, and the black orbs of his eyes bore into Tarpon.

The two ship's officers stirred uneasily at the threat to their captain. Jungling and Gonzalez snapped to quick readiness for combat.

Ussing spun unexpectedly toward the two mates. "How much salary do you make?"

"Ninety dollars a month and keep," said the first mate. His voice was strained, for he was not sure he liked what he was getting into.

"And you?" Wade queried the second mate.

"Seventy dollars and keep."

"From now on your salaries are doubled. Also, there will be a bonus for each successful voyage. Is that all right with you, Tarpon?"

"With this kind of cargo, we can surely afford that much," Tarpon said.

"Then all is agreed on, so let's pack our goods." Ussing pointed at a stack of empty wooden crates, partially full of straw. "Stow the objects gently and put layers of straw between them to prevent damage. Very gently now.

"Tarpon, come with me to my office. We have some papers to prepare and sign. You four finish here and then come and witness the documents. After that, we will load this on a wagon and go down to the ship."

Ussing checked his watch. "We have thirty minutes. Hurry it up."

Wade watched Tarpon sign the bill of sale giving him half interest in the *Wind Seeker*. With the captain's signature, all facets of Wade's plan were in operation. His brothel was busy and earning substantial amounts of money. The price he paid for stolen valuables was but a small portion of their true value. Now he had a ship to transport them to the States.

Ussing smiled inside his head. The American army had captured Vera Cruz, seemingly for his personal accumulation of wealth. Soon General Scott would overrun Mexico City. Ussing would then move his business to that fabulously rich city. The treasures there would be a thousandfold greater than in Vera Cruz. No man could stop Wade now. No man had better try.

Eight

The night wind came moaning down from the high crowns of the mountains and along the streets of Tacubaya. Chilton, lying on his bed, heard the breeze whisper as it entered the window. It washed pleasantly over his hot body, naked except for his bandages. He spread his arms and legs to the wind and listened to the tiles of the roof creaking and clicking as they cooled.

The chief surgeon, Campbell, had talked with Matt on the first day of his return to consciousness. He had explained the seriousness of his chest wound and the lack of knowing whether or not additional pieces of shrapnel might still be in his body and lie dangerously near Matt's heart. That discussion, and the presence of the never-ending pain in his chest, had cast a primal melancholy over him.

During the past two days he had partially climbed from under the gloom of the threat of death. He fretted about the slow passing of the hours and whether his wound would heal.

The night grew old, and sleep came late and uneasily. Nightmares of his men falling dead around him came. Their sightless eyes stared accusingly up at him from the ground. He tried to tell them he grieved for having led them to their deaths, but his lips would not open, and no words would come.

Matt came awake instantly at the crunch of boots upon the gravelly path leading to his room. He painfully reached out in the darkness for the two pistols on the table beside the bed. The Mexicans had sent a raiding party into Tacubaya and killed two sentries the night before. They might come again. He stared at the murky shadow of the doorway. A short range, he could easily slay a man with each gun.

The footfalls halted by the entrance to his room. "Lieutenant Chilton, this is Sergeant Stoffer. Are you awake?"

"Yes, Sergeant."

"Some of the troopers and I thought we'd come and watch the battle for Mexico City with you. It should start any minute now, for daybreak is near. If the Mexicans break through our forces, we can make our stand here and fight by you."

"I'm glad you've come." Matt lowered the hammers on his pistols. "Come in, Sergeant, and the men too."

Matt saw Stoffer's shadowy figure appear in the doorway. "Lieutenant, there's eleven of us who can walk, so that's too many for all to come inside. And besides, they've got their carbines and ammunition. Do you want us to move your bed closer to the window so you can see out over the city?"

"I would appreciate that. The surgeon says I shouldn't try to walk yet."

"It's been my experience that the men who walk the quickest heal best," responded the sergeant. "But Campbell is a good surgeon and knows what he's doing."

The sergeant raised his voice and called outside. "Four of you men who can lift, come in here and help me move the lieutenant's bed."

In the gloom of the room the sergeant and the other walking wounded of Chilton's dragoons gathered around the wood-frame bed.

"All right, now, all together, lift," directed the sergeant. "Take it right up against the window."

"Thanks, men," said Chilton. "From here I'll have the best view of all."

"Lieutenant, do you think we'll win?" asked a young voice from the window.

"I don't know, Darcy," answered Matt. "We have seven thousand men against sixteen thousand Mexicans entrenched behind heavy fortifications. However, our men are better fighters and better armed, I believe."

"What will happen if we don't take Mexico City?" asked Darcy.

Sergeant Stoffer spoke, his tone hard. "The Mexicans will kill us, as they did our wounded at Molino."

The troopers became silent. All but Stoffer went outside and found seats on the ground in front of Matt's window.

"Soon now," said Stoffer. "The sky is graying in the east."

"Yes," agreed Matt. He looked at his men, recalling their names one by one. Never had he felt so much a part of this group of warriors. He was immensely pleased that they had come on their own volition to be at his side in this dangerous time.

A tremendous boom broke the stillness. The twenty-four-pounders, situated a quarter of a mile down the hill from the town and trained on Castle Chapultepec, opened fire. A battery of the smaller sixteen-pounders merged their explosions with those of the big guns. The eight-inch howitzers and the ten-inch mortars joined in with their high-arching projectiles and bombs.

" 'Pears the battle has started for Chapultepec," Stoffer said.

Matt watched the flash of the large weapons. All were aimed at the castle sitting upon the narrow backbone of the high hill of Chapultepec. The projectiles of the cannon and howitzers were invisible; however, the lofting bombs of the mortars in their seven-second flights made giant arcs, fuses sputtering trails of fire in the half darkness.

The Mexican cannon at the castle began to return fire. They were slightly fewer in number than the American guns. The cannon in the city, two and a half miles from the castle, did not try to give assistance in the defense.

Matt viewed the continuous fire of the American batteries. Always there were shells in the air, so beautiful in their flight and so devastating in their fall.

Stoffer glassed the castle with a telescope. "I think our fellows are more accurate with their balls than the Mexicans are. I can see holes opening up in the walls."

"Our artillerymen have been in a lot of battles and have had a lot of practice," Chilton replied.

The incessant cannonade roared on. The storm of metal and explosives rained upon the castle. Clouds of burned powder smoke grew and drifted on the wind to the southeast.

Chilton grew weary lying on the bed and holding the telescope at the awkward angle. Gingerly he swung his feet to the floor and sat up. A black dizziness seized him, and he held on to the windowsill for support.

His body gradually adapted to the new, more upright position, and his head cleared. He laid his pillows on the sill and placed the spyglass on them. He sighted the magnified field of the telescope at the battle zone. Now and then he raised his view from the restricted area of the glass and examined the broad scope of the battle with his naked eye.

After a time, Matt tired and pain arose in his chest which grew in intensity. He lay down and closed his eyes. He dozed, and the booming salvos of the cannon and the thump of the mortars fell away to a distant, subdued rumble. The sun, like a giant golden cannonball that had escaped the battleground, moved far away to the west, sailing ever lower in a long, sliding trajectory.

Cavillin and his company of Rangers had watched the battle through the day. Their horses stood saddled in a Mexican grain field just below them. The Rangers were ready to ride in the event that the Mexican soldiers broke out from their fortifications or the enemy cavalry rode storming in from the nearby hills.

Shadows gradually came to life in the gullies and hollows and climbed out to fill the bottom of the valley, as if the dark ghost of the long dead lake was returning back across the aeons of time since it had been alive.

Night was near, and once again Tom could see the flaming trails of the bombs' high looping sky courses. The foreign, brown-skinned men in the castle had stubbornly withstood the massive and deadly barrage of solid balls and bombs for many hours.

Full darkness settled upon the valley and mountains. The American guns became quiet. The Mexican cannon also ceased firing.

"The Mex's made no effort to break out," Granger said. "They just hunkered down behind the walls and took all the iron balls we could throw at them."

"They've endured a lot of punishment, and still there was no white flag," Cavillin said. "In the morning General Scott will lambaste them again, for he doesn't want to make the same mistake as he did at the Molino. Still, taking the castle and Mexico City will be costly. Tomorrow we'll find out just how many of our men will die."

The long, shattering roll of American cannon awoke the dawn. Cavillin squatted beside his horse and raised his spyglass to observe the battlefield. The final contest had begun for Mexico City.

The Texas Rangers, grouped in two companies, were deployed a quarter of a mile east of the Belen Causeway. The dragoons, now all in one company directly under Major Sumner, were drawn up in formation a mile north at the beginning of La Veronica Causeway.

Neither band of mounted men would be of much assistance to the infantry on the narrow, raised causeways, crowded with stone arches supporting aqueducts running down the center. Further hampering the mobility of the horse soldiers were the drainage canals lining both sides of the causeways.

Cavillin's orders were to move east, paralleling Quitman's advance, and to act as a shield against a flanking attack by Mexican cavalry units that had been seen maneuvering by army scouts the evening before. Sumner would advance with Worth and give what protection he could there.

Cavillin noted that the enemy was responding to the American cannon fire with far fewer guns. The day-long Yankee fusillade of the previous day had significantly weakened the Mexican defense. Tom knew General Scott would also see the feebler resistance and would soon order the infantrymen to attack. He sighted out over the valley toward the Molino del Rey where the American force was poised.

An hour passed, and the bellowing guns abruptly stopped. An eerie silence fell.

A mile distant from Tom, a battalion of blue-clad soldiers burst out the Molino gate. Yelling shrilly, the men ran across the open field toward the cypress trees on the lower end of the castle grounds. A second group of Yankees came pouring through the southern wall of the Molino.

The Mexican infantry in the woods, pinched between the two American forces, soon began to fall back. Hundreds of red-uniformed figures broke from the grove of trees and raced in full retreat up the sloping green meadow in the direction of the castle.

The Americans, in hot pursuit, boiled out of the trees and faced the bare hillside that led to the great retaining walls of the castle terrace. Halfway up was the redoubt, to which the retreating Mexicans were running. On the terrace, Mexican soldiers, firing over the heads of their comrades, threw a murderous volley of grapeshot and musket balls at the Americans.

Tom watched the Americans charge bravely up the slope. Partway up, the assault was checked by heavy enemy fire, the Americans falling to huddle against the ground. Then they rose up from their scanty cover and charged forward again, flowing in a tide over the redoubt.

Mexicans and Americans mingled in hand-to-hand combat on the hillside.

The Americans overcame the defenders and, leaving red- and blue-clad bodies scattered on the ground, rushed toward the castle. They jammed up against the ditch at the base of the tall retaining wall. The Yankees crouched there, taking what protection they could by the ridge of the ditch while waiting for the men with the scaling ladders to come up. Now and then, when the firing slackened from above, they raised to pick off a Mexican gunner at one of the cannon.

Several soldiers ran up with the storming ladders. The ladders were flung as bridges to cross the ditch, then raised at a slant against the wall.

The first wave of men to mount the ladders were mowed down by a sheet of flame from the rifles of the Mexicans. Most of the second wave also died, falling like tiny dolls from the wall.

Fifty or more ladders were finally propped against the walls of the castle, and a few Americans gained the parapet unhurt. They began to fire at the defenders, then jumped down inside. A large body of American troops rushed over the walls and into the castle.

A large assemblage of men—Tom estimated it to be three regiments—had attacked the castle from the south. They veered left to avoid a Mexican battery firing point-blank at them, and ran onward to break through the southern wall of the castle.

The cannon inside Chapultepec fell silent, and a third group of Americans ran up the road and smashed open the main gate. They met the defenders trying to escape.

The Yankees shot mercilessly into the swarm of Mexican soldiers, dodging and running in wild fright. It was the Molino massacre in reverse.

"There it goes," cried Granger as the American colors floated over the castle. Chapultepec had fallen in less than an hour. Some men were saying it was impregnable. "Damn, what great fighting men we have. Now the drive for Mexico City can start."

"It's already begun," said Cavillin. "Look. General Worth and his men are moving north along the Veronica Causeway. Quitman is going east on the road toward the Garita de Belen."

The American infantrymen trotted close behind the horse-drawn artillery advancing swiftly toward the city. Miniaturized by the mile distance from Tom, the men appeared to be toy soldiers trailing their toy cannon. A Mexican battery of two cannon, firing straight along the road, halted Quitman's Americans. The answering Yankee fire failed to dislodge the Mexicans.

The infantrymen swarmed past their artillery and onward, directly into the muzzles of the enemy's cannons. The Mexicans abandoned their big guns and fell back to the Garita de Belen.

As the sun climbed to its zenith, the Americans continued to progress along the causeway, making swift, short charges, broken by hellish fire from the defending Mexicans. The Yankees would rest a moment and then rush forward once again. To Tom, the roadway looked to be paved with bodies.

A horrendous artillery barrage from Garita de Belen stopped Quitman and his infantrymen, killing them by the score. The soldiers tried to find shelters behind the arches of the aqueducts. But cannon fire from the side slew many who thought they were safe.

"My God. Our boys are caught," Granger said in a broken voice. "They'll all be killed."

"They have only one chance," said Cavillin, who had also

been looking at Belen. He shuddered as the Mexican cannon again belched fire. "They must storm the *garita* and silence the guns in front, or all is lost for them."

As if in response to Tom's statement, the Americans sprang forward and crashed open the mighty defensive *garita* gate. But they became penned there by fifteen cannon that began a savage barrage from a large fortified barracks beyond a wide and open park.

"They'll have to wait for darkness before they can go farther," Cavillin said.

"If they can hold on that long," replied Granger. "The *garita* is not much protection from cannon fire on the city side."

Tom shifted his attention to the battle in the north, some three miles away. The Yankees had already passed over the full length of the Veronica Causeway and turned east on Tacuba Causeway. The tall stone Garita de San Cosme had been breached.

Because of the long distance, Tom was precluded from making out the details of the fighting. But he could gauge the terrible intensity of the combat by the thundering rumble of cannon fire, the persistent pop of musketry, and a dense, thick mist of gray powder smoke more than a mile long.

"The battle will not be decided today," said Cavillin, pointing at the blood-red sun settling into the horizon. "The daylight is gone. Tonight there will be little rest for our artillerymen. The batteries of our big guns must be brought forward to support the final assault on the city."

"And our wounded must be found and carried to the hospital," Granger said in a sad voice. "There will be a lot of them. The surgeons will be busy all night, cutting off arms and legs with their saws."

Cavillin and the men were completely quiet as the sun sank out of sight behind the western mountains. The yellowish-red flame of the cannons and the tiny winking of muskets became visible.

Gradually, in a tired, ragged, tailing off, the firing ceased. Dusk fell upon the battleground and, thickening further, became black night.

"All right, men, we'll ride back to Tacubaya and see what our orders are for the night," said Cavillin.

"It's strange that the Mexican cavalry didn't get into the fighting," Granger said.

Tom agreed. The Mexican artillery and a portion of the infantry had put up a valiant defense. Still, there must be many thousands of fresh infantrymen in the city. They and the cavalry could yet make a major attack on the Americans, now exhausted after a full day of combat and terrible losses.

Chilton could no longer see in the stygian gloom of the night, but he could sense the walking wounded near him. During the day their numbers had increased threefold, coming on crutches from their beds and carrying carbines, sabers, and pistols. All waited for his orders.

"Sergeant, can you find one of our men who can ride and have him bring two horses here in the morning?" asked Chilton.

"Yes, sir. But why?"

"We'll either win or lose tomorrow. I intend to ride into the city and watch it surrender. If that is what happens."

"Are you up to riding?"

"I'll make it. I must be there."

"Then, dammit, I can also ride." Stoffer touched his injured leg. "I'll go with you. I want to see the faces of the Mexicans. I hope we can capture Santa Anna and hang him."

"Senior generals do not die in battle. Enlisted men and lieutenants are the ones who do the dying," Chilton said.

Nine

In the sour darkness of the night, Matt's ghosts returned. He and his dragoons were on a flat plain. The sun burned harshly down from a yellow sky, and all objects were vividly and starkly outlined. Mexican cavalry surrounded them, firing carbines and pistols, and stabbing with long, sharp-pointed lances.

Many of Matt's troopers lay on the ground, hideously, fatally wounded. They were calling out in a weirdly hollow sound, telling him they wanted to come and help him fight the enemy, but they could not because they were dying. Matt put out his hands to ward off the strange light that seemed to glow in their eyes.

He came away dripping with sweat, his hands thrusting out into the darkness. Slowly he lowered his arms. It was only a dream. However, the deaths and horrible injuries were not a dream. How could he ever repay his men for their gallant sacrifice?

Matt Chilton lay until the morning light pondering that most grave question.

Matt struggled erect from his bed, testing the limits of his strength. He staggered, but caught himself, and began to pull on his uniform. He looked across the candlelit room at Stoffer, standing in the doorway.

"I'll be ready soon, Sergeant," Matt said. "Tell me all that you know. Don't leave out anything."

"Yes, sir. A messenger from General Quitman just arrived at headquarters not more than fifteen minutes ago. The Mexicans have surrendered. A city official came to Quitman under a flag of truce at about four o'clock this morning. He told the general that Santa Anna had deserted the city with most of his troops. The Mexican official did not want us to fire on the town anymore. The gates were open wide."

"Scott has sent orders back to Quitman and Worth to advance cautiously. Worth is to move to the Alameda Park, and Quitman to the Grand Plaza, and take control of the National Palace. General Scott is preparing to ride into the city. Our dragoons are going to be his honor guard."

Matt smiled. The news helped to ease the ache in his chest. "The killing should soon be ended," he said. "Did you bring my horse?"

"Yes, sir. And mine too. Can you make it?"

"I'll ride into the city even if it kills me. I want to beat Scott there."

"We can do that, all right. The army band is moving out now. This ceremony will be complete. Do you want your pistols and sword?"

"When does a dragoon go anywhere without them?"

"Yes, sir, I understand." Stoffer lifted the saber from where it hung on a peg driven in the wall and handed it to the lieutenant.

Chilton put his pistols in their holsters and buckled the blade and firearms around his gaunt waist.

The two men led the horses up to the steps and, climbing from that height, tenderly drew themselves astride. Walking the horses, the men went down the grade of the hill to the El Camino Real and northerly toward Mexico City.

* * *

Cavillin, Captain Ripley, and Colonel Hays rode at a gallop along the Belen Causeway. Midway along the length of the roadway, they overtook a wagon used for gathering the corpses of the dead. It drew to a stop as they passed, and two privates climbed down.

In the scrub brush fifty yards away, several vultures were feeding on something the men could not see. The privates left the roadway and, carrying a stretcher, walked toward the carrion eaters.

"Damn ugly buzzards," Ripley said. "Already at their dinner before the dead can be found. But they do help locate the corpses after a battle."

The vultures raised their featherless heads up from their feast on the dead to look at the approaching soldiers. They craned their long red necks at the intruders, then scrambled away, flailing the hot air with thick wings. Their bloated stomachs, heavy with their gluttony, held them to the earth. The birds jostled each other as they ran awkwardly, trying to build speed. Pumping their wings fearfully, one after another became airborne, rising ponderously upward, struggling for distance and safety from the humans.

The privates waded into the brush and came back a moment later carrying a body slung between them on the stretcher. They placed the burden in the rear of the wagon.

The distant crackling of rifle fire sounded from inside the city walls. A cannon boomed half a dozen times. Then all became quiet.

"There are still some holdouts of Santa Anna's army that must be routed out," said Hays. "That kind of fighting will probably continue for several days. Guerrilla warfare on the road will go on for weeks. Let's get on into the city and to the palace."

The three officers guided a course along a broad avenue

toward a towering white building in the center of the city. Both sides of the street were lined with brown-skinned people, many with hate-filled eyes. The defeated people silently watched the victors parade past.

The National Palace was a massive stone building standing on the east border of the Grand Plaza. In the center of the great square, General Quitman's soldiers were formed up in orderly ranks facing the palace. The general paced back and forth in front of his ragged, bloodstained troops. He seemed not to notice he had lost one of his boots.

Cavillin and his comrades skirted the infantry and lined up with thirty-five or forty other officers in formation in a broad, open area in front of the palace.

Thousands of Mexican citizens stood nervously around the borders of the square. At the foot of the broad stairs leading up to the palace, Quitman had assembled those city and national government officials he could find. They fidgeted and glanced with frightened eyes at the terrible, savage Americans. Were those pale-eyed men going to execute them?

Loud cheers sounded a few blocks away. General Scott, mounted on a strong bay charger he used in battle, came into sight. A brigade of dragoons, their swords drawn and leaning on their shoulders, followed close behind him. The general was in full dress, epaulets gleaming gold against his blue uniform and the white plumes flowing from his cocked hat.

As the general entered the plaza the army band struck up "Yankee Doodle," followed by "Hail, Columbia." Scott reined his big horse in front of the troops. They greeted him with cheers that drowned out the sound of the band.

Cavillin did not cheer. Many unnecessary lives had been lost because of this man's poor judgment. But he had, in the end, won the war.

Tom saw Matt sitting his horse near his sergeant. The dragoon lieutenant's jaws were clenched, and his countenance was full of sadness. Cavillin thought he knew what lay so heavily

on the young professional soldier's mind. If Matt worried un-
duly about the dead, he was in the wrong profession.

The general listened another moment to the triumphant
shouts, then drew his saber and, in a grand sweeping swing
of the weapon, saluted his men. He lowered the blade and
began to speak.

"Brave rifles, you have gone through fire and come out
steel. You have fought a splendid battle and won a magnificent prize, one of the great cities of the world. No army ever
showed more courage. I cut you loose from all your supplies
at Vera Cruz and sent you marching inland. Never once did
you falter."

Scott looked at the barefoot General Quitman, standing
straight and motionless before his troops. "Your general and
you were to be merely a feint to distract and fool General
Santa Anna into thinking our main attack was coming from
the south. However, you accomplished much more than that.
You put Santa Anna and his men between two hammers and
did much to bring an early end to the battle. Because of that,
General Quitman is hereby appointed military governor of
Mexico City."

Thunderous applause exploded from the ranks of the soldiers. Scott waited for the tumult to end. He turned to the
gathering of Mexican officials.

"Your army has been defeated in battle. We Americans now
control the city. We'll pay for what we take and will not abuse
your women. However, I warn you, obey all my rules. My
men need shoes, blankets, and food. I hereby levy upon you
the sum of one hundred and fifty thousand dollars to be paid
as tribute to these grand American soldiers."

The general faced Quitman. "General, you will see that the
amount of money I've specified is collected by these men and
paid promptly to you. In the event that there's a delay, you
have authority to enforce payment. Use fifty thousand dollars
to purchase those supplies the army needs. I will send the

remaining money to Washington to construct a soldiers' home for the many wounded we've had.

"If there are attacks upon our patrols, I direct you to run up cannon and clear the streets with canister and grapeshot. When buildings are used by the enemy for protection, then use round shot and level those structures."

General Quitman saluted with his sword.

General Scott returned the salute. He dismounted and walked up the stairs and into the National Palace of Mexico.

Chilton and Stoffer rode along the Belen Causeway in the direction of Tacubaya. The lieutenant's face was pinched with pain, and he sagged in the saddle. A thought racing around in his mind diverted some of the ache.

"Sergeant, what did you think of the general's demand for reparation of one hundred and fifty thousand dollars from the Mexicans?"

"Good idea, but that's only a little over ten dollars for each soldier that landed with him at Vera Cruz. It should have been many times that amount."

"The family of a private that is killed will receive about three dollars per month," said Chilton. "Could a family live on that, Sergeant?"

"No. They would end up in the poorhouse. That's for certain."

"You're right. A family needs at least twenty dollars a month or fifty acres of good farmland."

They continued on without speaking, passed Chapultepec, and began to climb the hill to Tacubaya. When they came to the point where Sergeant Stoffer would turn aside, Chilton halted.

"Sergeant, I need time to do some thinking. After the evening meal, would you come to my quarters and talk with me?"

Stoffer stared at the lieutenant for a long moment. Chilton believed the man had some inkling of what his thoughts were.

"Certainly, sir," Stoffer said.

Matt slid one of the two Paterson Colts from under its holster and ran his finger along the cold iron barrel. He pointed the gun out the window.

"A beautifully balanced weapon," he said to Lieutenant Cavillin. "Thank you very much for the gift. How did you happen to have an extra pair?"

"We've lost some Rangers. The Colts are always kept as spares when needed. Today I saw you in the city with your single-shot pistols stuck in your belt and thought you could use a better gun. I knew you'd like these."

"My old pistols have served me faithfully in many battles. But these Colts are by far the better weapons."

"I brought you some powder, balls, and caps for them. You really need more than that, since you'll want to practice quite a lot. But we're short of ammunition. We'll bring back thousands of rounds when we return from Vera Cruz."

"You're going to the coast? I thought you were up for court-martial. When is that going to happen?"

Cavillin smiled his rakehell smile. "I was in direct disobedience of orders to enter the fight. But Major Hays testified in my behalf, stating his belief that I could not have stood by and let the whole regiment of dragoons be destroyed. And you, too, my friend. Then your Colonel Sumner stood up and made the damnedest speech you ever heard. He said I deserved a medal and not punishment. That Sumner would make a hell of a lawyer.

"Scott isn't about to give me a medal, but no court-martial, either. He told me that since I liked to fight so much, he would personally see that I get into every battle and skirmish we have in the future. That is why I'm going to the coast."

"How soon?" asked Matt.

"In two days. Scott has ordered General Lane and three thousand men to relieve the siege of our garrison at Puebla. Colonel Hays is taking four companies of Rangers. I will command one of them. Then, after we relieve Puebla, we'll continue on and attack any organized group of Mexicans and stop guerrilla raids on the King's Road. I estimate that we'll be gone at least five, maybe six, weeks."

"Tom, the war is about finished, and I'm glad for it."

"Soon as we can run Santa Anna to ground, then it will end."

A knock sounded on the doorjamb. Both men glanced around. Sergeant Stoffer stood in the entrance.

"Shall I come back later, Lieutenant Chilton?" asked the sergeant.

Cavillin thought he detected, just for an instant, a silent, secretive interplay between the two dragoons. Then it was gone. He must have been mistaken. What secret could they have? "No, Sergeant, don't leave," Cavillin said. "I must go now. My Rangers didn't get much fighting the last two days, and so Scott has ordered us to patrol Mexico City and rout out any Mexican guerrillas that fire on our men. Also, Santa Anna released all the convicts in the National Prison, more than thirty thousand of them. They'll cause a lot of trouble."

Cavillin rose and moved out the door. Stoffer stepped aside to let him pass, then entered.

Cavillin looked back. Matt's face was haggard, his eyes clouded. Cavillin believed the dragoon lieutenant was tormented by the death of so many of his men. In battle there was death. The living must not anguish too much over that. Dying, after all, was but a one-man job. Tom almost turned back to tell Matt that but stopped himself and went off along the path.

Neither Chilton nor Stoffer said a word until Cavillin's footsteps had died away. Then Chilton said, "Please be seated. There's something I want to discuss with you."

The two cavalrymen talked through the evening and late into the night. At the end, the lieutenant put out his hand. The sergeant grasped it and they shook, each man's eyes locked on the other's.

Chilton picked up the pair of Colt revolvers. He slid one holstered gun off the belt and handed it to Stoffer. "Take this. You'll need it, for our most dangerous battles may just be starting."

The horse soldiers, infantrymen, and one hundred and eighty supply wagons of General Lane's army stretched two miles along the King's Highway. Steep, brush-covered hills reared hundreds of feet high on both sides. The heat of the burning sun was captured by the hillsides; repeated, magnified, and thrown back upon the men and animals.

Cavillin led his company of Rangers through the choking dust that lay like a dirty brown river in the valley bottom. The shapes of his men and horses, wavering and indistinct, wrapped in streamers of dust, were like particles themselves. The sun overhead was only a hazy red disk.

The army had been on the march for four days, and it was twenty-five miles west of Puebla. Captain Sam Walker, with his four companies of mounted riflemen, rode in the vanguard, scouting for guerrilla concentrations. Cavillin's contingent of men was close behind.

A running horse carrying one of the mounted riflemen broke from the dust and sped up to Cavillin. The man pulled the horse to a halt on its haunches beside the lieutenant.

"Captain Walker has had a report of a guerrilla garrison at the town of Huamantla, a mile ahead. There is a big supply dump there. The captain is moving immediately to take the town before the guerrillas have a chance to organize. He asked that you bring your Rangers up quickly to support him."

"What is the number of guerrillas?" asked Cavillin.

"We don't know. A few hundred was the scout's best estimate."

"Walker should wait a few minutes for the infantry to come closer."

"The captain is already riding upon the Mexicans. I must go now and report to General Lane." The rifleman lashed his mount and disappeared into the dust.

Cavillin turned to Sergeant Granger. "Walker has begun action. He's depending on us. Pass the word back along the column. We'll advance at a gallop."

Gunfire erupted ahead and echoed between the hills. From the number of weapons firing, Cavillin knew a major battle had begun. He looked back, signaled his men, and kicked his horse into a run.

The Rangers crested a small rise and Huamantla lay in front of them. The town was long and narrow and strung along the King's Highway for half a mile or so. Four or five streets paralleled the road. Walker's riflemen were sweeping down every avenue.

Cavillin saw hundreds of Mexican cavalrymen racing on the cross streets to intercept Walker's forces. Withering musket fire was pouring down from the rooftops of the buildings and onto the Americans. Walker's men were being hard hit, several falling from their saddles. Horses were down, kicking and squealing as they died.

Walker was dangerously outnumbered. Cavillin's Rangers alone would not change that sufficiently enough to turn the direction of the battle. And the infantry would require at least fifteen minutes to come up and enter the fight.

Cavillin swiftly surveyed the battleground. The greatest concentration of enemy was at a giant warehouse structure on the northern edge of town. He would fight his way there, but he would not divide his force as Walker had done. That would be suicide in the face of such superior numbers.

He shouted out above the roar of gunfire. "Stay together! Always!" he commanded. "I see a company of riflemen penned down near the large warehouse. That's probably the supply dump. We'll help those men and remain there until Lane gets here with the infantry. Follow me."

They charged up the narrow street. Cavillin killed a sniper who was aiming a rifle from a rooftop. Another man, more a boy, raised up to shoot. Tom shot him in the face. The revolvers of the other Rangers were crashing, hurling lead projectiles up at the sharpshooters on the rooftops. At such close range, the Rangers hit many targets.

The immense fire of the Mexicans emptied two Ranger saddles, then another and two more. Cavillin looked back and saw wounded Rangers clinging to their mounts, and riderless horses running with the rest. *Damn you, Walker. Because of your fool move, I'm losing good men.*

A hot pain seared Cavillin's flesh as a bullet creased his ribs. His crooked battle grimace twisted more fiercely. He shot a Mexican from the rooftop, and then a second.

A speeding bullet exploded the right ear of his mount. The poor beast screamed and shook its head, almost tripping itself. Tom fired swiftly up at the rifleman and saw him tumble backward and out of sight on the roof.

The charging Rangers broke the ring of Mexican cavalrymen surrounding the remnant of one of Walker's companies. The Rangers were halted by the other Americans and spun about to add the shots of their revolvers to the fire of the riflemen.

The Mexicans, taking heavy punishment, reeled backward. They regrouped in the mouths of several streets ending near the warehouse.

"Dismount!" Cavillin ordered in a full-mouthed shout. "Use your horses as protection!"

The Rangers swung down and started to shoot over the

backs of their nervous mounts. Horses commenced to fall in greater numbers as the Mexicans lowered the point of aim of their firearms. Cavillin hated to see the animals die.

A storm of rifle fire roared on the west side of the town. Cavillin recognized the crash of the American muskets. The Yankee infantry had arrived and entered the fray, but they were still a half mile away.

"Ration your shots. Make them last," Cavillin called out to his men.

He rotated completely around, looking for Walker. He could not locate him. One of the riflemen saw Cavillin's questioning search.

"Captain Walker is dead." He pointed at the body of a man slumped on the ground at the edge of the group of Americans. "He was lanced in the side as we charged. He has bled to death."

"Where's your lieutenant?" questioned Cavillin.

"He was killed early, back up on the border of the town."

"All right," Cavillin said. He was now the senior officer of all the men here. "Pass the word, slow up your firing. Pick your targets. Make every shot count. We may be here quite a while before help arrives."

The crack of the guns slackened. Both Rangers and riflemen were using only their carbines. One of the companies of Lancers retreated. Another group saw the first leave and they, too, turned and rode away. In a moment the Americans stood alone with their dead and wounded.

The last of the stretcher bearers filed up to one of the field-hospital surgeons. The surgeon ran experienced fingers over the bloody body on the stretcher.

"Dead," he said. "Put him there." He pointed at a row of corpses.

Inside the nearby operating tent, the chief surgeon deftly

drew a sharp-toothed steel saw across the bone of a soldier's arm, below the shoulder and just above the shattered end of the limb. Two heavyweight orderlies gripped the soldier. Though unconscious, the wounded man jerked and quivered with the pain.

General Lane stomped up and down the street in front of the eight tents containing the injured. He often cast a piercing look in at the opening of the operating tent to gauge the progress of the last operation. His officers stood nearby, nervously fidgeting as they waited and watched the general. Never had they seen him so angry.

The surgeon pulled a flap of flesh and skin over the end of the bone and sewed it in place. The orderlies gently lifted the unconscious soldier, laid him on a stretcher, and carried him to one of the hospital tents. Lane looked at the surgeon. The man nodded in the affirmative.

General Lane faced his officers. "Our wounded have been tended to. Our dead have all been found. This has been a costly battle. Captain Walker and many of his men have died. Santa Anna led the attack and has escaped again. But we'll catch him."

The general hesitated and swept a piercing glare over the gathering. He pointed at the formations of men drawn up in long rows both ways along the street. His voice crackled with implacable hatred. "This town belongs to your men. They've conquered it and may take whatever they want. The women, the gold, the silver. Anything at all. I want this place to remember the day they helped Santa Anna. Go tell the men exactly what I said.

"This town is theirs and yours."

Ten

Cavillin listened to the blood roar of the male hunting pack, deep and savage, coming from all parts of Huamantla. It had continued for better than an hour now as the Americans stormed through the town, destroying and pillaging. He heard a pistol shot now and again, a soldier firing in exuberance of his license to sack and plunder, or a Mexican dying while defending his possessions or his woman.

Cavillin lay on a bed in the dimly lit room of some unknown family's home. Where had the people gone? Had they run from Santa Anna, or later, during the attack of the Americans? It didn't really matter. Men and women were expendable during combat. But General Lane had been wrong in his deliberate violence against civilians after the battle had ended. Tom scowled at himself; that was a fine line to draw. However, he wanted no part in further hurting the people of Huamantla.

The door of the room was shoved abruptly open. Tom's hand snaked out for his pistols, lying on the bed beside him.

Sergeant Granger came in smiling and dragging a young woman hardly more than a girl, by the hand. He spoke not a word, simply flinging the girl toward Tom and leaving, slamming the door.

The young woman staggered a few steps before she could catch her balance. She backed away from Tom, hesitatingly, a step at a time. Suddenly she sprang to the door and yanked it wide. She jumped to the ground and hurriedly looked back to check Tom's action.

Cavillin did not stir. The fear on her face saddened him.

A man shouted nearby and Tom heard running feet drawing nearer. The young woman flung a glance in the direction of the call.

She hurried back inside, closed the door, and shaking, huddled against the wall.

The man hit the door with his shoulder. It slammed open, half torn from its leather hinges. One of Walker's mounted riflemen stormed inside.

Tom stood up swiftly, his pistol in hand.

The man slid to a halt. His face blanched. "Goddamn! I'm sorry, Lieutenant Cavillin. I didn't know you were here." He backed speedily out the door and was gone.

Tom spoke in Spanish to the girl. "You may go." His command of the language was good. As a lawman in Texas for six years, he had by necessity learned the tongue of the Mexicans.

She watched the redheaded American and listened to the cries and noises outside for a few seconds. Then she shook her head in the negative. "I will remain here for a short time if I may," she said.

"Certainly," replied Tom. "Please shut the door." He evaluated her as she moved to comply with his request. She was pretty in a dark, square-faced sort of way. Beneath the printed calico dress, her body was full and rounded.

He lay back down, propping his head up with a pillow. She took a seat on a chair and sat tensely, poised to dart away if he should move toward her.

Weariness from the battle rode heavy on Tom, and the wound on his chest pained beneath the bandages. Lulled by the heat and the softness of the feather tick on the bed, he half dozed off.

The young woman examined him through slitted eyes. His revolver lay loose in his hand. Was he truly asleep or merely trying to trick her? She hated those horrible Yankees, but she was not sure she could grab this man's gun and kill him with it before he woke up.

The great General Santa Anna had ridden up and down the street shouting, to warn the people of the town that the Americans would kill and rob them. He had not told the whole truth. Things were much worse than the general had said.

The door swung ajar quietly. Sergeant Granger peered inside. He looked at the young woman on the chair, and Cavillin asleep on the bed.

"Go to his bed or I'll take you to other men," the sergeant whispered in a threatening voice.

He held out a bottle of tequila. She came hesitatingly and took it. The sergeant winked at her and left.

Tom snapped awake with the movement of the bed. The young woman sat beside him. She had a bottle in her hand, offering it to him.

"Tequila?" she said.

"Where did you get it?"

"Your friend brought it." She tried to smile.

She is a woman trying to survive in a time of war, thought Tom as he saw the timid, fragile smile. He recognized the momentary curve of her lips as a signal from a woman to a man, an unspoken offering in exchange for safety. He accepted the offering and the condition attached to it. In this time and this place of savage violence and death, it was the only thing to do. Tom reached up and pulled her gently down on the feather tick beside him.

"Count my legs, Lieutenant Chilton. Please raise the sheet and count my legs," pleaded the wounded dragoon. "I can't feel them and I think this surgeon is lying to me." He swung his feverish gaze from Matt to Campbell and back.

Matt lifted the white covering and then lowered it. "You have two legs and two feet, Culberson," he said.

Chilton sensed the eyes of the other injured troopers in the large room on him. He turned to the pallid, longtime wounded. "You all will soon be going home. General Lane and several of our regiments are on the march opening the road to Vera Cruz. When they return, you will be taken to the coast and shipped out to New Orleans and on home."

"And what then?" asked a man. He held up a stub of an arm, his hand and forearm missing. "How do I harness a horse or hold a plow with this?"

"The army will take care of its own," Matt said.

"Like hell," growled the man.

Campbell walked to the door. Matt followed.

"The heat makes them grouchy," said the surgeon as he stepped outside.

"No. Being mutilated in pain, and fearful of the future makes them grouchy," Matt said. "Why couldn't Culberson feel his legs or move?"

"A bullet has severed his spinal cord. He will never recover. How is your injury? How do you feel?"

"The ache in my chest is continuous. Sometimes worse than others. However, my strength is slowly returning."

"I saw you riding earlier today. Don't overdo it."

"Just into the city and back. Never more than that. Thanks for taking care of my men. If there's ever anything I can do, just tell me."

"Come and visit them often. Sometimes they feel they've been forgotten."

"They'll never leave my memory." Matt tapped his forehead with a finger. "I'll be back."

* * *

Matt sat on a wicker chair in the shade beneath the tree near his room. He waited, his eyes closed, his head resting on the high back of the chair.

The leaves of the tree started to flutter against the hazy blue sky as a breeze came puffing up the hill. A scent of dust reached Matt. He raised his head and saw Stoffer riding a horse and leading another, coming up the street.

The sergeant stepped down and found a seat on the ground and leaned against the base of a tree. He straightened his leg, making a wry face at the pain. He began to fan himself with his hat. Neither man spoke.

The sun walked slowly down along its ancient path, disappeared behind the lava mountains, and the big stars came out in the evening dusk. The sweltering heat began to leak away into the darkening sky. An orange glow formed on the eastern horizon, heralding the rise of the moon.

"Are you ready, Sergeant?" asked Matt.

"Yes, sir." Stoffer got up awkwardly, favoring his leg. "How many miles tonight?"

"Want to try for twenty?"

"I'm game to try that many."

Matt ranged his view down the hill. Others of his walking wounded, in pairs and in threes, were riding in the direction of Mexico City. The number of men who could ride had grown to fifteen.

Chilton and Stoffer climbed astride and headed into the new darkness toward the city. Matt tried to relax, to adjust to the rhythm of the horse's step. With every hoof fall, a twinge of pain ran through his chest.

The night deepened on the land, and the black bats came and began their tumbling dance in the darkness. Matt traced one's erratic flight in the pale moonlight for a brief time before it vanished in the gloom. He felt a cooler breeze on his cheek.

He reviewed the recent days. Following his long conversation with the sergeant, every one of his company of dragoons had come, one at a time, to talk with him. He had explained a daring and perilous plan to them, a strategy to benefit all the injured and crippled of the company. To a man, they took his hand in a vow of secrecy and mutual agreement to help him accomplish it.

Every night they saddled and rode into the city. However, they did not linger at the attractions there but continued onward, crossing the plain of the old lake bed and traveling far up into the mountains. Their bodies, weakened by injury and inactivity, had gradually grown stronger with the long rides.

The dragoons always sought new routes for their journeying. Soon they would know the terrain nearly as well as the natives. Darkness would not hamper their travels, for the immense heat of the day and the necessity to conceal their true destination had made Chilton and his men into mostly nocturnal animals.

Matt knew that in a very few days the rides of his dragoons would have a different and hazardous purpose.

Cavillin walked beside the two parallel lines of wagons that crowded the Vera Cruz street and stretched six blocks to the waterfront. The strong oaken beds of the vehicles were heavily laden with military supplies and covered with tarpaulins lashed down with rope. Sentries with muskets on their shoulders constantly patrolled around the wagons to prevent theft.

Tom estimated the number of wagons at one hundred and fifty. That was only half the quantity that would be required to haul all the medical supplies, ammunition, and other provisions needed by Scott's army in its occupation of Mexico City, and in keeping the El Camino Real open.

General Lane's regiments had arrived in Vera Cruz weary from two major battles, many skirmishes, and three weeks of hard marches. The siege of Puebla had been lifted after three days of fighting. Of the two thousand and two hundred soldiers of the garrison, only four hundred were still fit for combat.

Tom was amazed that such a small force had been able to hold control of the city of eighty thousand people, the second most important population center in Mexico.

General Lane's army had remained in Puebla three days. The Rangers and the mounted riflemen were in the saddle from daylight to dark, scouting ahead along the road to Vera Cruz and into the surrounding mountains. They had encountered five bands of guerrillas that stood and fought. The Americans won every battle.

By the fourth day, the general was satisfied that Santa Anna's shrinking forces were no longer a threat to the garrison at Puebla. He ordered the advance toward the coast, and the troops and wagons again strung out on the El Camino Real. He continued to send his mounted fighters out to attack every concentration of enemy resistance the scouts could find.

In Vera Cruz, Cavillin found quarters for his men and released them from duty until the wagon train would leave for Mexico City. He had one more task for himself before he relaxed, and that was to make certain the .36-caliber ammunition for the Rangers' revolvers was included in the supplies being transported inland.

Tom walked down the sloping street, past the wagons, and toward the warehouses on the waterfront. Craftsmen, wheelwrights, blacksmiths, and carpenters bustled about, making last-minute repairs on the vehicles. Civilian teamsters and soldiers with nothing to do loafed on the sidewalk. Tom spoke to those men he recognized.

The man walking in front of Tom abruptly halted. "God Almighty," he exclaimed. "Ain't that a beautiful sight."

Tom angled up to the side of the fellow and gazed ahead. A woman wearing a yellow dress was approaching on the sidewalk. She wore a wide-brimmed yellow hat, the same color as her dress. Both matched the golden yellow of her hair.

She moved with a measured, gliding step, and from time to time she fanned herself with a tiny Chinese fan hardly larger than an open hand. Her face was finely, delicately sculptured, with flawless skin. There was a slight flush to her cheeks. From the heat of the sun, thought Tom.

"Where did she come from?" Tom asked the nearby man. "Why is someone like her in Vera Cruz?"

"She takes a little stroll most days," said the man. "Ussing brought her. She's one of his women."

"What do you mean, one of Ussing's women? Who's Ussing?"

"Where have you been for the past few months?"

"At Mexico City and thereabouts."

"Then you left before Ussing arrived in Vera Cruz. He's a whoremaster. Got himself a big house near the waterfront. That there gal is his favorite, so I'm told."

The man scrutinized Tom's worn and sun-faded clothing. "She's not for the likes of you and me. It'd take your whole month's wages just to touch her. Only officers can afford her price."

"That high a price, eh?" Cavillin said.

"Ussing is getting rich with all the army and navy officers here. And late at night, I've also seen some mighty fancy-dressed Mexicans going into Ussing's place."

Cavillin started to walk on, his eyes lingering on the woman.

"Wait a minute," said the man. "Ussing has a sideline. Maybe you picked up some gold or silver trinkets, or some jewels there in Mexico City. He'll buy them from you. The soldiers and Mexican thieves bring him things. However, let me warn you, he only pays a small portion of what they are really worth."

"He buys stolen things?"

"Don't call them that to his face. He says he only buys lost objects that have been found. He's a hard man, and he has some hired help that's also tough." The fellow looked at the two Colt revolvers on Cavillin's belt. "I take it you're one of those Texas Rangers, but Ussing would take you too."

Tom grinned crookedly at the man and lengthened his stride to pull ahead.

Sophia walked leisurely up the sidewalk of the street. The men stepped aside to allow her to pass unimpeded. She smiled at those who touched their hats in greeting.

Her health had been stable during the past week, and there had been no recurrence of the severe bleeding from her lungs. If she walked slowly and did not breathe deeply, she seldom coughed. Today she felt moderately strong. Her spirits were high, and she thought that was because of the presence of all the young faces of the soldiers who had returned safely from deep inside the hostile land of Mexico.

She noted the vast array of wagons on the street. Their numbers were growing swiftly. Soon all would be loaded and rolling up through the mountains to Mexico City. Ussing and she and the other women would be accompanying the wagon train.

Sophia had tried to persuade Wade to remain in Vera Cruz. Their business was very profitable. In another two months she would have enough money accumulated to book passage on a ship and return to New Orleans. There she could live comfortably and, with the proper medical treatment, perhaps be healed of her consumption. Further, she was not certain she could withstand the long trek over the mountains to Mexico City.

Ussing had rejected her pleas to stay on the coast. He was adamant that much greater wealth awaited them at the fabulous city deep in the interior of Mexico.

She could not live and work in Vera Cruz without the protection of Ussing. So in the end she had agreed to accompany Wade to Mexico City.

A man shoved himself away from the wall of a building where he had been leaning and trailed a few paces behind Sophia. He raised his head and pulled in a breath of air. As he caught the pleasant aroma of Sophia's perfume, left floating in the air in her wake, he smiled broadly at his friends. They laughed good-naturedly.

Sophia glanced back at the man. His smile widened. "Most pleasing, that rose water you have on, ma'am," the man said.

Sophia nodded her acceptance of the roughly worded compliment. Some women were afraid to be among large gatherings of men. Sophia knew that men in a group were the most chivalrous. Men were the most dangerous when they were in a small band and knew each other, for then the primeval male instinct sometimes took control of their emotions and a woman was at risk.

A redheaded man in battered, dusty clothing and wearing two big pistols came into Sophia's view. He was reflectively rubbing the stiff stubble of beard on his chin. Then their eyes met and he whipped his hat off.

Above the demarcation line where his hat had protected his forehead from the sun, his skin was startlingly white. His eyes were colored a pale, grayish blue. For some unexplainable reason Sophia wondered what shade they would be in combat or while making love.

He smiled. In it there was an expression of understanding, as if he had read her thoughts. She blushed, the very first time in a long, long time. She quickened her pace and passed him by.

Eleven

The three infantrymen came from the dim interior of the Cantina el Pescador. They halted on the street and stood blinking in the bright sunlight.

The fat man, Seplow, belched loudly. "A gallon of beer sure makes a man feel good," he said.

"It doesn't help much against this damn Mexican sun," said Sickels, raising his hand to shade his eyes. "Let's cross over and walk on the shady side of the street."

The third soldier wiped the back of a hand across his coarse lips. His head was long and horselike, and set on thick shoulders. His bleached blue eyes were sullen and bored as they ranged up and down the street.

"I need me a woman or a good fight," growled the man.

"There's a sight of difference between fighting and loving," Sickels said.

Seplow laughed deep in his fat chest. "Sickels, you haven't seen how Langrell treats his women." He looked at Langrell. "What kind of woman will it be? White or brown?"

Langrell reached into a pocket and brought out some silver and copper coins. He counted them on the palm of his hand and shoved it all back into his pants pocket. "Looks like it'll have to be a brown-skinned gal this time," he said.

"Then away we go up to the hilltop, where the cheap whorehouses are," said the fat man.

The three soldiers stepped into the street and wound a course through the columns of wagons. Langrell stopped abruptly as they drew near the opposite sidewalk.

"Damn it all to hell," cursed Langrell. "I stepped in horse shit. I can't make love with stinking horse dung on my boots." He raised his boot to show his comrades.

"Well, now, I expect you could if you wanted to pay an extra two bits." Seplow chuckled.

Langrell glowered at Seplow. "Don't laugh at me or I'll mess up your mug."

Seplow's smile faded. "Hell, don't be so testy," he said in a mollifying tone.

Sickels pointed at a wheelwright and his helper, working on an army wagon. "There's a kid with some rags in his pocket. Get him to clean your boots."

A short, square-built man and a youth in badly soiled clothing with grease smudges on his face labored at the rear of a loaded wagon. A corner of the vehicle was jacked up, the axle supported on a square of timber. The man held a heavy, iron-rimmed wheel ready as his young apprentice smeared grease from a tin can on the axle. A wad of cotton cloth hung from one of his back pockets.

As the three soldiers watched, the wheelwright hoisted the six-foot wheel and impaled the hub on the axle. The locking burr was made fast to hold the wheel in place. The man moved to throw his weight on the end of a long pry pole and raised the bed of the wagon slightly. The boy kicked the block of wood aside. The wagon was lowered to the ground.

Langrell stalked forward. He called out, "Hey, kid, bring some of those rags and wipe my boots. I'll give you two pennies."

The youth glanced quickly at the wheelwright. The man shook his head in the negative and motioned for the boy to gather up the tools.

"Fellow, tell your boy to wipe my boots," Langrell called

again, his tone turning surly. He continued to advance, his feet tramping hard on the ground. "I'll raise my price to three cents. That's a fair price."

"I'm teaching him to handle iron and wood and be a wheelwright, not a bootblack," replied the wheelwright, facing the soldiers more directly. He looked at Langrell's boots and continued speaking in a mild voice. "You can use a piece of rag to clean your boots if you want. Les, give the man a strip."

"The hell with that," barked Langrell, his eyes narrowing like those of a sniper with a target in view. "You civilian contractors think you are better than us soldiers. You follow the army around and get paid ten times what we do. We do the fighting and you get rich."

The short man cast a calculating look at the soldiers. "Well, maybe you fellows have done some fighting," he said with a doubtful expression, "but I've got work to do and must be going." He gestured at the boy to gather the tools.

Langrell's face reddened as he understood the implied slur in the wheelwright's words. His voice stabbed out. "I'll tell you what you're going to do. Tell the boy to clean my boots or I'll kick the hell out of you and then wipe my boots all over him."

A fearful expression washed over the face of the slightly built youth, and he backed away nervously.

The wheelwright's jaw was ridged beneath sun-browned skin. His calloused, work-hardened hands folded into bony hammers. "That might take some hard doing, soldier boy," he said.

Langrell stepped forward and reached out for the boy. The wheelwright moved swiftly to intercept the man.

Langrell's long arms, which had been stretching to catch the boy, suddenly shifted direction. A hard fist lashed out to slam the wheelwright on the side of the head. The smaller man staggered and fell to his knees.

The soldier drew back his leg and kicked at the dazed man.

The wheelwright, speedily recovering, rolled to the side, avoiding the blow. He sprang instantly erect.

The wheelwright shook his head once, then, with astounding swiftness and strength, bore in from the side. His arms pumped as his fist pummeled the big soldier. Two blows thudded into the man's ribs, then a flurry smacked against the long horse-face.

Langrell reeled away from the punishing blows. Blood gushed from his broken nose and cut lips. "Help me!" he bellowed at his cohorts.

Seplow and Sickels leaped to aid Langrell. The wheelwright pivoted and sprang to meet them. He crashed into Sickels, caught him over a shoulder, heaved mightily upward, and flipped him behind to land on the ground with a bone-jarring thump.

Before the wheelwright could turn, Seplow lunged in and clasped him around the chest in a powerful embrace. The wheelwright began to struggle to break free, his muscles straining and bulging.

"Hurry and help me, you bastards," yelled Seplow. "He's strong as an ox."

Sickels scrambled to his feet, rushed in, and struck the wheelwright a brutal lick over the heart then immediately gave him another savage wallop in the same spot.

Langrell bounded forward. "You son of a bitch, I'll gouge out your eyes," he roared at the wheelwright.

The slender youth dashed in front of Langrell. His hands were thrust out as if he could ward off the big soldier. "No, don't," he cried in a scared, high-pitched voice. "Leave him alone. I'll wipe your boots clean."

"Too late," snapped Langrell. He slapped the youth left and right on the face, then, with a harder blow, boxed him aside, and the boy fell on the hard earth.

With a pleased, grim gleam in his eyes, Langrell marched

upon the struggling wheelwright, now held pinioned between Seplow and Sickels.

Cavillin walked down the gentle slope of the street past the lines of wagons. His heart was pounding pleasantly in remembrance of the beautiful blond woman. A man should see such a pleasurable sight every day. It was doubly satisfying in a land so far from home.

Ahead of Tom, some soldiers and a few civilians left the shade near the buildings and began to congregate around men fighting near the wagons. Tom heard curses and shouts from the combatants, and dust puffed up from under their stomping boots.

He drew closer and saw that three men were in soldier's uniforms. The other two fellows were dressed as civilians. One was small, not yet a man.

As Cavillin watched, the boy sprang in to halt the attack of one of the soldiers upon the older civilian, held tightly and powerless to defend himself. The youth shouted out something about cleaning boots. The soldier hit him several times.

The fight was damn uneven. Tom wondered why none of the surrounding circle of men were trying to stop it.

Tom did not consciously decide to enter the lopsided brawl. His blood began to cascade through his veins, hot and swift. He found himself moving in long strides. A soldier was shoved out of the way. Tom heard him cursing behind. Then Tom was grabbing for the man who had hit the boy.

He clamped hold of a handful of long hair and yanked backward. The soldier whirled partway around as he was propelled to the rear. His fist began to swing a haymaker at his new opponent.

Cavillin punched the man in the face, a vicious blow. He felt a wonderfully satisfying vibration run up his arm as the blow landed. Maintaining his hold on the hair, Tom again bashed the man solidly with his fist.

The soldier's eyes closed. Cavillin released the hair, stepped back a short distance, and knocked the soldier flat on the ground. Quicker than Seplow and Sickels could release the wheelwright and defend themselves, Cavillin was upon them. Seplow was closer, and Tom battered him ruthlessly, first the face, then his body, and back to his face when Seplow dropped his guard. The soldier collapsed.

Tom spun around to meet the attack he expected from the third soldier. The man was retreating, backing away from the civilian, who was pounding him unmercifully with hard, rapid blows.

Cavillin went to kneel beside the boy. "Are you all right?" he asked as he caught the boy by the shoulders and sat him up.

The youth wiped at the blood trickling from his lips and mixing with the grease smears on his chin. "Yes," he replied in a husky voice.

Tom released the youth and reared back on his haunches. Beneath the grease smudges, the tanned face of the young person was extremely smooth and without a sign of a beard. The thick brown hair was cut quite short and lay close to the scalp, like a fine, luxurious pelt of a prime high-mountain otter.

He recalled the feel of the youth's shoulders in his hands. Though firmly muscled from work on the wagons, those shoulders had been slenderly built and without the bone mass and muscle hardness a young man would have under similar labor.

Deep within his male being, Tom felt his instinct telling him without a doubt, that a girl—more, a young woman—sat before him.

"Well, I'll be damned," he said softly. The smears of grease were deliberate. So, too, was the short haircut and stained, baggy clothing that camouflaged the femaleness of her in this dangerous, war-torn land.

She climbed to her feet, backed away from Cavillin's intense examination, and looked past him.

Tom twisted to glance in the same direction. The wheel-wright stood close on his side. He studied Tom as if trying to read his thoughts.

"The boy does not appear to be hurt much," Cavillin said.

The worry lines lessened in the wheelwright's face. Apparently the man had not recognized Les's true sex. "Thank you for helping me. They had me a little outnumbered."

"So I noticed." Tom held out his hand. "I am Lieutenant Thomas Cavillin of the Texas Rangers." He knew he would never have introduced himself with so much detail if it had not been for the girl standing wide-eyed and watching so interestedly. Tom laughed silently at himself for his behavior.

"Carl Hampton." The man shook his hand with a viselike grip. "This is my son, Les."

"Hello," said Tom, and extended a hand.

The girl hesitated and then gave her own.

Cavillin pressed the small, firm hand. "I'm pleased to know you," he said.

"Thank you for your help," she replied. "Those mean men would have hurt my father." She withdrew her fingers from Tom's grasp.

"Glad to be of assistance." Tom smiled at her.

Les stepped back, her hand rose, and the ends of her fingers touched the short hair on the side of her head. Such a natural feminine gesture, thought Tom. How could anyone misinterpret the lightly chiseled features of the young woman, even under the dark stains of grease, as that of a male? Looking closely, he could see where the mounds of her young breasts pressed against the shirtfront.

Tom swung his sight to Hampton. "You are a contractor for the army?" he asked.

"Yes. I signed a one-year contract to keep the wagons rolling. The army shipped my wagon, forge, tools, and me and Les from New Orleans. My contract ends in January. The war has taken longer than I thought it would. I may extend for two or three more months."

"The Mexican army is beaten, but there are still considerable guerrilla forces to whip," Cavillin said. "There are many thousands of pounds of supplies to transport to Mexico City, and then all the armaments and injured soldiers to bring back to Vera Cruz to return to the States. Hundreds of wagons will be needed."

"We'll go inland with the wagon train," said Hampton. He stared along the columns of vehicles on the street. "That's where I'll be needed. And also, I don't want to leave Mexico without seeing Mexico City."

"Where do you plan to go after the war?" questioned Cavillin.

"We'll probably go back to New Orleans. However, since I've been here I've heard a lot about Texas. You being from there, tell me about it. Is the country as rich and growing as fast as people say?"

"It's truly filling up with people coming from the East. There must be a quarter of a million there now. Once the Mexicans are beaten and the threat of them marching back north is ended, Texas will grow even more rapidly. A skilled wheelwright would find plenty of work. Any of the larger towns should be a good place to start a business."

Seplow groaned, mumbled a few curses, and sat up. Half conscious, he stared around.

"Hampton, it may be best if you and Les leave now," Cavillin said. "I'll stay here a little while, and when these fellows come all the way to their senses, I'll have a little talk with them. After that I believe they'll leave you alone if they run into you again."

"I greatly appreciate that," replied Hampton. "Les, let's be on our way." He spoke to Cavillin. "Are you going inland with the wagon train?"

"Yes."

"Then we might see you again."

"Perhaps so." Cavillin watched after them as they loaded their tools into a light wagon, clucked the team of horses into motion, and went off on one of the side streets.

Tom saw the girl look back at him as the wagon turned the corner. He felt again the pleasant increase in tempo of his heart from a woman's direct, interested gaze. A grease-smudged face crowded the blond woman's memory for space in his mind.

Twelve

Cavillin came to the street fronting on the Bay of Campeche and angled off on the wide, stone-paved area between the piers and the warehouses. The waterfront was crowded with ships' officers, Mexican merchants, and squads of stevedores loading thirty or more horse-drawn wagons. The warehouses, with doors opened wide, were speedily being emptied.

An army supply lieutenant, aided by a supply sergeant at the entrance of each warehouse, was attempting to direct the stevedores and warehousemen and at the same time negotiate with the many merchants trying to sell a wide variety of goods.

All the pier space was full of ships unloading. Other ships, their captains weary of the long wait in the harbor and wanting to turn over their cargo to the army, had sailed in closer to the beach and dropped anchor. Harbor lighters, each rowed by several dark-skinned Mexicans, were transporting the ships' freight into the docks.

Tom drew close to the supply officer. He called out above the voices of the other men. "Have you loaded the .36-caliber ammunition for the Texas Rangers' guns?"

"What?" said the officer, ignoring the clamoring Mexican merchants and focusing his attention on Tom.

Tom shoved in nearer to the officer and raised his voice. "I say, have you loaded the pistol ammunition for the Texas Rangers?"

"Not yet. Come over here." The officer broke free of the throng around him. "Are you one of the Rangers that came in with General Lane?"

"Yes. I'm Lieutenant Cavillin."

"Then as far as I'm concerned, that gives you preference over these storekeepers. Your .36-caliber ammunition is on my manifest. It is not loaded yet, but we'll get right to it."

"How many rounds has the general's quartermaster ordered?"

"Thirty thousand."

"That's not nearly enough."

"Maybe so, but that's all I'm to load."

Tom pulled his revolver and held it out for the lieutenant to see. "This holds five rounds. I can easily empty it with aimed shots in three seconds. There are almost five hundred Rangers. Thirty thousand rounds would not last us long. How much ammunition do you have in stores?"

The lieutenant's gaze lingered on the Colt revolver for a few seconds. Then he ran his fingers down the listing of items on several pages until he came to the correct entry. "Enough powder, balls, and caps for one hundred and twenty thousand rounds."

"We need most of that sent inland. How about one hundred thousand going on the wagons and leaving the remainder warehoused here?"

The lieutenant looked back at the manifest. His pencil moved briefly.

"I'll be damned," said the lieutenant. "That's a strange coincidence. I must've misread the amount that was ordered. It's exactly what you said you needed. I'll load all of it this afternoon. I'll put everything in wagons numbered one hundred eight-three and eighty-four. The numbers are painted on the sides of the wagon beds. You can keep an eye on them yourself."

"That's a favor I owe you," said Tom. "Call it in when you want to."

"Then I'll do it now. I've been hearing some mighty powerful tales of how good those Paterson Colts are. You Rangers seem to have nearly all of them to yourselves. I'd like one to replace my single-shot Army-issue pistol."

"All right. I can have it for you tomorrow morning. Where will you be?"

"Right here. It'll take me another day to load all these provisions. My name is Herrington."

"Good. I'll see you then. Where is the nearest bathhouse and laundry?"

"Four blocks that way to Morales Street," Herrington said, pointing. "It's outside the restricted area. You can get anything you want there. The bathhouse is one block to the left on Morales."

Cavillin paid for a bath and the washing of his clothes. For two bits more he had his garments pressed and dried with hot irons. He soaked leisurely in a tub of sun-warmed water until the laundryman called to tell him his clothing was ready. In the same block a barber shortened his shaggy hair by four inches and shaved off his three-week growth of beard.

Tom stepped from the barbershop onto the street. He stretched, feeling the cleanliness of his body and the freshly pressed clothing caressing his skin. A powerful feeling of well-being swept over him. It was wonderful to be alive and strong. A little entertainment with a pretty woman and all would be complete.

He checked the height of the sun above the mountains to the west. Two more hours of daylight were left. He ambled toward his quarters. A short nap, and then he would find the blond woman with the nice smile.

* * *

Tom woke to night and the plaintive wind song of the city. He buckled his pistols around his waist and went out on the sidewalk. A streetlight showed as a yellow pool in the darkness four or five blocks toward the center of the city. The immediate area was lit only by the pale light from the stars and the moon low on the wet horizon of the sea. A breeze was blowing from Campeche Bay, damp and somewhat cooler than the walls of the buildings, which still held memories of the heat of the day.

Men's voices and the crunch of their boots on the cobblestone street drifted out of the heavy gloom. Weaker but still discernible, the music of a piano came from the far-off waterfront. Cavillin walked unhurriedly in that direction, moving silently through the night shadows of the foreign city.

Five sailors, laughing and talking among themselves, passed in the middle of the street. They never sensed Tom's presence on the sidewalk. Their voices faded away behind him.

Cavillin heard men's voices raised in a harsh argument. He slowed and peered ahead. Against a lighter shade of gray near the whitewashed wall of a building, two men stood facing each other. One of the taut figures burst into swift action, drawing some object from inside his coat and slashing at the second. That man tried to dodge away. Tom heard the whack of iron upon the man's skull. The man with the weapon violently struck his opponent twice more, hammering him to the ground.

Staring hard into the weak light, Tom thought the man being beaten so savagely was in an officer's uniform, and the assailant in civilian dress.

"Stop that!" bellowed Cavillin. He sprang forward, drawing his revolvers.

The attacker's head lifted abruptly. His sight flicked out at the man rushing at him in the murk. In one lithe bound, he was ten feet away and in a streaking run. Instantly he was swallowed up by the night.

Tom stared into the darkness after the man. The fellow had moved effortlessly, leaping out of sight like a big cat. Tom was certain that the man was dressed in civilian clothes, dark suit and white shirt.

Cavillin squatted beside the man on the stone pavement. He rolled the slack body to its back and pressed his fingers to the side of the throat, probing for the pulse in the carotid artery. The face of Herrington, the army supply officer, gazed up with blank, dead eyes.

Tom removed his hand. Herrington would not be wanting the Paterson Colt now. There was nothing to be done for the man except report his murder. But why had he been killed?

Skillfully played piano music flowed from the large, stone-walled house occupying the corner of the block. Two glowing lights hung from iron hooks in the patio that led to the front entrance. A lieutenant commander of the navy entered Ussing's brothel as Cavillin approached.

Cavillin had reported the murder of Herrington to an army lieutenant, the duty officer of the day, at his office near the docks. Then, after obtaining directions from the man as to the location of Ussing's establishment, Tom had proceeded there.

He entered the patio, strode across it, and shoved open the door. At the right end of the long room seven officers, a mixture of army and navy men, were in resplendent full dress uniform. Only their swords were missing. They sat with drinks in their hands and talked with three blond women. One was the woman Cavillin had seen on the street. She was facing partially away and had not noticed his entrance.

An eighth man, a young ensign, leaned on the end of a piano, listening to a fourth woman playing a light, airy piece of music. The musical selection came to a close, and the ensign caught the woman's hand. She smiled, stood up, and led him from the room.

Tom moved toward the remaining group of people. He marveled at the women's elegant dresses. *I must appear to be a vagabond in comparison with these men in their fine uniforms,* he thought. He began to smile at that notion.

The woman he had seen on the street looked past the officers surrounding her and saw Tom as he drew closer. She was very quiet as she watched him. Then she excused herself and walked to meet Tom. He doffed his hat and half bowed to the woman.

The woman's rouged lips formed into a gracious smile. "I am Sophia. I welcome you." Tom grasped the soft hand she offered, enclosing it within his own. It was quite warm, almost hot to his touch.

"I am Thomas Cavillin."

"May I have your hat, Thomas?" Sophia asked.

Cavillin started to give his hat to Sophia when movement at the far end of the room caught his attention. A man had entered and was crossing toward the officers and the women.

Tom's smile fell away. The man wore a black suit and a white shirt. He walked strongly, with a supple grace. His face was the exact shape of the one that had risen up over Herrington in the night. Though Cavillin had not been able to see the details of the killer's countenance, he knew with certainty that this was the same man.

Ussing sensed the man near Sophia staring at him. He switched his view to look. He hid the shock of discovering the tall man who had shouted at him and charged out of the dark when Herrington had died.

Wade knew the man had recognized him. He raised a hand to clasp the coat close to his shoulder holster. He might have to kill the stranger.

Wade cursed silently to himself. Herrington was still causing trouble, even after death. It had been bad luck to have to do business with such a man, but there had been no alternative. Wade had not known when General Scott's army would break through the bands of guerrillas infesting the El Camino and appear at Vera Cruz. To anticipate the event, Wade had scheduled Captain Tarpon to return at regular intervals to pick up the gold and silver as it accumulated. With the worst of luck, General Lane had arrived when Ussing had acquired a substantial quantity of treasure, and Tarpon was not due in port for another ten days. Lane was departing on his return to Mexico City much sooner than that.

Planning to trail the army inland, Ussing could not wait for his own ship to haul the valuables to New Orleans. He had gone to Herrington, the supply officer in charge of all the transfer of cargo into and out of Vera Cruz. The lieutenant agreed to transport four of Ussing's crates in one of the army's chartered ships.

Herrington had examined one of the containers and discovered the nature of Ussing's freight. The foolish lieutenant had demanded a higher price for his crooked work. However, that had been after the ship had already left port on its voyage north, a time when he was no longer needed. So he had died.

Sophia saw the redheaded Cavillin look past her, and his eyes become frosty and hard. His hands swung to hover near the butts of the pistols on his belt.

She twisted to look in the same direction. Ussing was poised on the balls of his feet. His face and body held that deadly tenseness that Sophia knew preceded violent, ruthless action. She did not know why the men were enemies, but she feared for Cavillin. She glanced at him, intending to try to divert him from Wade's wrath.

Cavillin's smile was tight-lipped. He showed no worry or alarm. He was as ready to fight as Ussing. Maybe more so. If either man made a sudden gesture, guns would be drawn and someone would die.

"Who is that man?" Cavillin asked in a flinty voice.

Sophia jumped slightly at the sharply worded question. "Wade Ussing," she replied in a tone hardly above a whisper.

"I thought it might be," Tom said. The lawman in him felt disappointment. As an experienced Ranger, Cavillin knew he could never convict Ussing in a court of law for killing Herrington. A man such as the whoremaster and thief would have men to swear he was somewhere far away when Herrington was murdered.

Sophia sensed Tom mentally rein himself in. Some of the tautness left him. He shifted his eyes back to her.

"Pour us a drink and talk a little to me," Cavillin said. He knew the evening was spoiled for him in this place, even with the presence of the beautiful blond woman. But he would not allow the man to drive him away before he was ready to leave.

They sat and talked about meaningless things. In a short time Tom became restless. He climbed to his feet.

"Sophia, if I stay here, there will surely be trouble between Ussing and me. Perhaps you or one of the other women might get hurt." He held out his hand. "Good-bye," he said.

She clasped the broad hand, feeling the hard, strong bones inside their sheaths of muscle and tendon and the rough calluses on his palm. He smiled broadly at her.

"Perhaps we shall meet someday in a more friendly place," Cavillin said. He released her hand, turned, and left.

In the green meadow east of Tacubaya, the army had buried its dead. Mounds of brown dirt, one hundred in each row, precisely spaced, marked the shallow graves of the soldiers.

Chilton walked among the graves, reading the names and ranks carved into the six- by thirty-inch wooden planks driven into the ground at the head of each excavation. About fifty graves were yet to be identified.

He found the section of the cemetery containing his dragoons. He stood in contemplation of the many names so familiar to him. Once he had thought a man who had no fear could do anything he wanted. How bitter was that thought today, with so many of his men lying buried around him. A lump of sorrow rose in his throat, a lump that choked him. Tears welled up, overflowed, and coursed down his cheeks. The tears were for this place and this time, for what his men had meant to him.

A wagon drawn by a pair of mules rattled its way into the edge of the cemetery. An old Mexican man, stooped and bent, his bones close to the skin, drove the team. A young American infantry corporal sat beside him. They climbed down and began to fill their arms with grave markers from the rear of the wagon.

The corporal referred to a map of the burial ground and started to distribute the wooden planks according to the notations on the paper. The Mexican went to the vehicle and, load by load, brought the rest of the monuments to the American. Methodically they placed a single marker at the head of each mound of dirt.

The corporal took a hammer and drove one of the wooden planks upright in the end of a grave. He pointed at all the other markers. *"Todo el mismo."* "All the same."

The old man nodded his head in understanding and began pounding a monument in place. The corporal watched the man finish and go to the next one. Then, certain that his instructions were properly interpreted, the corporal strode off toward Tacubaya.

The Mexican completed the task, climbed upon the seat of the wagon, and with a slap of the reins on the mules' rumps, set the team in motion. He guided the animals near Matt and reined them to a stop.

In Spanish the man said, "I'm an expert stonecutter." He held out his gnarled, but muscular, hands. "I could have made beautiful granite headstones for all these brave men. That durable stone would have lasted for a hundred, two hundred, years. Yet your army buyer hired my skill to carve only soft wood. Why is that, *señor?*" His face crinkled with deep, questioning furrows.

"The soldiers will be removed from the graves here in a few months and taken to their homes and buried with much ceremony. Therefore only temporary markers are needed now," Chilton replied.

"Now I understand, and it's a logical thing to do. I'm glad I have found someone who speaks my language sufficiently well to answer my question." The old man hesitated, then, seemingly overcoming some reluctance, spoke again. "Why, my friend, do you look so sad?"

"I knew many of these men."

The web of wrinkles in the Mexican's old face creased more deeply as he smiled with an enlightened expression. "The dead body goes into the ground," he said. "The real man lives here." He touched his forehead. "In the mind and memory of his friends. He is not truly dead until all those that knew him are also dead."

"But I am not their friend," Chilton cried out in an anguished voice. "I led them to their deaths." He spun around and hastened from the burial ground.

Thirteen

The big gray horse crossed the wide lake bottom with long, swift strides. Matt rode easily to the soft step of the animal. He had recaptured a major part of his strength, and the pain in his chest was but an annoyance.

He had left Tacubaya, passed through Mexico City, and was headed north on the deeply worn King's Highway. The sun, still three hours above the horizon, burned its way across the heavens. It was a time of day much earlier than when Matt normally made his rides. However, this day he had many miles to travel, and tomorrow, a town to rob.

The heat-warped air shimmered and danced, distorting vision and distance. Mirages quivered and fumed in the hot, rising air. A hunting hawk up high gave a keening cry. Foolish bird, thought Matt, it must be young or very hungry to hunt in this temperature, for all prey would be hidden safely away in some cool underground burrow.

The cultivated areas of the farmers slid by, deserted in this hour of the siesta and rest in the shade. In a bean field, irrigation water in the ditches caught the sun and reflected silver arrows. On the road, a man riding a cart pulled by a lone oxen went toward the city.

By late evening, Chilton had passed beyond the farmland. Not wanting to be observed by any Americans beyond this point, he veered off El Camino Real and headed cross-country over a grassy plain studded with clumps of waist-high brush. By early dusk, he reached the border of the lake bed, where the flanks of the mountains rose abruptly upward.

Sergeant Stoffer and fourteen dragoons sat on the ground in the shade of a large cypress tree. Nearby, their horses lowered their long necks and nibbled at the grass. Now and then, as the animals chewed, their teeth rattled upon the iron bits in their mouths.

The sergeant saw the lieutenant making his way toward them. He spoke to the men, and they all climbed to their feet and stood waiting.

Chilton rode into the shade and stopped. He wiped sweat from his face and ranged his view over the men. "I'm glad you're here. It's time for our plan to be put into operation. So let's be about it. Mount up."

"Yes, sir," replied Stoffer. He stepped to his horse, swung up into the saddle, and fell in on the right side of his lieutenant.

All but one of the remainder of the troopers, riding two abreast, took up position behind Chilton. The last man, leading a horse with an empty packsaddle, brought up the rear.

The column of horsemen began to climb along a narrow, winding footpath that hung precariously on the mountainside. From some of the outward bends of the trail could be seen a well-used road, far below them in the valley bottom between the feet of the mountain.

Through the long, hot evening hours, the dragoons labored upward on the twisting pathway. The brush grew in height and density and became a forest. The massive lower body of the mountain swelled outward, obscuring the men's view of the road, now miles away.

The valley filled with purple shadows as the night came flooding in from the east and overran the riders. Matt halted his troop in a saddle separating two tall, stony peaks to let the horses rest and catch their wind.

The dragoons sat silently as a bright, full moon sailed up

over the mountaintop. The huge shining globe drifted westward across the black sky, bathing the land in its silver rays. Long black shadows came to life behind every horse and rider. The only sound on the mountain was the creak of leather as now and then a man shifted his weight on his mount.

Matt spoke to his horse and led off following the trail, its trace easily discernible in the moonlight gilding the trees and grass. When the moon was at its zenith and the path started to slope steeply downward, Chilton stopped. The men climbed down from their mounts and stood weary and stiff in a small group in the dark.

"Bed down," Chilton called quietly. "The night is half gone."

The troopers moved apart and staked their horses on the end of rope tethers in a meadow of mountain grass. Bedrolls were untied from behind the saddles and carried a few yards to a nearby grove of trees.

"Sergeant, set two sentries," directed the lieutenant. "One with the horses and one there in the dark shadow under that tree where he can't be easily seen. Not much sleep time is left, so change the sentries every hour so we can all get some rest. Call me an hour before daylight. I'll take one of the watches for the last period."

"Yes, sir."

Chilton started to walk away, then turned back. "Tell the men to shake out their second uniforms and hang them over a bush so some of the wrinkles will fall out by morning. We want to look military tomorrow."

"Yes, Lieutenant," replied Stoffer.

Matt rolled out his blankets off by himself near the trunk of a big tree. He lay on his back, tuning himself to the sounds of the night and the mountain. He pondered what danger the coming day would bring.

The slow wind stirred and whispered the leaves of the tree above him. Down the hill, the horses stomped around and made low tearing sounds as they cropped the wild grass. Some of the men talked briefly to each other as they selected spots and bedded down. Then all conversation ceased.

The wind died away, the leaves hung without a rustle, and the horses quit feeding. Complete quietness reigned. Matt held his breath to better hear the rare moment of utter stillness.

Several seconds crept by. The only thing that moved was the moon gliding noiselessly through the sooty sky.

A series of melodious bird warbles, sweetly trilling and quavering, sounded from the treetop directly over Matt's head. He cocked his ear to listen to the tuneful song.

It stopped for a few seconds, then came again, an enchanting medley beginning low, rising to full-throated volume, then sliding delightfully downward in a succession of perfect, lovely notes. And lower still, until it could only be heard in Matt's memory.

Did birds sing in their sleep at night? Matt wondered. He raised up on his elbow and waited, hoping for the lovely song to come again.

The wind began its rustling passage through the treetop. The horses started to tear at the grass. One of the men called out something unintelligible in his sleep. His voice trailed off to a low mutter and then silence.

Matt sank into sleep. Some subconscious part of him waited for the nightmares of his dead men to commence. He felt the nearness of his ghosts, but they did not come into view. Were they, too, waiting to see what would happen when the new sun rose?

Chilton sat on a point of the mountain and watched to the east as a blood-red dawn slowly increased. The orb of the sun crested the curve of the earth and pierced the haze in the sky. The bright rays stabbed into the deep valleys and burned away the lingering purple shadows of the night.

Three miles distant and half a mile below Matt, the town of Coyoacan became visible. It lay in the center of an oval-shaped basin a mile long and three quarters of a mile wide. The meandering course of a fair-sized live stream divided the town into approximately equal parts. The cultivated fields of farmers ringed the town on all sides.

The waste dumps of half a score of gold and silver mines were dark brown wounds on the green mountainsides. Chilton had heard that the mines were very profitable and the town rich. He hoped it was true.

"Uniform inspection in ten minutes," called Stoffer. "Look sharp and have your gear packed and horses ready to ride."

"Damnation, Sergeant, we came her to rob a town, not to go on a parade," growled one of the dragoons.

"No griping, Coyle," the sergeant said. "This is a military outfit, and will be until we are all dead or discharged. Now move your ass."

Chilton heard the troopers talking, and he rose to return to camp.

"Here comes the lieutenant," said Stoffer. "Form a single line so he can look you over."

Chilton walked along the row of men. They wore the pants and boots of the dragoons. Their shirts and shoulder insignia were those of the Missouri Riflemen. Pennsylvania Infantry black shako caps with short-billed visors crowned their heads. The disguise was good; the uniforms could be traced to no particular regiment.

Chilton was dressed similarly. On his shoulders were the silver bars of a captain.

"We mustn't be identified," Chilton said to the men. "These mixed uniforms will help confuse those who search for us. And there will be many men trying to determine who we are. Be careful that you show no sign of being wounded, for that would lead them straight to us. Those of you who limp, do not dismount within sight of anyone. Obey orders promptly, and address each other only by rank and never by name."

The lieutenant saw the uncertainty in several of the men. He had doubts himself. Was he leading the men into an action that would get them killed or caught, to spend long years in a military prison?

He pointed into the valley of Coyoacan. "That is a rich mining town with both gold and silver. See the mines on the mountainsides? We're going to take part of that wealth for the families of our dead comrades and for the wounded that can never work to make a living. They must not be forced to spend the rest of their lives in poverty. Not after the sacrifice they've made.

"It is not too late to change your minds about this action. Any man wishing to leave should do it now. Simply ride back over the mountain to Mexico City. Those who remain with me will depend upon you never to tell what we plan to do here."

No man stirred. All the faces became set with determined expressions.

"Very well, it's decided then." He stepped to one of the troopers. "Towell, here are lieutenant's bars. Put them on your shoulders. You speak Spanish very well and do not limp. I want you to act as the company lieutenant. Stay beside me and help interpret what is said."

Towell took the bars and grinned. "I always wanted to be a lieutenant." He fastened the strips of metal to the tops of his shoulders.

"Sir, if there is resistance, what do we do?" asked Darcy. His young face was drawn. "The war is supposed to be over."

"We will use force, Darcy. But only as little as possible, and still take the gold. If we're attacked, we'll shoot back and fight our way out. Mount up."

All the men climbed astride and, with their dragoon garments hidden within the bedrolls, rode at a gallop down the long, slanting side of the mountain toward Coyoacan.

* * *

The troop of dragoons swept into the main thoroughfare of Coyoacan. The pounding, iron-shod hooves of the trotting horses, rebounding in multiple echoes from the fronts of the buildings lining the street, sounded like the rumble of distant cannon fire. Dust puffed up in little geysers at each hoof fall and trailed after the riders in a brown cloud.

Lieutenant Chilton twisted to call out behind. "Draw carbines and hold ready. Watch all side streets and rooftops. I want all of us to leave here alive."

The men swiftly pulled out their rifles and held them, butts resting on thighs and cold iron barrels pointing threateningly at the sky. The dragoons held close formation, and wary eyes probed everywhere.

The people on the street stopped to stare at the Americans. Many drew back from the riders and pressed against the walls of the building. A woman grabbed the hands of two tiny girls and darted into a clothing store. A tall, hard-looking man, dressed in tight leather pants and heavily armed with a pair of pistols in his belt, glared at Chilton as he passed.

The lieutenant looked back stonily. This was the type of man who could cause trouble.

Matt's sight ranged far up the avenue, down the cross streets, and into the open windows and doors. He had observed Coyoacan twice, but only from a distance on the mountainside. He knew nothing of how well the town was mobilized for defense. If one citizen fired on the Americans, the odds were great that hundreds more would join in the assault.

More dangerous than the townsfolk were the organized bands of guerrillas. From their headquarters in remote mountain villages such as Coyoacan, the guerrillas rode down to attack the American wagon trains on the valley roads. They searched for the opportunity to strike at a weak force of the hated invaders. Chilton's small troop of sixteen would be cut to pieces if they should stumble into a concentration of the unconquered Mexican fighters.

Chilton evaluated the prosperous-appearing town with its well-built and -maintained homes and businesses. New construction was under way. A two-story building was going up on the right side of the street. The exterior walls of stone were nearly complete. Three dozen or more private dwellings of pretentious dimensions lined an avenue on a bench above the town. Two more residences were being built up there. Matt could see the workmen moving around. It seemed that the war had bypassed Coyoacan. Until this day.

Chilton brought his fighters to a clattering halt on the stone-paved town plaza. Sensing the tension of the riders, the horses tossed their heads and pranced nervously, sending sparks flying from under their hooves. The men held the animals with tight reins.

A village constable in a brown uniform ran across the plaza and entered a building. The sign over the door read, ALCALDE DE COYOACAN, Mayor of Coyoacan. Chilton noted the man's speedy departure. He rotated to scan every section of the plaza.

Half a block to the left of the Alcalde's office was the Pantoja and Campins Bank. Though the day was still early, the bank's door was open. Other business proprietors also had their establishments ready for customer trade. Several farmers had arrived from the countryside and were placing baskets of produce out to be inspected by potential buyers. A meat wagon had taken a shady location beneath a tree, and the butcher stood ready with his long knife to cut off any piece wanted by a patron.

All the people on the plaza turned to focus their attention upon Chilton and his men. He would have preferred there be fewer witnesses to his action. However, it was too late to draw back now.

"Sergeant, face your men outward from each other in a defensive formation," ordered Chilton. "Return fire if fired upon. Send two troopers up on the bench to watch for Mexicans concentrating on the streets, or riders approaching the town."

Stoffer turned and gave the necessary commands to the columns of dragoons. Two men, Templeton and Corlett, peeled away from the troops and spurred up the slanting hillside to the bench two hundred feet above.

The alcalde came out of his office, fastening the yellow and blue sash of authority over his right shoulder and under his left arm. The constable walked beside him. They stopped in front of Chilton.

Chilton saluted the town officials and spoke in Spanish. "I am Captain Charles Gilchrist of the United States Army. What is your name?"

The alcalde drew his short, square body together. "I am Luis Runuel, the alcalde of Coyoacan. For what reason are you here, Captain?"

Chilton asked his own question. "How many banks are in your town?"

"Only that one owned by Pantoja and Campins." The alcalde's black eyes took on a suspicious expression. His lips compressed into a thin line.

The constable started to back away slowly. Chilton spoke quickly in English to Towell. "Take the lawman's pistol. Turn him over to the sergeant to be kept under guard."

Towell swiftly pulled his handgun and aimed it at the constable. In Spanish he said, "Give your pistol to the sergeant."

The constable hesitated, glancing at the alcalde for a sign as to what action he should take. Runuel raked his view over the armed riders and then back to the American captain. He saw the intensity in the blue eyes of the officer, a steely purpose in the set of his jaw. This man could be dangerous if opposed.

"Do as the lieutenant says," Runuel told the constable.

The man reluctantly reached for his weapon. Stoffer did not like the angry, calculating glint on the brown face. He lowered the barrel of his carbine to aim directly at the man's chest. He held out his hand for the pistol.

"Lieutenant, tell this jasper to do it slow and butt first, or I'll shoot him where he stands," Stoffer growled.

The constable read the meaning of the sergeant's words without interpretation. Fear replaced hate as he realized how near he was to death. Cautiously he drew the pistol from his belt and passed it to Stoffer.

"Lieutenant, come with me," Chilton ordered.

"Yes, Captain." Towell sprang to the ground.

"Señor Runuel, please accompany me to talk with the bankers," Chilton said.

Runuel did not move. "I have no authority over the bank," he said.

"Once I have explained things, I think you *will* have authority equal to the banker. Come with me." Chilton took hold of the Mexican's shoulder. Runuel was afraid. He knew the outspoken objective of the American and didn't have a way to stop him. He stepped forward under the firm pressure of the American's hand.

At the steps of the bank, Runuel found himself drawn to a halt and spun around to face south. The captain spoke. "Alcalde, I suppose the bankers live up there on the bench in those big houses. Which ones belong to Pantoja and Campins?"

"Pantoja lives in that large two-story overlooking the town. Campins owns the long one on the west end of the street."

"I see the homes you describe," said Chilton. "Lieutenant, do you also know the ones he means?"

"Yes, Captain."

"Good. Remember them. Let us go inside now." Chilton again prodded the alcalde forward, and they entered the bank.

A tall man with gray hair rose from a desk and walked

toward the three arrivals. Two other men were behind iron-barred teller windows. One was counting out paper money to a customer. That man picked up the bills and left.

Towell spoke in English. "Captain, those bank men will surely have guns and know how to use them."

Chilton spoke in the same language. "Yes. Go stand where you can see what they do. We will disarm them in a moment."

The gray-haired man drew close, and the alcalde spoke to Chilton. "This is Señor Campins, owner of the bank." His voice was an angry growl.

"Señor Campins, I am Captain Charles Gilchrist of the United States Army. Where is your partner, Pantoja?" While Matt waited for an answer, his eyes examined the heavy iron door of the bank's vault in the far wall of the room. It was closed.

"Señor Pantoja is in Mexico City," Campins said. "What can I do for you, Captain?"

Chilton stared hard at the bank owner. "You know the Mexican army has been defeated by the United States. All Mexico is under martial law." It was a statement and not a question.

Campins turned to look through the front window at the armed troopers on the plaza. Then, once again, his eyes settled on Chilton. They had narrowed to mere slits and were full of hostility.

"General Scott has demanded a tribute from Mexico City of one hundred and fifty thousand dollars," Chilton continued. "My orders are to collect additional tribute from Coyoacan. You have a rich town. I demand fifty thousand dollars. Please open your vault and allow me to inspect its contents. I'll give you a receipt for the amount I take."

"Show me your orders," demanded Campins. His despair was not fully hidden.

"My orders are verbal. Do not waste my time. Open the vault."

"I will not. The money in this bank belongs to hundreds of people. Many are poor. It is their money, and I will not give it to you."

Chilton spoke quickly in English to Towell. "Lieutenant, disarm those two men and take them to the sergeant for safe-keeping."

Towell had been awaiting the command. He speedily pulled his pistol and pointed it at the tellers before they could act. "Hand me your weapons, slowly and carefully," he ordered.

Chilton stood ready to draw his revolver and assist Towell if there was a need. Both tellers grudgingly relinquished their pistols to Towell.

Chilton spoke out in Spanish so everyone could understand. "Lieutenant, tell two of our men to go burn Señor Campins's and Pantoja's homes. Also the alcalde's office. So they will burn swiftly, get a couple gallons of coal oil from the general store on the side of the plaza."

"Yes, sir." Towell motioned the tellers ahead of him to the outside.

"You would not do this thing," said Campins in a weak voice.

"Surely I would. You are a conquered nation. The victors can do whatever they want."

"Now, Señores, let us go outside and watch those buildings burn. After that, we will find something else of value to burn or otherwise destroy."

Chilton pulled the revolver given to him by Cavillin and aimed it at the two Mexicans. Desperate men sometimes took desperate chances, and Matt wanted to prevent these two men from gambling that they could somehow beat him. He wanted the gold of the town and not men's lives.

"Walk in front of me," Matt commanded.

Two troopers rode to the entrance of the store. One swung

down and went inside. In a moment he came back outside, carrying a bucket. He pulled himself up on his horse, gingerly balancing the bucket to keep from spilling its contents. He looked at Chilton.

Fourteen

Campins drew back from the cold stare of the American captain. The alien blue eyes followed the banker, boring in with evil intent. The gringo began to speak with his harsh, crude accent, his words almost unintelligible. But the grim threat was easily understood.

"Señores, do you open the bank vault, or do we begin this costly game?" questioned Chilton. "In the end you'll comply with my request. Otherwise you won't have a town, for I will burn it to ashes. Talk it over between yourselves." He turned away from the two Mexicans and went to stand by Stoffer.

With uneasy expressions the men and women on the plaza watched the Americans. They did not know what was happening, only that it must be very bad. For what other reason would the alcalde and Señor Campins appear so afraid?

Chilton heard the increasing grumble of the townsfolk. He pivoted slowly, raking his cold view over them. The men and women stirred fearfully when his eyes fell upon them.

"Sergeant, do you hear that?" Matt swept his hand over the throng of people in the plaza square. Their voices had grown to a growling storm wave. "Something will soon break. Because they outnumber us so heavily, they will think we can be driven away."

"I think so, too, sir," replied Stoffer.

The man in the leather pants Chilton had seen along the

street was on the opposite border of the plaza. A second man, similarly clothed, was with him. Both of their dark faces held angry scowls. Matt had a premonition that he should kill the men to forestall trouble from them. But he could not, unless they tried to stop the taking of the gold.

He spoke to Stoffer. "Those two men with the pistols in their belts on the far side of the square—watch them. Shoot them if they make a wrong move."

"We see them, sir," said the sergeant. "They are dead men if they start anything."

Matt glanced at Campins and Runuel. They were talking earnestly together. Matt would give them a few seconds more. He lifted his hat to wipe his sweating forehead. The sun was still low in the morning sky, and already it was hot.

"I will open the vault," Campins said to Chilton. The banker's jaws trembled with rage. "You Yankees are devils. You have stolen Texas. Then you murdered many thousands of our soldiers. Now you rob us of what wealth we do have. You are truly one of Satan's people."

Chilton did not respond to Campins's harangue. The loading of the money must proceed without wasting time. The longer the dragoons remained in Coyoacan, the more likely the citizens would become organized and attack. Matt walked over to Towell.

"The banker will now give us what's in the vault. Tell those two troopers at the store to forget the fire. Send one up to the bench and have him bring back our fellows from there. I want to leave this place as soon as possible."

"Yes, sir." Towell hurried across the plaza toward the general store.

"You two come with me," Chilton directed, pointing at men who could work without showing that they had old wounds. "Bring the packhorse up to the bank steps."

Chilton spoke to Campins. "Lead the way to the vault."

The bank owner did as commanded. He bent, spun the dial to a series of numbers, and yanked wide the heavy iron door.

The six-foot-square stone-walled room was lined on three sides with shelves. Thirty or so canvas bags filled part of the shelving. Eight bars of gold glowed a rich yellow straight ahead. Matt estimated the dimensions of each bar as two by four by six inches. Identifying numbers were stamped into their tops. On the left side of the vault were many bound packets of paper money.

"Damnation! What a hoard of money," exclaimed Towell, coming up behind.

"Load all the gold," Chilton told his men. "Those bags there will probably hold silver, but check to be sure. If so, don't fool with them, for they will be too heavy for their value. Take all the paper money ten pesos and larger. Lieutenant, see that no one interferes with the removal of this money."

"Yes, Captain."

Chilton went through the bank door and started down the steps to the plaza level. Something tugged at the top of his left shoulder. He heard the whizzing of a bullet and instantly the crash of a pistol.

He flinched to the right. A second bullet burned the outside curve of his arm. Matt changed his flinch to the right to a fall to get out of the line of fire.

The corner of one of the wooden steps of the bank thudded into his ribs as he crashed down. He lost his breath at the lance of pain in his chest.

Several carbines cracked almost simultaneously. Matt heard Stoffer's Colt booming. Skittish horses stomped the pavement with a rattle of iron hooves.

"Hold formation!" shouted Stoffer. "Damn you all! Hold formation."

"Got them! Got the sons of bitches," Darcy cried out.

"Lieu—Captain, are you hurt?" Stoffer called.

"Just a scratch." Chilton clambered erect, catching his breath. "Was it the two men we talked about?"

"Yes, sir," responded the sergeant. "They are both down. Not moving, and I judge hard hit or dead. At this close range they took a lot of lead balls."

Towell and the two men helping him ran from the bank. Each carried a heavy bag in one hand, a pistol in the other. They looked around swiftly.

"Back to your task, Lieutenant," commanded Chilton. "Everything's under control here."

The men jumped down the steps and dropped the bags into one of the pockets of the packsaddle. They spun around and raced back inside the bank.

The three men who had been stationed as lookouts on the bench came speeding in on running horses. Their pistols were drawn and ready. The three clustered around Chilton.

"A bunch of Mexicans, maybe two hundred or more, are gathering on the main street," Corlett said.

"How far away?" questioned Chilton.

"Six or seven blocks from here."

"All right. Get into rank."

Towell and the men helping him came from the bank with bulging leather bags and loaded them on the pack animal. The flaps of the packsaddle were hastily tied shut.

"All loaded, Captain," Towell called.

Chilton pointed at their horses, and the men leapt astride. Matt sprang upon his own mount. He felt his heart throbbing. A prick of pain pulsed through his chest with each beat.

Campins hastened up with a sheet of paper. "Captain Gilchrist, you have taken the equivalent of forty-eight thousand American dollars. Please sign this receipt for it."

Chilton laughed out loud at the outrageous idea of signing the paper. The money was being stolen, and a large band of Mexicans waited to ambush and kill him and his troopers for taking it.

He took the offered quill pen. Campins held up an inkwell. *It is much more gold than I'd reasoned we'd get,* thought Chilton. He dipped the quill. In a large, bold hand he wrote the name Charles Gilchrist, Captain, United States Army. *Now, General Winfield Scott, let's see what you think of your new captain.*

"Form ranks two abreast and follow me," Matt shouted at his dragoons. He spurred, and his big horse bounded from the plaza and back along the main street.

The route in front of the dragoons was empty, but Chilton knew the enemy was there somewhere close ahead, around the bend of the street. The Mexicans would be able to easily hear the sound of the dragoons running horses on the hard ground.

Matt yanked on the reins of his mount and swerved left on a cross street. He glanced behind him. The column of men followed faithfully. Three blocks later he turned back to his original direction, west toward Mexico City.

Stoffer shouted, "There the Mexicans are, Captain. They were fooled. They thought we were coming right past them. See them hustling to get within range for a shot at us?"

At an intersection Matt saw bands of men running pell-mell on the parallel avenue on his right. He spurred, and his valiant horse lunged ahead in full stride. He threw a look to the rear at the packhorse. The dragoon leading the animal had thrown a dally of lead rope around the pommel of his saddle and was towing the loaded beast. So far the trooper and the packhorse were keeping pace.

On the edge of town, Matt angled back to the right and again struck the main thoroughfare of Coyoacan. He led onward at a run for a mile, then slowed to a gallop. In the confined, canyonlike streets of the town, his dragoons would have been in a very hazardous situation, running a gauntlet through the Mexican gunners behind the protective walls of the buildings. Here in the open valley bottom he did not fear the untrained townsmen.

The riders reached the beginning of the mountain trail and began to climb. An hour later they reined their horses to a halt on the shoulder of the mountain where they had camped during the night. All the dragoons twisted in the saddle and closely scrutinized the path back toward Coyoacan.

"I see no pursuit," Chilton said to his men. "Our objective has been accomplished, and we have forty-eight thousand dollars in gold and Mexican paper money."

Sergeant Stoffer raised his head and shouted out with relief and triumph. The other troopers joined him in a happy chorus. The echoes of their cries struck a rimrock above them and, bouncing back, added that volume to the original shouts and, thus doubly strong, went sailing off down into the valley toward Coyoacan.

Chilton's lips curled into a somber smile. He looked to the west in the direction of Mexico City and the graveyard there. *Rest more easily, my dead dragoons, for soon we'll have much money for your families.*

The army wagon train, three hundred and fifty wagons strong, snaked up the long climbing grade of the El Camino Real. The sweating teamsters popped their bullwhips and cursed the heat and the steepness of the mountain. The wagons had nearly reached the pass lying on the high shoulder of the mighty volcanic mountain, Ixtacihuatl.

Several companies of General Lane's foot soldiers marched in the lead of the wagon train. Lane had deployed his mounted riflemen and the Rangers to ride along both sides of the train, giving protection from possible flanking attacks.

Three teams of horses strained to pull each heavily laden vehicle. Blood leaked from the backs of the laboring beasts and mixed with the sweat, to course down their sides and dribble onto the ground. The red liquid oozed out from beneath the thousands of large black flies that clung like a living blanket to the horses' hairy backs. A low drone arose from the insects as they pumped with their wings to gain purchase on the air. They drove their sharp, probing snouts ever more deeply into the flesh of the horses, sucking greedily at the warm blood.

Desperate for relief from the torment of the biting flies, the horses frequently rippled their skins, causing a sharp fluttering sound. At the jerk of the muscles the bloodsucking pests would swarm up in a dark fog to hang over the horses, then settle back onto the bleeding bodies almost immediately, with a contented hum.

Cavillin rode down from the bulging shoulder of Ixtacihuatl, where he had climbed to a vantage point to search with his telescope for Mexicans ambushes. As he galloped his mount past the wagon train, he saw the fierce assault of the flies on the teams of horses. But there was nothing he could do to halt the unending torment.

However, within one day, the train would be above the lush, tropical coastal zone, and the flies would be left behind. Then, in another nine or ten days, the army would reach Mexico City.

Tom scanned to the southeast. Giant thunderheads were crowding the heavens and scudding up fast. He shifted his sight along the creaking line of wagons to measure the distance of the approaching storm against the nearness of the vehicle he sought. He wanted to ride by the wagon of the wheelwright, Carl Hampton, before the storm struck.

Tom grinned. Perhaps if he timed it just right, he would be invited to take shelter from the storm in the wagon with Hampton and his daughter. He admitted to himself that the young woman had been much in his thoughts these several days since leaving Vera Cruz. However, constant patrols scouting for guerrilla ambushes had prevented him from seeing her, except for once, and that had been only at a distance too far to speak.

He often wondered how pretty she would be in a dress and with a freshly scrubbed face.

The wagons of the army civilian contractors, blacksmiths, harness makers, gunsmiths, and other skilled craftsmen brought up the middle of the train. That group of wagons was still half a mile from Cavillin. At the tail end of the train and separated from the last army wagon by a distance of three hundred yards or more were approximately thirty additional wagons. Those were the uninvited camp followers and hangers-on, whoremasters and their women, mistresses of some of the soldiers, whiskey peddlers, gamblers, and others of like ilk that the army tolerated to trail along under its protective umbrella.

The thunderheads of the storm front were rushing speedily upon the caravan. The wells of sunlight in between them were winking out as the heat of the afternoon sent masses of moisture streaming upward to tower fifty or sixty thousand feet into the sky. The mountains lying in the direction of the coast began to disappear, devoured by the cloud monsters.

As Tom passed a string of horses, a few flies lifted up from the bleeding backs. In a second more, all the pests rose with a buzz of wings, hovering there as if testing with some primeval instinct the omens of the oncoming storm. Then, in a fraction of time, the horde of flies dispersed like an evaporating black vapor, speeding away to find some safe refuge from the threatening storm.

Lightning flashed among the clouds, setting whole patches of sky aflame. Splinters of lightning shot down to the earth and skipped over the rugged land. The heavens roared, thundering in Tom's ears. Static crinkled in the supercharged air, and he felt his hair twisting and flaring as each strand tried to separate itself from the next.

The first faint puffs of a damp, cold wind stirred the air. Quickly it strengthened and charged upon the wagon train with a roll of dust and shrieking a wild song. The canvas covering on the arching hickory ribs of the wagons billowed and flapped crazily.

The wind buffeted Cavillin and tore at his clothing. Above him, the sky was an ocean of swift wind churning and boiling the water-laden bottoms of the dark gray clouds.

The wagons halted. Drivers sprang down over the tall wheels to the ground and began to unhook trace chains from single trees, and breast chains from the wagon tongues.

Cavillin spotted Hampton pulling his teams of horses up to the wheels of his wagon and tying them there with short, stout ropes. One of the animals tried to pull free to bolt away. Hampton subdued the beast and snubbed its head close to the iron rim of a wheel.

The wheelwright was a small man, smaller than Tom had remembered him from the day of the fight in Vera Cruz. But some look in Hampton's face and eyes and something inside him made him seem a big man. Tom knew he was fearless.

Les tugged at the flaps of the canvas to close the rear of the wagon. The wind fought against her. As she secured the last knot, Cavillin came into her view. She felt her heart lift in a happy flutter. She had not known how badly she had wanted to see the young, redheaded man.

Hampton glanced at his daughter to see how she was faring with her tasks. Les was staring off through the wind at something. A small, tender smile lit her face. She is a girl almost grown to womanhood, thought Hampton. Soon she would be leaving him. A feeling of sadness washed over him at the imminent loss of her delightful company. But he could not keep her with him forever. One day she would take a man and leave. Hampton ranged his eyes to the side to see what she watched so intently.

Texas Ranger Cavillin sat his long-legged horse and gazed at Les. He was smiling in a pleased way. He jerked off his hat in greeting to Les.

Hampton flung an apprehensive look around to see if anyone

was noticing the strange action of a man removing his hat to a young person in grease-stained clothing. The attention of the men at the nearby wagons was fixed upon their chores to prepare for the growing storm, and saw nothing that was happening elsewhere.

Tom nodded once at Les. The wind caught his long hair and sent it dancing and flicking. His smile widened as he thought of the ridiculous sight he must make with his hair streaming out and half covering his face. He turned to the blast of the wind and jammed his hat back on to capture his red mane.

Hampton raised his hand in greeting to the lanky Ranger. Tom returned the salute and waited for the wheelwright to speak. But Hampton lowered his head and began to work on a knot holding one of the horses and studiously ignored Cavillin.

Tom read the clear sign. There would be no invitation to stop and take shelter with the Hamptons, no pleasant conversation with the girl. Tom grinned ruefully. That was all right for now. She was still young. However, one day Tom would come again, and he would not ask permission to court her.

Tom touched his hat in farewell to the girl and pressed spurs against the flanks of his horse. Les's eyes were wide as she waved back, half bashfully and half boldly. Tom lifted his mount to a gallop along the wagon train.

The wind was filled with the smell of rain. Already the tail end of the wagon train was obscured by the sheets of falling water. Tom heard the pounding of billions of raindrops beating on the hard earth.

The cold wetness surged over him in a roaring, irresistible wave. Lightning struck somewhere very close. An animal screamed in terrible anguish. Cavillin could not tell if it was a man or a horse. The air was filled with the odor of burning sulfur for a moment before the rain washed it clean. Tom hoped the lightning had not hit any of the thousands of men hunkered down under their rain slickers out there beyond sight in the deluge.

Cavillin dragged his cayuse to a stop at the covered wagon where he stored his bedroll and extra clothing. He leapt down and tied his mount. Carrying his carbine, he scurried into the rear of the wagon and up on the boxes and crates filling the bed.

The vehicle was deserted. Tom judged that the driver had gone to some adjacent wagon to wait out the storm with a comrade. That was good, for he appreciated the solitude.

The torrential rain flogged the canvas above his head, creating a mighty din. Though weighted down with a heavy load, the vehicle rocked and swayed. Tom trusted the brakes were firmly set and the wheels chocked with rocks against the steep grade of the hill. This was no time to ride a runaway wagon.

Cavillin sat for several minutes listening to the turmoil of the storm. Lightning crackled, flashing its impossible brightness through the canvas covering. Thunder rumbled incessantly, like great boulders rolling down the mountainside.

Tom warmed as he began to dry. He dug into his food supply and fished out a can of sardines and some raisins. Slowly he ate.

Finishing the food, he stretched out and spread a blanket over himself. He was like the gray squirrel; he liked to lie and muse to himself when his stomach was full and it was raining. Today he would think of the future. A smile drifted across his heart at the thought of the girl called Les.

Fifteen

The sun had aged and lay flaming weakly upon the far western horizon when Chilton and his dragoons came down from the mountain trail leading to Coyoacan. Southwest of them ten miles or so distant lay Mexico City. To the southeast, tall storm clouds were pushing against the high, stony crowns of Popocatépetl and Ixtachihuatl.

Lightning flared sulkily, trapped within the towering cloud masses and lighting them internally with a smoldering, infernal glow. Misty fingers of the storm were already thrusting between the two mountains and flowing down toward the valley bottom and the city.

The weary horses plodded slowly through the short, dry grass and brittle brush. The air was full of the chatter and chirp of thousands of grasshoppers swarming up from the ground and whirring away with the swift beating of their wings. A flock of ravens flew up in a black, screaming explosion of sound from the shade of a large cottonwood. The tired mustangs merely pricked their ears in that direction and gave no further notice.

Chilton shifted the hang of his arm to ease the pain of his wound. He felt the bandage, stiff and dry. Gently it was removed and tossed aside. He would wash and mend the bullet hole in the clothing. No aid from a doctor would be sought. No one must find out he was freshly wounded.

"It'll be storming soon, Lieutenant," Stoffer said, pointing at the cloud banks tumbling down the sides of the far rim of the valley.

"I agree," responded Matt. "And within the hour. That's good. We'll wait for that and for the night, and then we'll ride on across the city and to camp at Tacubaya. Until then we need a place to be out of sight and rest. Let's take a look at that old hacienda. It appears to be deserted."

"There are weeds in the yard, and some of the roof has fallen in," said Stoffer, closely examining a long, low adobe structure straight ahead.

Chilton tied his mount and entered the open portal of the deserted building. The old adobe house was cool and musty, with dark shadows in the corners. All the windows were open to the outside. A slow breeze blew from the southeast, probing out ahead of the storm.

His men came inside and scattered about the room. They slumped, silent and exhausted.

Matt sat on the earthen floor of the large central room and leaned against the wall. He rested, watching out one of the windows.

The daylight drained from the sky, leaving behind a blue-gray heaven. The dusk became night. With the blackness, a mist-like rain came in to run as softly as the feet of spiders across the housetop.

The rain thickened to a muted drum on the rooftop. Water leaked through the aged roof in half a hundred places and fell to puddle on the dirt floor with little plopping noises.

The storm built in intensity. Lightning flashed and cut the sky; peals of thunder shook the earth. A horse snorted in fright. The clouds opened to dump a torrent upon the old hacienda.

All the energy had seeped out of Matt. He twisted to lie flat on his back and lay quietly. While the storm raged, the dragoons should be safe here. He would not even post a guard.

He went to sleep listening to the storm gathering in madness and violence as it walked the dark world outside.

For the very first time in many days he felt no ghosts on his shoulders.

Chilton and Stoffer, leading a laden packhorse, halted in the deep darkness of the grove of trees below the Catholic Church, La Piedad. They remained motionless for several minutes, listening to the sounds of the town of Tacubaya on the high ground above them and watching the orange squares of lamplight in the windows and doors of the houses.

This was the third time they had come to the church with gold and pesos stolen from Mexican towns lying in the mountains beyond the valley of Mexico City. After Coyoacan, they had ridden upon San Augustin. Early this morning Cuernavaca had been hit. Sadly four Mexicans had died in this last raid. The most ever. All had been young men, daring and determined to stop Chilton and the dragoons from robbing their village. The Mexicans had been terribly outclassed by the fighting skill of the professional American cavalrymen. The brave Mexicans would not turn back, so they had died.

The low mutter of men talking reached Chilton as they sat in the cool of the evening. One fellow shouted out good-naturedly, his voice rising above all other talk. Someone called back a rejoinder. A ripple of laughter rose, then died away.

A horse nickered somewhere off around the hill. Chilton knew that would be the cavalry mounts that had been brought in from grazing and would be kept under guard until daylight.

"The hospital in the church is quiet," said Matt. "Wait here for my signal."

"Yes, sir," Stoffer said.

Chilton touched his horse with spurs, and the animal moved up the grade. The courtyard of La Piedad was deserted. The surgeons' quarters in the house immediately east had one small light visible in a window. No one stirred.

Chilton whistled three warbling calls. Stoffer answered and came out of the trees and up the hill to the church.

Matt stepped down from his horse. He staggered and caught hold of the saddle.

"Are you all right?" questioned Stoffer in alarm.

"Too much riding. But I'll be okay." Matt released his grip and stood erect.

He moved to ten grain bins, each as high as a tall man and equal that dimension in diameter, that were attached to the rear wall of the church. They had been constructed in some long-time past and for many years had been stocked with corn and other grain during times of harvest plenty. During lean periods the priests had doled out the grain to the poor and needy. Matt wondered why the church had ceased that charitable sharing.

Over the years of neglect, gaping fissures had ruptured the adobe walls of the storage bins. Rain and dust found entrance. Mice and bugs had gleaned the last grain and crumb of food. One bin contained three feet of moldy corncobs.

Chilton pulled open the sagging wooden door that covered a hatchway near the bottom of the bin that held the corncobs. He felt for the spiderweb that he had placed back across the opening the last time he had been there. The silken thread was in place. Some industrious spider had stretched other strands of its net across the hatch.

Matt plunged his hand into the cobs. His fingers encountered the leather of a satchel.

"All is safe," he whispered to Stoffer. He raked aside the cobs to form a cavity beside the gold and paper money already there.

"Bring the sacks," Chilton told Stoffer.

The sergeant hoisted two small, heavy bags and a large light-weight one from the packsaddle of the horse and carried them to Matt. He brought a second load. Matt stowed the valuables in the hole beside those pouches already there and covered all with the corncobs. He reattached two strands of the spiderweb. The door was closed and latched.

Chilton brushed the ground to remove all signs of boot prints at the grain bin. "It's finished," he said. "Let us leave at once."

Leading their mounts, they walked around the hill sixty yards until they were directly below the house where Matt had his room. They started to climb, then stopped abruptly. Above them, a man called out Chilton's name, and a minute later a lucifer flared.

Cavillin halted his cayuse in the dark near the house on the hilltop in Tacubaya. He sat his saddle, relaxing his tired body and letting the wind that was rising up over the ridge cool his sweaty face.

General Lane's army, with its hundreds of wagons, had arrived in Mexico City in mid-afternoon, ending the long trek from Vera Cruz. Tom and his Rangers had joined with the other military detachments in unloading the tons of supplies and storing all in warehouses confiscated by the army in the city. Finishing that chore, he had ridden to Tacubaya. Now, after a bath, a bite of food, and a hello to Chilton, Tom would sleep the clock around.

He dismounted and moved to the doorway on the right end of the house. He rapped on the wooden panel with his knuckles.

"Chilton. Matt Chilton, this is Cavillin. Are you there?"

No response sounded from inside the room. Tom lifted the latch and shoved open the door. An odor of dry clay from the earthen floor and adobe walls filled his nostrils, as if the room had been closed for a long time.

"Matt," Tom called again, staring into the black rectangle

of the door. There was no answer, only his voice echoing back, hollow and empty, at him.

Chilton had been gravely injured. Had he failed to recover and now lay buried with the hundreds of other dead men in the cemetery? Tom dug a lucifer from a pocket and struck it into flame.

The single bed and rocking chair were still there. So, too, was the small table where Matt laid his pistols when he slept. Now a washbasin and pitcher occupied that space. Looking farther, Tom saw two cavalry uniforms hanging on the pegs driven in the wall behind the door. It was a bleak room with little sign a man had lived there for weeks.

Matt probably had gone into Mexico City for some amusement, thought Tom. It would be a fine thing if he was indeed well enough to have found a woman.

The lucifer burned close to Cavillin's fingers, and he shook it out. He stepped to the outside and picked up the reins of his horse from where they dragged on the ground. Wearily he walked down the hilly street in the direction of his quarters with Sumner and Ripley.

Chilton and Stoffer listened to the footfalls of Cavillin and his horse fade into the night.

"That is Tom Cavillin," said Matt in a low voice. "That means General Lane has returned from Vera Cruz. The El Camino Real must now be open."

"The wounded will soon be leaving on the long journey home," Stoffer said.

"Yes. We must gather our gold more swiftly before we're ordered to the coast."

"Your friend, the Texas Ranger, could be very dangerous to us," said Stoffer in a worried tone. "He might stumble on to what we are doing. I would never want that man hunting me."

"I agree. He's a lawman and would not understand why we

must do this thing. We've robbed three towns and have accumulated over a hundred and twenty thousand dollars. Twice that amount should be enough for our purposes. We shall continue with our plan. I've selected the next town for us to ride on. In ten days, two weeks at the most, we should have reached our goal and be finished. We must be more cautious than ever before."

"I have a bad feeling about Cavillin," said Stoffer. "I believe he'll do us great harm."

"We'll take more roundabout routes to assemble our men for our raids. Also, when we're in camp, we will post a lookout to watch the grain bins from a distance. We must always be ready to do what is necessary to protect our men from being found out and arrested. Now it is time to rest."

"When shall we ride again?"

"Soon. A day or so. Don't let the men go into the city. I'll talk with Tom and learn the latest news of Lane's campaign to the coast and back. Then I'll decide and let you know."

"We'll wait and be ready," Stoffer said.

"Good night, Sergeant."

"Good evening, sir. I'll feed your mount and rub him down." Stoffer lead the horses off in the darkness.

Chilton entered his room and threw open the wooden shutters of the windows. He looked out at the muted glow of the distant lamp and candlelight of the great capital of Mexico. *I'm taking part of the wealth of your land,* he said silently to the city. *Allow me just a little more and then I'll stop. Never again will I rob or kill one of your people.* Matt's face twisted with an ironic smile at his queer thoughts and he turned from the window.

He dropped onto his bed. All his strength was wrung out of him. Some knowledge deep within the core of his being told him his last days were running out. Only raw nerve kept him moving. Those secret things that all men dream of doing in some later period of their lives never would be accomplished. His heart yawned, empty and bare.

Chilton woke to the sweet, golden sunlight of early morning. For a couple of minutes he lay without moving, watching the sliver of blue sky visible through the window.

Gingerly he swung his legs down and sat on the edge of the cot. A pain began in his chest. The fall on the steps of the bank in Coyoacan had done something bad to him. His heart often ached, and his strength was failing, never fully recovering between the long rides.

He rose and poured water into the washbasin. Slowly he shaved and cleansed himself. *I'll go talk with Tom,* he thought as he pulled on a fresh uniform.

The angry voices of a man and woman erupted in a heated argument. Matt cocked his head to listen. The quarrel seemed to originate from the room at the far end of the very same house where he lived.

Matt could not decipher the rumbling growl of the man. The woman's voice, higher-timbered and insistent, was demanding something be given to her.

Chilton went to the door and outside. He was drawn along the wall. A woman speaking English without an accent intrigued him.

The loud wrangle ceased. A tall man burst from an open door. He saw Matt and instantly stopped.

The man pivoted toward the lieutenant, and his hand rose near the open flaps of his jacket. In a swift, hard stare, his piercing eyes measured Chilton.

He stood poised, leaning slightly forward. His lips compressed to thin lines, and the ends of his fingers disappeared inside his jacket. Then his view jerked away. He spun around and moved off in long, gliding strides.

Chilton knew the man had challenged him in that short interval, had dared him to intervene in the controversy. Matt felt his blood rushing in response to the threat. He did not know what the dissension was about, but already he felt himself on the side of the woman.

Sixteen

"Goddamn you, Ussing, you're a thieving bastard," the woman shouted at the man as he passed in front of the open window of the room.

Ussing ignored the shrill tirade. He swung astride his mount, raked the animal cruelly with sharp spurs, and left at a fast gallop.

Matt heard the woman begin to cough, a long series of racking hacks. Had the man hurt her before he left? Matt hurried to the doorway.

A blond woman, frail and wan, lay on a bed in the room. A handkerchief was pressed tightly to her mouth as she strove to stifle her cough. Tears were shiny rivulets down her face onto the pillow.

A small, breathless moan of agony escaped her. Then she saw Matt in the doorway. She subdued her coughing and became very still.

Her lids fluttered down and veiled her large, stricken eyes. A moment later when she reopened her eyes, they were under firm control and showed only an interested watchfulness.

"May I help you?" Matt asked.

She raised a hand, so thin that the veins stood out in a fine blue network. "Only if you can hold off death," she whispered.

Then she abruptly laughed, an honest laugh that her eyes

joined in. The sound was pleasant to Matt's ears, yet strange, such a rapid change from anger and sorrow.

"How so very unfair of me," she said in a low, gentle tone. "You come as a friend and then I behave so badly. Come in. I am Sophia Carleton. Who are you?"

"Matthew Chilton. I have the room just over there." He pointed.

"I understand these rooms are for the wounded, so you must be recovering from some injury."

"Yes. But it is nothing."

Sophia evaluated his haggard face and gaunt body. His wounds had been major ones.

"Please draw up a chair and sit awhile. That is, if you have time."

"I have all the time in the world," Matt replied. "Where have you come from?" he asked, wondering about the woman as he seated himself.

"I came in yesterday on the wagon train from Vera Cruz. I was very ill. Your Major Campbell was most kind to me. He had be brought here so I could rest."

"Why were you with the wagon train?"

"I was traveling," she responded curtly.

"Yes. I suppose you were." It was none of his business why she was here.

"I have been ill for several months and should not have left Vera Cruz. The constant jarring of the wagon made my condition much worse. Do you know Mexico City?" she questioned, abruptly changing the subject.

"I have ridden through it several times."

"Would you describe it for me? I may not get to see it for a time."

"I would be glad to," replied Matt. She was not going to tell him what the conflict was between her and the man she called Ussing.

"It is a great city with magnificent buildings and broad

boulevards. There are scores of large churches and hundreds of fine restaurants. It is a very ancient city, perhaps thousands of years old. Much of the land of the city has been claimed from the lake and marshes that surround it on three sides. A long maze of canals, hundreds of miles of them, has been dredged by hand through the marshes. Boats too many to count and brightly painted are sculled and rowed along the canals for travel and to transport foodstuffs and manufactured products."

"It sounds like Venice, the beautiful city built on the water in Italy. I must see Mexico City soon. Will you take me?" she questioned, and smiled a delightful smile.

"I would be glad to. And there is something else we must see. Thirty miles northeast are the ruins of the religious city of the ancient Aztecs. It is called Teotihuacán, which means House of the Gods. Two great pyramids, one more than two hundred feet tall, exist there. The Spanish conqueror, Cortés, found a large stone diaz on top of the largest pyramid. It was heavily stained with much blood from human sacrifice made to Quetzalcoatl, the Serpent God. In his righteous Catholic anger, Cortés destroyed all the temples at the sacred city of Teotihuacán, as he also destroyed the many lesser temples in what is now called Mexico City. Here in this city he built churches for his own religion on the very foundation of the Aztec temples."

Sophia and Matt talked for a long time about many aspects of the city and its people. She laughed now and then as Matt described something that particularly caught her interest. In those moments he saw the prettiness in her thin face brighten to true beauty. He watched Sophia keenly, enjoying every trait and mannerism of the woman.

"Miss Carleton, I am Corporal Swanson," a young soldier spoke from the door. He held a small covered tray in his hands.

"Come in, Corporal. What may I do for you?"

"I am a medical orderly, Miss Carleton. Major Campbell

said I should bring this fresh fruit for your breakfast. There are oranges, mangoes, grapes, and some warm bread fresh from the oven."

"That was very thoughtful of Dr. Campbell, and kind of you to carry it to me."

"I shall go now," Matt said, rising. "I have a friend to see. Good-bye, Sophia."

"Good-bye, Matt. Please come again."

"I would like that," Matt said.

Matt waved and crossed the officers' mess to greet Tom. "Damn glad to see you," Matt said.

"Sit and have some food with me," Tom said. "We've much to talk about."

"Indeed we do. Tell me about the campaign to reach Vera Cruz."

Tom took a bite of his food and chewed thoughtfully, reflecting upon the battles to reach the coast. "Huamantla and Jalapa were both hard fights. Too many men died. Many more than should have."

"So it seems in most battles."

"Sam Walker was killed at Huamantla. Santa Anna was there with the remainder of his army, and they put up stiff resistance. Lane held the people of Huamantla responsible for Walker's death because they harbored Santa Anna. Some of the townsfolk helped him fight. After the town was captured, General Lane turned the army loose on the people. Bad, bad doings. But the road to Vera Cruz is wide open. Our patrols had two skirmishes on the way back. Nothing serious."

"That last part is good news," said Chilton. "Mexico City is fairly well under control. There are snipers now and again. The gunman gets away most times. At night there are usually two or three killings in fights between the Mexicans and our soldiers. Almost always it's the Mexicans that die. The El

Camino Real north toward the Rio Grande is often attacked by guerrillas. Our next fighting will be in that direction."

"How is General Scott succeeding in getting a treaty from the Mexicans?" asked Tom.

"He's been prevented from accomplishing that. Each time a group of Mexican officials tries to form a recognized government and have someone who can negotiate with us, the coalition falls apart from internal bickering and power struggles. At the rate the talks are going, it could be weeks, perhaps months, before a treaty is signed and the army goes home."

"I am ready to leave for Texas now," Tom said. "I'd rather earn my thirty-two dollars a month chasing outlaws than fighting the tail end of this war. How about you? Are you ready to go home?"

"I should be able to travel in a couple of weeks."

"I stopped by last night to see you, but your room was empty."

"I rode into town. Sometimes I spend the night there," Matt replied.

"Sounds like you've found yourself a woman," said Tom. "That always helps a man to heal. How about riding into the city with me this evening, if you feel like it. We can find a place that serves good food and wine."

"That's a good idea."

"I have duties until this afternoon. I'll stop by then."

"Good, I'll be in my room."

Tom rose. He remembered his brief moment of sadness of the past night when he had thought that Matt had died. He reached out and touched the shoulder of the dragoon officer. "I'm glad to see you up and walking around, old friend." Tom turned and walked away.

Would we be friends if you knew I had killed and robbed many people of their gold and silver? wondered Matt.

* * *

Cavillin finished his meal of wine, roast mutton, beans, warm bread thick with fresh butter, all topped off with a large bowl of crushed oranges and figs smothered with wild bee honey. The fruit and honey was an odd concoction, but delicious.

Chilton had already shoved his plate of food back half eaten. He was staring out the window of the restaurant and onto the Zocalo, the great plaza in the center of the city.

The late-evening sunlight bathed the one-eighth-mile-wide plaza in a soft yellow-orange glow. Scores of native vendors hovered protectively over merchandise they had displayed for sale in open stalls, or spread on brightly colored blankets on the stone pavement. Cavillin was amazed at the tremendous variety of foodstuffs and manufactured goods, ranging from nuts, fruits, and candies to clothing and children's toys. One man was trying to sell a donkey and another a hawk that threatened with shrill cries anyone that came near.

A mighty throng of townspeople and country folk milled about, talking to friends or stopping to inspect some merchandise that caught their interest, to haggle and then buy, or move on.

"It's Friday, the busiest marketing day of the week," Chilton said, gesturing out at the crowd on the square. "While you were gone, General Scott imposed regulations prohibiting price increases and also levied a duty on all merchandise to help pay for maintaining the American army."

"Wars are costly," replied Cavillin. Here and there he caught sight of Americans in uniform or two or three Texas Rangers mingling with the Mexican shoppers. A squad of soldiers led by Lieutenant Barclay marched across the plaza and left on patrol duty toward the south part of the city.

Directly opposite Tom on the far side of the Zocalo, the brown-and-red-stone Governor's Palace lined the whole eastern border of the plaza. On the northern boundary was a dark

stone cathedral with soaring towers and domes, and crosses
capping all the highest points.

A Ranger hurried from the mouth of the street that ran between the two massive buildings. He called out to another
Ranger. They talked together for a few seconds, then separated
to hasten through the gathering of people. Cavillin saw them
stop to confer briefly with several other Rangers.

The Texans began to congregate at the opening of the street
near the Governor's Palace. Some of the men were on horseback; most were afoot. Some of those walking sprang up behind riders. Riding double or trotting to keep up, the pack of
Rangers plunged down the street.

In less than a minute the crashing explosion of many firearms violently jolted the air. The crowd on the plaza swayed
fearfully back from the harsh noise.

"That's the revolvers of your Rangers," Chilton said.

"I know," agreed Cavillin, also recognizing the rapid banging of the Colts.

"I don't hear any return fire. Who in hell are they killing?"

"No one, I hope. Let's go and see what's happening."
Cavillin dropped silver coins on the table and hastened from
the restaurant. Both men swung astride their mounts.

The booming of the guns rose to a crescendo. Like a body
of water struck by a high wind, the frightened townsfolk rolled
back in a wave from the side of the Zocalo nearest the shooting. The vendors were left behind, isolated islands on the broad
expanse of the square. Swiftly they flung their wares onto carts
or bundled all in the ground clothes that they could cling on
their backs. They lifted the heavy loads and rushed after the
others, speedily abandoning the plaza.

Tom and Matt reined their cayuses through the crush of
people. Those individuals directly in front of the horsemen
dodged and scuttled aside to avoid the pounding of iron
hooves.

The two Americans left the Zocalo behind and sped past a

stretch of small warehouses and a block of older homes. They turned a corner and entered one of the brothel districts of the city.

Ahead of them, the pistol shots slackened to a sporadic popping. A man yelled a high, clear call of warning. The firing stopped. Men on foot and horseback streamed out of sight into the alleyways and cross streets. In a short moment not a man stood in the street.

"God! Look! It's a massacre," Chilton cried out.

Bodies by the scores lay sprawled on the street and sidewalks for a distance of two blocks or more. A man hung half out of a window. Several were slumped in doorways, as if they had tried to take shelter there. A woman lay unconscious on the cobblestone. Blood spurted from a hole in her throat, widening in a dark pool beneath her head.

Cavillin saw no weapons with the dead Mexicans. They appeared to have been gunned down without giving any resistance. He caught movement from the corner of his eye and spun, drawing his revolver with a lift of his hand.

Seventeen

"Just like a shooting gallery, Cavillin!" Felmers shouted. He was hanging head and shoulders out of a second-floor window and laughing drunkenly. "I watched it all from right up here in the grandstand. What a show, what a beautiful show. You should have been here, Lieutenant."

"Get your ass down here, Felmers," ordered Cavillin.

"Right, Lieutenant. Wait there for me. I'll be down. If my legs will work."

Felmers withdrew from the window opening and stumbled noisily down the stairway. He staggered out onto the street and stood tottering. He grinned at the two officers and chuckled wickedly.

"What in hell happened here?" Cavillin questioned grimly.

"Just target practice," said Felmers. "The Mexicans played mean and rough, and then our boys taught them how killing is really done. You should have seen the greasers trying to get away when our fellows opened up with their Colts. This little killing helps pay for the Americans Santa Anna murdered at Goliad and the Alamo. And for Allsens being dead. It's a fitting payment, Cavillin. You should be happy too."

Tom kicked his horse close to Felmers, reached down, and grabbed him by the shirtfront. He shook the drunken man roughly. "Damn you, Felmers, sober up. Tell me quick what went on here."

"Cavillin, you don't have to treat me this way. They were only greasers. Let me go so I can tell you."

Tom released his grip. "Do it fast."

"Right. One of our Rangers, Allsens, got in an argument with a brown-skinned whore. He wasn't being real mean to her, just slapping her around a little. Some of the Mexican men who protect the whores came to help her. Allsens didn't listen when they told him to stop. Damned if they didn't cut him up awfully bad, and he fell on the street and bled to death in a minute. He's laying down there half a block or so. Well, Allsens's buddy runs up to Zocalo and brings back nineteen or twenty Rangers. They shot the hell out of anybody that looked like he might be guilty of doing Allsens in."

Felmers teetered and caught himself against the wall of the building. He laughed inanely. "I just wish I had had a chance to help. But I couldn't hold my gun steady enough to hit anything."

A rhythmic cadence of many feet pounding the stone pavement at a double-quick march drummed along the street.

"Barclay and his patrol are coming on the run," Chilton said. "They'll arrest Felmers if they catch him, whether or not he's too drunk to have killed anyone. Scott will put somebody before a firing squad for these killings."

"Felmers, climb up behind me," Cavillin directed. "We'll ride double."

"Sure, Lieutenant," Felmers said, shoving himself away from the wall.

"Move, man, move!" Cavillin snapped. "Once the patrol turns the corner and sees us, it'll be too late to run." He slid his foot from the stirrup nearest the Ranger so he could use it.

Felmers huffed and grunted as he tried vainly to pull himself up on the rear of the horse. He failed and sagged limply on the horse's flank.

Tom bent, clamped Felmers by the belt, and hoisted mightily.

"Strong as an ox. Strong as an ox," Felmers said as he was swung onto the rump of the horse. He clutched Cavillin around the waist.

"Spur! Lieutenant, spur! I don't want to get shot by any firing squad."

In the early darkness of the night, Cavillin and Chilton reached the quarters of the Rangers in Tacubaya. They stopped at one of the houses occupied by the Texans. Cavillin slid from the saddle and helped Felmers to the ground.

"This won't take long, Matt. Wait for me," Tom said.

Mostly carrying the intoxicated Ranger, Tom shuffled him through the door and dumped him unceremoniously on a cot in the dark room. "Felmers, it would be best if you forget you were in Mexico City today," Tom said, staring at the dim outline of the man. The only response was a ragged snore.

Cavillin retreated from the house. Chilton had dismounted, and together they silently walked, leading their horses along the street.

They climbed to the ridge top and veered right in the direction of the hospital. Ahead, Chilton saw Sophia's door open and lamplight running out to fall on the ground in a yellow mist.

Matt slowed. "Tom, I see a friend of mine is still awake. She's ill. I think I'll stop and talk with her and help her pass the long evening."

"Okay. I must find Sumner and Ripley. The Rangers are in bad trouble. We must plan a strategy to keep our men from facing a court-martial."

"Good luck. You'll need it. See you in the morning."

"Right." Tom strode on and was lost in the night.

Chilton moved to Sophia's door and knocked softly on the casing. "Sophia, it's Matt Chilton. Do you want some company and conversation?"

"That would be most enjoyable, Matt." Sophia's voice had a happy lilt. "Come in."

He stepped inside. Sophia sat in a chair near the bed. The room was warm with lingering memories of the heat of the day.

"Let's go outside where it's cooler," Matt suggested.

"I may need someone to lean on to walk," she said.

"That is easily arranged. Here, sit on the bed while I take your chair outside and get my own. I'll be right back."

They sat late into the night beneath the tree near Matt's room. The black, sooty sky settled around them, close and soft. They talked of many things. And the lights of the city in the valley of Anahuac grew dimmer and dimmer as the hours aged and the tired citizens of that ancient place sought their sleep.

"Let us go inside, Matt," Sophia said. "I'm getting chilled."

"Certainly."

As Matt lowered Sophia onto her bed, she whispered to him, "Will you hold me and warm me? I am terribly cold."

Gently, he pulled her close.

She and he made their own brief-lived world wrapped in each other's arms.

Chilton stepped from his room in the gray morning dusk. He leaned wearily against the wall of the house and gazed down at the city, lying in a valley half full of night shadows. He waited impatiently for the first light of the sun.

The yellow orb crested the eastern mountains, and its bright rays evaporated the last traces of the night in Tacubaya. Chilton drew his Colt revolver and in the new light began to rotate the cylinder. Carefully he scrutinized the loads. One firing cap was less than perfect. He flipped it off and pressed on a fresh one.

"Good morning, Matt," Cavillin called out as he turned from the street and came up the pathway to the house.

Chilton glanced toward the call, raised a hand in acknowledgment, and turned back to inspect the firing pin of his weapon.

"Matt, I'd like for you to act as a lawyer for my Rangers if they have to go before a court-martial board," Tom said as he drew near. "Sumner and Ripley and I would help you prepare the defense, but we want you to present it."

"Sure," Matt answered shortly. "But I have no time to talk about it now." He shoved the Colt into its holster. He drew his single-shot pistol from his belt and began to check it carefully.

Cavillin saw the tautness in Chilton, the jaws clamped and rigid. "What's happening, Matt? You act like you're getting ready to kill somebody."

"It may come to that."

"Well, hell, tell me about it," exclaimed Tom.

"A man named Wade Ussing refuses to give Sophia the money he has been holding for her. That's eight thousand dollars and a lot of money. She needs it badly."

"I'll be damned," Tom said in surprise. "This Ussing, is he a tall hombre and dark?"

"You know him?"

"If it's the same man I'm thinking of, I saw him kill an army officer in Vera Cruz. He ran a whorehouse down there. Now, what is he doing here in Mexico City?" In consternation, Tom stopped speaking. Sophia had been Ussing's favorite whore. What relationship existed between her and Matt?

"I know what she was," Matt said in answer to Tom's unasked question. "Ussing says he won't give her the money until she comes back to work. But she's not going to return to that business. She plans to rest a few weeks to recover from her illness and then go to New Orleans. The money must be gotten for her."

"Matt, I have seen Ussing move. He will be very quick Maybe faster than you."

"Maybe he is and maybe not. It doesn't make any difference I'm going to make him give the money to Sophia."

"Most likely he will have other men with him. These whore masters know they are in a tough business and are prepare for the worst."

Matt shrugged his shoulders. He put the pistol in his belt.

"Do you believe she tells the truth that Ussing owes he that much money?" asked Tom.

"I'm certain of it. I heard them arguing about it."

"Then I'll ride along with you. Perhaps I can keep hi friends busy while you deal with him."

"I'd be very pleased to have you do that," Matt said grate fully. With the Ranger's help, he just might survive the nex hour.

"Where does Ussing hang out?"

"He's rented a large house in the city a couple of block east of the Alameda Plaza."

"Then let's go and brace the fellow."

"He'll give us the money either alive or dead," growle Matt, his anger very cold, hard, and determined.

The big stone house had luckily escaped the bombardmen during the battle for Mexico City. It was very old but wel maintained and strikingly handsome. A wide porch with a ornately carved railing ran the full length of the front.

A large, powerfully built man sat on a chair on the porch He was reared back, with his shoulders and yellow-thatche head resting on the wall. He had been on guard since midnigh and was in a foul mood.

From under hooded eyelids Jungling sourly watched the tw riders approaching between the rows of houses lining th streets. Their undeviating course pointed straight at the hous of Ussing. The damn fools must know the women would be resting and the bar closed at this time of day.

Jungling stood up as the men drew rein and stopped. One of the men was in the uniform of a cavalry officer. The second wore civilian clothing, and Jungling judged him to be a Texas Ranger. Jungling saw the pistols on their belts. The men dismounted and tied their horses to iron rings fastened to an iron post embedded in the ground.

"Gents, we're all closed up until this afternoon," Jungling said.

"We came to talk to Ussing," Chilton said. "Call him."

Jungling stepped to the edge of the porch so he could tower over the men. "He's sleeping. Your business can wait. Come back later."

With a vigilant eye Tom watched the man and the doors and windows of the house. He let Matt talk. It was his game.

"It can't wait," growled Chilton. "You wake him or we will."

"I said he was asleep. He'd be mad as hell if I get him up this early." Jungling saw the hard set of the men's faces. He let his hand swing near the revolver on his hip.

"Ussing! Wade Ussing! Come out here!" Chilton's shout rebounded from the perpendicular sides of the houses and went echoing down the street.

"Damn you, stop that bellowing," Jungling ordered. He started down the steps toward Matt.

"Stop. Stand where you are." Cavillin's words were like steel darts flying at Jungling.

The yellow-haired man swung his attention to Tom. The tips of his fingers touched the butt of his revolver.

"You had better be damn good with that gun, or you're a dead man," warned Cavillin.

Jungling saw the deadly intent of the Ranger to draw upon him. He was jolted by the readiness of the man for combat. He had been in gunfights and had killed many men, but he always chose those battles heavily in his favor. Some animal instinct warned him that this time the odds were wrong and death was very near.

The door behind Jungling opened, and Ussing stalked out. A small, swarthy man followed behind. He took a position on Ussing's left.

"All right, Jungling, hold it for now," Ussing ordered.

He had seen the two men before. The dragoon officer only yesterday, and the Ranger weeks ago in Vera Cruz. They meant trouble, and trouble was bad for business. His women were set up in this fine house. The first day's trade was finished, and he had made a bundle. He had even made a very profitable purchase of jewels from a captain of the Kentucky volunteers. Wade's reputation for buying stolen objects had followed him from Vera Cruz.

"What's your problem?" Wade questioned.

"You have eight thousand dollars that belongs to Sophia Carleton," Chilton said. "She has asked me to bring it to her. I have a written authorization from her to do this." He pulled a piece of paper from his shirt pocket. "If you care to see it."

Ussing did not answer. He swept his glance over both men, plotting his strategy for shooting them. The dragoon was gaunt and looked ill. But his hand rested on his pistol. He would surely fight. The eyes of the Ranger were those of a confident animal sure of its skill to kill.

Cavillin stared into the calculating glance of the whoremaster. He felt the savage emotion growing in him to do battle with this man who used women so meanly and who had killed an army officer. At the thought of blasting a bullet through Ussing, Tom's mouth twisted into a reckless, lopsided grin that showed his teeth.

A hot urge rushed through Ussing to grab his pistol and shoot the grinning, bastard Ranger. He raised his view and looked along the street as he fought the dangerous passion. A workman walked toward the Alameda. A woman left her house, bellowed across the avenue, and started a conversation with another woman.

Wade's gimlet eyes were suddenly devoid of life, as emotionless as a blind man's. The dragoon and Ranger could not be slain here and now. He would be mad to let them provoke him into a fight where people could see.

Ussing knew of the fierce vengeance the Rangers had taken the previous evening when they had murdered nearly a hundred Mexicans for the death of one of their company. The Rangers would wreck his establishment with the same relish for killing this man. The regular army would investigate the death of their lieutenant. Ussing must keep the goodwill of both the Rangers and Scott's regulars if he was to stay in business and accumulate the fortune he so desired.

"So I owe Sophia eight thousand dollars, do I? Let me see her signature on your paper."

Chilton extended the paper. Ussing examined the writing for a moment. "You will get it, but I don't carry that kind of money around as pocket change. I must go and open my safe. Wait here."

Cavillin was instinctively suspicious of the whoremaster. He was a treacherous man, and such an abrupt switch was most likely a trick.

"Matt, I'll go with Ussing. You keep watch on these two."

"Good idea," Matt agreed.

Ussing led the way to a back room of the house. He knelt in front of a heavy safe and dialed a series of left and right numbers. With his body he shielded the contents of the safe from Tom's view.

"Here is eight thousand. Now leave while you can," Ussing said in a tightly controlled voice. "I may change my mind."

"Walk back outside with me," replied Tom. "I don't want you behind me."

Ussing, his back stiff, stalked through the house.

Tom nodded at Matt. "I have it."

They mounted, warily watching Ussing and his gunmen. Tom and Matt left at a slow walk.

"Señor Ussing, why did we not kill them?" the Spaniard Gonzalez asked in a puzzled tone. "We could have done it easily."

Positive of the swiftness of his hand, Wade also believed Sophia's friends could have been killed. But it would not have been easy.

"I want them both killed," rasped Ussing. "But not here in the street. Follow and find out their names and where they are billeted. Tonight they die."

Eighteen

General Scott growled low in his chest. His normally ruddy face was pale with his anger. "Eighty-one men and two women were killed in the city last evening." He leaned forward over his desk and glared at Major Sumner. He swung his scalding view to rake Ripley and Cavillin.

Tom remained straight and stiff at attention. He looked directly past the general and into the wall. Scott was just getting wound up. He had much more to say.

"Our investigation has shown to my complete satisfaction that the Rangers did the killing. They were seen entering the street where it occurred, and that was just seconds before the shooting."

The general slammed his hand on the desktop. A pile of written reports bounced into the air and fluttered like crippled birds to the floor. Scott glanced down at the scattered papers. "Goddamn," he said.

His face raised, and there was a look of hopelessness on it for an instant before he masked it. "How in the grace of God can I get a properly ratified treaty from the Mexicans with this kind of action against the population? Why can't you so-called Ranger officers keep your men under control?"

"Those men that I have questioned swear that the Mexicans fired upon them first and the Rangers merely defended themselves," replied Sumner. "That is permitted by your own orders."

"Don't play games with me, Major. Only eleven handguns and no rifles were found on the dead. Just one of those pistols had been fired. Does that sound like the arms of an attacking party?"

"Then someone must have hidden the weapons to make my Rangers appear guilty," Sumner said.

"Bullshit," thundered the general. "Lieutenant Barclay and his patrol were there within three or four minutes after the shooting. He swears that nothing was bothered or removed."

"I know what the Rangers tell me."

"And you want to believe them, to protect them. That is a laudable action, but it won't suffice here."

"In a court-martial hearing, if all the men stick to their version of this incident, not one will be convicted of any crime."

"Don't tell me how a court-martial would decide," snapped the general. He paused. "We are running out of time here in Mexico. The enlistments of the volunteers are rapidly expiring. One hundred Pennsylvanians go home this week. Five hundred Kentuckians leave next month. By early spring I'll have only the regular army units here. That's less than three thousand men to maintain military control of a nation of millions. An uprising with any degree of popular support could drive us into the sea, or worse, trap us here in the mountains. You Rangers are destroying the very victory we fought and bled for."

He rubbed his jaw, and a flinty glimmer came into his eyes. "Your men will not be brought up on charges. I have a different solution. Never again will you Rangers have liberty in Mexico City. In fact, I want them out of my sight permanently. Since you like to fight and kill Mexicans, then that is what you will do every day you are with this army. You will prepare immediately for a long campaign. No later than noon today, you and all your men will march north on El Camino Real. I want

that route swept clear of all guerrillas, all the way to Matamoros on the Texas border.

"I will notify the supply officer to issue sufficient ammunition and supplies for your needs. When you return, I want
a report that the road is open. Immediately after that, every
man jack of you will continue straight to Vera Cruz on the
coast. I will have ships waiting there to transport you to Texas.
Do you have any questions, Major?"

"No, sir."

"Then carry out my orders."

The three officers saluted and started to turn.

"One additional thing, Major Sumner. Several of your Rangers were law officers before they joined us for the march
against Mexico. I have a special task for your best detective."

The Rangers stopped in surprise. "What is that, General?"
asked Sumner.

"I want a band of robbers caught."

"I have heard of an officer with a squad of men collecting
tribute from some of the outlying towns," Sumner said.

"Tribute, hell. He has no orders from me. It is simple robbery. He has fifteen or so mounted men. They go straight for
the bank, threatening to burn every building in the town if the
bankers and town officials refuse to open the vault."

"The officer calls himself Captain Charles Gilchrist. He always signs a receipt for the contents of the vaults."

"This Captain Gilchrist is not one of my men," Sumner said
with certainty.

"No one said he was," snapped the general. "The bandits
are very disciplined and military in every way. That eliminates
the Rangers."

Sumner did not rise to challenge Scott's comment on the
Rangers. "You are certain the bandits are Americans?"

"The people of the towns are certain. They heard the men
speak fluent English. They were white men."

"Were they in uniforms?"

"Yes, but as they were described to me, not in uniforms that I could identify. They wore pieces of clothing from different army units. I want the attacks on the towns to cease. Now who will head up this operation?"

"Cavillin should be the man," Sumner said. "He was a fine lawman before the war. Captain Ripley and I will command the Rangers on the campaign on the El Camino Real."

"Very well, Cavillin, the task is yours," Scott said. "How many men do you want?"

"Before I can answer that, I need more information," Tom said. "What towns have they hit?"

"I will show you." The general unfolded a map and spread it on his desk.

Cavillin examined the map quietly. It represented an area some eighty miles across. A score of towns were located along the roads radiating out from Mexico City. The major elevations and drainages were depicted.

Scott spoke. "I had our army engineers prepare this from existing Mexican maps and their own surveys. The first town robbed was Coyoacan, about eight days ago." He stabbed the map with a finger. "Here. That was a rich mining town. Three days later they hit San Augustin, here. The last one was Cuernavaca, twenty miles out along this road. The alcalde of Cuernavaca just left this office not an hour ago after complaining of his town's loss of all its money. He holds me responsible for the robbery. In a way I guess I am, since I'm sure the bandits are American."

"What are these?" questioned Cavillin, pointing at one of several small, widely spaced squares with names written beside them.

"That symbol represents the locations and names of several of the large ranches that lie in the mountains. None of them have been bothered. Not yet."

Cavillin pondered the job before him. He made his judgment. "I'll need fifty Rangers and a map like this one," he said.

"Fifty men," ejaculated the general in surprise. "There are but fifteen or sixteen outlaws."

"Perhaps that is correct. Counting the ranches and towns, the bandits can hit any of dozens of places. I need to post men at many locations to spot their movement."

"What is your plan?" asked General Scott.

"I want everybody to think I've gone north with Major Sumner and the Ranger companies. After a day I'll turn aside with my men. The hardest part of the operation will be to find this Captain Gilchrist and his band of men."

"Major Sumner, give Lieutenant Cavillin his fifty men." The general faced Cavillin. "Catch the bastards. If you come upon them in the act of robbing a town, shoot the hell out of them. I'd just as soon bury them as have a trial. Do you understand me?"

"Yes, sir."

"Good. You are dismissed. I don't want to see any of you again until you've carried out my orders."

Cavillin heard the complaining grumble and grouch of the Rangers behind him. The men knew they had been ordered to clear the El Camino Real of guerrillas as punishment for the shooting spree in the red-light district in Mexico City. In their minds the revenge they had taken against the Mexicans had been well justified and they resented any opinions that it had not been.

The company of the Rangers rode north in loose formation, two abreast in a long line on the broad boulevard, San Juan de Aragon in Mexico City. The people, thick on the street, drew back from the clatter of the hundreds of iron-shod hooves on the stone pavement.

A Mexican youth, carrying a shallow tray at his waist, stood on the street. The container was supported by a leather strap around his neck. In a pleasant tenor voice he hawked his wares, bragging of the delicious taste of the hard candies in a wide array of colors and piled in individual partitions on the tray.

"I got to feed my sweet tooth," one of the Rangers in the last rank said. He reined out of the column and rode up to the candy peddler.

The youth smiled uncertainly as the rider leaned from his horse and scooped up a large handful of candies. The Ranger wheeled his mount and galloped after his comrades.

"Tres centavos," called the peddler. "You owe me tres centavos for that candy."

The Ranger did not slow or look back. He popped one of the sweets into his mouth.

"Tres centavos, you Yankee pig," the peddler said, lashing out in a furious voice.

The youth hastily lifted the strap of the tray from his neck and set the candy on the street. He snatched up a chunk of broken cobblestone from the pavement, cocked his arm, and hurled the missile.

His aim was true. The projectile hit the American in the back with a solid thump.

Almost too fast to see, the Ranger dropped the candy, drew his revolver, and whirled toward the rear. The gun cracked. The bullet struck the young Mexican in the chest. He staggered backward and fell heavily to the hard surface of the boulevard.

All the Rangers spun to look in the direction of the shot. Pistols appeared in every hand. The Americans jerked the reins of the horses tight in preparation to shoot or ride quickly.

Cavillin spurred back along his column. He swept a swift glance at the Mexican peddler sprawled on the ground, and the Ranger solemnly reloading the fired chamber of his pistol.

"What in hell happened here, Wardlow?" Cavillin questioned.

Wardlow looked up from his gun.

"The son of a bitch hit me with a rock. For half a second I thought I had been shot again. Felt that same way."

"Why would he throw a rock at you?"

"I just took a little candy. Nothing serious."

"You stole his candy and then wouldn't pay. Is that the way it was?"

"Hell, yes. Every soldier in this army has stolen more valuable things than that. I've seen them rape and kill too. So have you, and only just days ago."

"There have been times and places when all that happened. This wasn't one of the right times. Damn you, Wardlow. Scott said we would pay for what we took. We want peace with these people. The war is over in this city."

"It'll never be over for me," rasped Wardlow, finishing the loading of his pistol. "And don't cuss me again."

"The war in this city is over, Wardlow, even for you, as long as you ride in my Ranger company. If ever you cause trouble again, you'll answer to me personally. Do you hear me plain?"

Wardlow's grip on the pistol tightened, and his thumb rested on the hammer. His eyes battled with Cavillin's.

"Do you understand me, Wardlow?" snapped Cavillin, his voice cutting the air. "Answer, yes, sir, or use your gun."

"Yes, sir," Wardlow said in a guttural, malevolent voice. With a shaking hand he shoved his pistol into its holster.

"Get back into rank," ordered Cavillin.

Tom regretted the death of the young candy peddler. He turned toward the crowd of sullen-faced Mexicans near the body and shouted out loudly in Spanish, "I'm sorry for this man's death." He repeated, "I'm sorry," and meant it.

Cavillin spurred and galloped his mount to the head of the column of Rangers. He glanced back at the hard countenances of the riders. Wardlow was correct. The hatred between the Texans and the Mexicans would not end during this generation of men. Too many dead lay blocking that possibility.

* * *

Cavillin sat in the shade beneath a large tree on a hilltop ten miles northwest of Mexico City. Methodically he worked a telescope to scan the broad valley the Aztecs called Anahuac.

It was the afternoon of the second day after General Scott had commanded Cavillin to capture the American marauders robbing the Mexican towns. Thirty-three of his men lay lazing on their bedrolls in the shade. The remaining seventeen Rangers were stationed at strategic, hidden lookouts on the roads fanning out from Mexico City to the outlying villages in the mountains. Tom waited patiently. Soon now one of his sentinels would come with word that the renegades were riding. The Rangers would run them to earth.

Tom allowed his view to wander to the city and forty miles beyond to the snowcapped peaks of Popocatépetl and Ixtacihuatl, stabbing four miles into the sky. A gray tendril of vapor, hardly visible at the long distance, climbed into the sky from Popocatépetl.

Some of Cortés's men, exploring the mountain, had found sulfur precipitating out of the volcanic gases. When the Spanish commander had run short of gunpowder during his battle with Montezuma, he had ordered some of his soldiers to scale the mountain and descend into the crater. There they had scraped the pure yellow sulfur from the rock walls and carried it back to Cortés. The Spanish gun masters mixed the sulfur with charcoal and potassium nitrate to produce gunpowder. With firearms once again charged, the Spaniards had marched upon the inhabitants of the city and conquered them.

Overhead the dome of the sky was a faded blue, bleached by the intensity of the sun. To the east lay Lake Texcoco, its salty brine a brilliant turquoise. North of Texcoco rested the dry, yellow clay bed of a lake dead for a thousand years.

A wind blew from the southeast, sweeping the hotter air of

Anahuac toward the mountains. Heated unevenly by the baking sunlight, the wind in places was losing its smooth, laminar flow and beginning to eddy and rotate. The swirls grew and pirouetted like invisible dancers, and then, as their strength increased, birthed giant dust devils that dizzily spun yellow dust around and upward in vortices of counterclockwise-rotating turbulent pools of air three to four hundred feet deep. The ghostly columns, like giant dancing worms, wiggled and zigzagged along to the northwest with the wind.

Tom lowered his glass and sat for a long time staring out over the land with its aged civilization. Such a beautiful place, too beautiful for so much savagery and death.

He looked down at the swarm of eight or nine dust devils. A horse and rider, made small by the long distance, were speeding over the dry lake bottom. A ground cloud of dust like a yellow tail followed the swiftly approaching horseman as he swerved and curved around to escape the gyrating dust.

Soon Tom recognized the form of Ken Macy, one of his Rangers, on a running horse. Macy's arm was rising and falling as he lashed his steed.

Cavillin climbed to his feet. "Get ready to ride," he called to the slumbering Rangers. "The chase begins."

The sweat-streaked horse was dragged to a halt near Tom. Macy sprang down.

"They are riding," Macy said. "They were widely scattered out along the road. It took them two hours to pass where I was hiding. I counted sixteen Americans. If I hadn't known what to look for, I'd have thought they were just soldiers out for a ride. But they rode businesslike and did not look around like someone out sight-seeing. Though I was some distance away, all looked like they were wearing uniforms of dragoons."

"Maybe they were and maybe not," said Cavillin. "It's easy to get the uniforms of another regiment now that the supply train is in from Vera Cruz."

Tom spread a map. Granger and Macy knelt to lean over it with him. Other men crowded close to see.

"Macy, you were stationed here." Tom pointed at a spot on the map where a road from Mexico City entered the foothills of the mountains. "Which direction did the men go?"

"The bunch of them gathered here in some woods on the side of a hill"—Macy touched the map—"and went off across country paralleling this road."

"It appears they are heading for Xalostoc," said Granger.

"Yes, and that means they have about twenty-five miles to ride," said Cavillin.

"It is very late in the day for them to travel so far. The gang will find a place close to Xalostoc and spend the night. In the morning they will hit the town just as it is waking up."

"What now?" asked Macy in an expectant voice. "Do we try to catch them in the town?"

"No," replied Cavillin. "They will surely have a lookout posted and we'd never slip up on them. We'll waylay them after they get the money and are on the trail back to Mexico City."

Cavillin studied the map, evaluating the mountainous terrain, the roads snaking over the land, and the few ranches widely located between Xalostoc and the capital city.

"If I had robbed Xalostoc and was trying to get back to Mexico City without being seen, I'd climb up from the town and ride this long strip of benchland on the side of the mountain. Then drop down through the foothills in the late evening and into Mexico City in the dark. We will ride to here on the flank of the mountain about five miles from Xalostoc. If I have our bandit leader figured correctly, he will lead his men right to us."

Cavillin folded his map. "Mount up," he called. He felt the rising exhilaration of the hunt. "We've many miles to cover before it turns night."

The Rangers rode down the brushy slant of the hill and

came out onto the lake bed. The pace of the horses was lifted to a ground-devouring gallop.

The madly twirling dust devils spun away, as if knowingly and deliberately leaving the course of the Rangers clear.

Nineteen

Chilton halted the swift flight from Xalostoc and flung his squad of dragoons in a skirmish line across the main road leading from the town. If the citizens wanted a fight, then let it be here, for he did not want a long drawn-out pursuit as had occurred at Cuernavaca, then still in the end to have to kill some of the townsfolk to turn them back.

Mexican horsemen moved on the streets, gathering into a crowd of forty or so at the edge of Xalostoc. Matt called out an order, and the dragoons trotted their mounts back a hundred yards toward the town. Show the Mexicans that the dragoons are willing to fight, thought Chilton. Perhaps he could bluff and scare them from venturing out to challenge the Americans and in this manner prevent a battle.

Matt brought his men to a standstill facing the town. They sat their prancing mounts and held their carbines ready.

The dragoons waited, letting the slow minutes pass, and no men of Xalostoc rode out to do battle with them. Chilton knew there was a second reason that the Mexicans held back. What untrained horsemen wanted to fight sixteen heavily armed cavalrymen for a measly six thousand pesos, and that money probably belonging to other men?

Chilton cursed his damn dismal luck. The vault of the rather sizable bank had contained only the pitifully small amount of Mexican paper money and not one gold coin. Yet the town of about three thousand folk was prosperous, that was evident. Many of the buildings were quite large and well built, and the shops around the plaza were full of merchandise. The soils of the farms were deep and rich. So where was the money that men used in trade and as a form of wealth?

"Form up," Chilton ordered. "Let's ride."

For some instinctive reason Chilton could not have explained, he guided his band of dragoons down from the surface of the plain into an arroyo, hiding them there as they fled Xalostoc. They ran their steeds, splashing the water holes and flinging dirt from the sandbars.

The ravine, flat-bottomed and steep-sided, extended southeast across the valley. Matt judged that it should reach the mountains two miles south of where he had camped with his men during the night. That was good, for he did not want to return to Mexico City along the route they had traveled before.

The arroyo began to shallow, then abruptly ended. Matt spurred his horse in a scrambling run up the precipitous dirt wall to the flatland above. Behind him, his men shouted encouragement to their mounts. Leather whips slapped sharply on sweating flanks.

Pawing and tearing at the bank, the beasts surged up from the depths of the ravine in a pall of newly spun dust. Matt cast a quick look back. All the riders had safely made the ascent. He raced them across the two hundred yards to the dense woods on the flank of the Sierra Zoltepetl Mountains.

The dragoons fought upward, tearing a path through the thick tangle of brush growing on the stony side of the mountain.

An hour later, with the horses laboring mightily, the riders came onto a lightly used wagon road. Matt stared to the southeast along the way. Out there, thirty-five miles or so and beyond the mountains and foothills, lay Mexico City. He heard the strenuous breathing of the horses around him. If the dragoons held to the brush, the animals would soon be totally exhausted. Matt turned to follow the easier route toward the city.

The road showed signs of recent use, the weeds crushed and the barren spots of earth containing imprints of horses' hooves and narrow, iron-rimmed wheels. A small wagon or buggy escorted by several riders had passed.

"Not older than early this morning," said Stoffer, also observing the hoof and wheel indentations. "They came from the direction of Xalostoc. Do you suppose they are hauling the gold that we could not find?"

"Long odds against that being the case. But it's going in the direction we want to go, so we'll follow along and check it out."

"Seven riders and two men in the wagon," said Chilton. "They are not caballeros but men in uniform and armed with muskets for a fight. That man on the gray horse is an officer in the Mexican army."

The dragoons had overtaken the cavalcade of horsemen and wagon on a stretch of winding road. The Americans had quickly veered aside into the trees before they were seen. Matt studied the Mexicans thoughtfully. What was one of Santa Anna's officers doing here with a patrol? What were they transporting?

"Do you think we should attack them, Lieutenant?" asked Stoffer. "I'd like to see what they are hauling."

"I would also like to know," Matt said. He watched the soldier on point guard fifty yards in front, and the rear one an equal distance behind, warily scan the terrain in all directions.

"Whatever it is, it's heavy," said the sergeant. "I can see the wagon jar as the springs bottom out on the axle every time a rut is hit."

"Let's get closer," Matt said. He led off through the trees beside the road.

The woods fell away, and the road came out into a broad meadow. The Mexican patrol turned up a lane toward a large stone-and-wood hacienda set at the upper end of the opening. A circular corral of an acre or so and a long, narrow barn were set off to the right side. Matt saw several horses tied in stalls within the barn. On the opposite end of the house were an ungrazed field of grass and a garden. More distant, perhaps a fifth of a mile away, was a cluster of small, one-room structures, the homes of the ranch peons. Matt heard the slender tinkling of children's laughter.

The wagon stopped at the front of the house. Six of the guards lifted heavy bags from the wagon and carried them inside. The last guard took the reins of the mounts and went off with the pair of men in the wagon to the barn.

"Only gold would be that heavy for its bulk," said Towell.

Chilton ranged his view over the hacienda with its massive walls. Heavy wooden shutters hung at every window, ready to be slammed shut. He could make out gunports in the shutters.

"That's a damn strong fortress to protect the gold if that's what they have," Stoffer said. "What do you think, Lieutenant?"

"We know the money of Xalostoc has been moved. Perhaps it is here. We can go take a look, or continue on to camp at Tacubaya. What say you all? But consider this, I believe those soldiers will certainly fight."

"You call the tune, Lieutenant," said Towell.

The remaining men nodded in agreement. Stoffer said, "Yes, you decide."

Chilton remembered how once he could have hurled his men without hesitation straight into the flaming muzzles of enemy cannon to capture a gun emplacement or a strong redoubt. Now, today, he sensed the weakness of that daring resolve to gamble their lives. However, he must not let them know that.

They must remain strong in their belief in him until their goal was reached.

"We go in," Matt said in a flat tone.

"From here and spurring like crazy, it'll take twelve to thirteen seconds to reach the hacienda," Stoffer said.

"We don't do it in a charge," Chilton replied. "See that area of tall grass stretching out across the hillside? Then comes the garden that goes up near the house. The horses will walk quiet in those places."

"The Mexicans will see us and shoot the hell out of us out here in the clearing," exclaimed Towell.

"They will surely hear us if we come pounding in. There will be no surprise, and some of us could die. But instead we'll walk up silently on the end of the house where the men in the barn can't see us. The troopers in the house will stay inside long enough to have a cold drink and talk a couple of minutes before they're organized into guard details. We'll catch them before that happens and they come outside.

"Now, no more delay in discussing it." Chilton's voice was firm and confident. He kicked his horse out of the protective cover of the trees and started over the meadow.

He tensed for the crash of a rifle or a cry of alarm. There was only the chitter of the insects in the grass of the meadow and the faint laugh of the distant children in innocent play.

Chilton whispered over his shoulder to Stoffer. "Pick four men to go with you. Once the rest of us are inside, you continue on and keep the Mexicans in the barn from joining in the fight."

"Right, sir." The sergeant dropped back to tell the others of the plan.

The band reached the middle of the tall-grass area. Then the edge of the garden was made good. The hooves of the horses crunched through long rows of green and red peppers, and a patch of late-growing melons.

Against the wall of the hacienda, Chilton swung down from

his mount. "Darcy," he whispered, "hold the horses. You be here if we need to leave in a hurry."

"I'll not budge," Darcy responded.

"Towell, take those four men," Matt said, "and go in the rear door. You five come with me. Sergeant, get ready to do your part."

Chilton pulled his pistols as he moved around the corner. The door was forty, fifty feet away beyond two windows. The space to cross was exposed, dangerous, and seemed immensely long. The barn was in full view past the house. Anyone there could easily see the Americans.

He heard the soft steps of his men behind him as he moved. The first window was passed. Then the second. The door was ajar. A man speaking Spanish was giving orders, setting watch periods for the guards.

Matt sprang through the door in a headlong rush. He darted to the side to allow those behind to enter unimpeded. His pistols lifted, the open black bores of the barrels swinging to find targets.

The Mexicans stood near the center of the large room. An old man who had not been with the soldiers was beside the officer. They all whirled in astonishment as the Americans poured in. Their hands grabbed for pistols.

"Hold it," Matt cried out in Spanish, "and you shall live."

His words were far too late. Already guns had been snatched up, cocked, and were rising to point.

Matt began to shoot. A heavily bearded man was very quick. Chilton shot into the center of him. The man's bones melted and he collapsed. The officer fell at Matt's second shot.

Then many pistols were banging beside Chilton. Others exploded from the rear door. A fierce wind seemed to strike the Mexicans, spinning them, whipping them backward, to fall crashing down.

One of the dying men fired into the floor as he fell. Another man, preparing to shoot, was whirled around by the strike of a bullet. He shot a comrade in the side.

Matt began to breathe again. Not one bullet came close to the dragoons. The surprise had been complete.

He stepped to the side to see past the cloud of gray gunpowder smoke boiling and eddying in front of him. One of the Mexican soldiers, shot through the neck and spinal cord, began to buck and roll and twitch like a berserk marionette.

A dragoon revolver exploded. The man on the floor jerked and then lay crumpled and still.

A rapid rattle of gunshot sounded from outside. A half minute later Stoffer, with his pistol cocked, came cautiously in the door. His glance swept over the dead men and then rested on Chilton.

"All secure at the barn, Lieutenant," Stoffer reported.

"My God! Look at this," Towell croaked in amazement. "Gold!" He was peering into one of the leather bags the soldiers had carried inside. He sprang to another one and ripped off the tie. "More gold!"

The Americans gathered around. The men nearest Towell plunged their hands into the throats of the bags and scooped up quantities of yellow coins to show to their comrades.

"No town the size of Xalostoc ever had this much wealth," Stoffer muttered in a weak yet elated voice.

"What's this?" Darcy asked, holding up a small pint-sized pouch he had extracted from one of the larger sacks. He jerked the tie loose and poured part of the contents into the palm of his hand.

"Jewels! Holy heaven! Jewels of all colors and sizes." His young voice cracked and broke.

"This is Santa Anna's private treasure hoard," Chilton said, staring at the great fortune. "That explains why the officer was here. He must have been one of the general's trusted staff."

"Maybe we won't have to rob any more towns," Darcy said in a hopeful tone.

"I'd say you're correct," replied Matt. "There is sufficient wealth to more than satisfy our needs. Sergeant Stoffer, let's get out of here quickly. The shots could be heard a long distance over the mountainside."

"Shall we take the wagon to haul all this weight?"

"No. Rig three of the horses for packing. We want the ability to travel wherever it's safest, the deep woods or the steepest mountain slopes. Make sure the horses are loaded lightly so they can keep up regardless of how fast we ride. Use four of them if needed."

Stoffer jabbed a finger at the two men nearest to him. "You and you, come with me." They trotted out the door.

"Carry all this outside," ordered Chilton.

Darcy hoisted one of the bags. "Heavy, but oh so lovely." He laughed gleefully.

The dust boiled up, a small brown cloud against the green of the valley floor. Cavillin's eye caught the sudden appearance of new color. He lifted his spyglass. At the end of a long ravine nearly two miles away, a string of riders raced over a short strip of open land and disappeared into the woods on the side of Sierra Zoltepetl.

"There they go," Tom called to his men and pointed. "They are returning on a different route."

"That mountain is hellish rough going for horses," observed Granger, looking up at the range of tall volcanic peaks.

"There's a road someplace near where they disappeared," said Cavillin, recalling the symbols of the map. "Perhaps they will follow it. They have nearly forty miles to go to reach Mexico City. We must catch them before dark sets in and they mingle with all the other soldiers in the city. We could never sort them out. The shortest way to overtake them is to go up and over the mountain."

Cavillin surveyed Sierra Zoltepetl, rising up steeply from

deep valleys. The topmost thousand feet was bare lava rock. Below that, the mountain was dark green with trees, brush, and a few grassy parks. It was about twenty-five miles long and ran southwest.

"There must be good grazing up on the mountains," Cavillin said. "That means there will be sheep and cattle trails nearly to the top. We'll circle to the south until we find one. Then up and over, holding below the rocky crest. We'll spot the sign of the outlaws somewhere on the other side. The tracks of sixteen horses can't be hidden from us."

The Rangers climbed Sierra Zoltepetl along a narrow, stony pathway on the spine of rock between two ravines. They passed over the crown and worked downward. In the evening, with the slanting sun rays baking the southern face of the mountain, the Rangers found the trail of the outlaw Americans on an old wagon road grown full of weeds.

Cavillin kicked his cayuse to a run along the fresh sign. *I have you now, Captain Charles Gilchrist.* The wind created by the racing steed sang past Tom's ears.

The Rangers swarmed over the ridge of the hill. Ahead, the road lay in the bottom of a winding canyon lined with brush. A mile distant on the road, a knot of horsemen broke from a gallop to an all-out run.

"Yahoo!" bellowed Granger. "There they are. They've seen us, but we'll catch them." His voice rose in the wild, keening battle cry of the Rangers.

The others picked up his shout, sending the devilish cry rolling in loud waves down the canyon toward their prey.

Cavillin leaned far forward over the neck of his running mustang and watched the band of outlaws, like a cluster of black ants, hurtling away. He felt the powerful muscles of his big brute of a horse working easily as its leg reached for the maximum distance. It was the strength of the mounts that would determine whether or not he caught the robbers.

Matt Chilton and his dragoons rode across the evening at the top of their speed. Clotted sweat foam flew from the straining necks and flanks of the running horses. Yet the Rangers, on their stronger mounts, toughened by the long campaign to the sea, had gained half a mile and were closing inexorably upon them.

Matt had recognized the Rangers by the ragtag, multicolored outfits they wore. Of all the possible squads of men that could have been sent to hunt him, the Rangers was the most skilled and dangerous.

He cast a look to the west. The sullen red eye of the sun rested its half-open eye on the horizon. If Matt could in some way hold a lead until dark, his men might possibly escape.

The road left the giant hulk of Zoltepetl and came down into the rolling foothills. Faraway Mexico City was visible now and then through gaps between the hills. Matt dared not head directly to the city while there was still daylight. At the rate the Rangers were gaining on him, they would catch him on the open valley floor.

He guided to the right, heading south toward a broad area of swampland. He had once ridden past the border of the zone of stagnant water, cane grass higher than a man's head, and a few islands of firm ground covered with dense brush. The place was hazardous to travel in but still could hold safety for the hunted.

His horse was weakening rapidly. Its stride was becoming uncoordinated and wavering. The suck and blow of its lungs was a hoarse, ragged saw. It was a splendid beast, an excellent runner, but Matt was killing it.

The other dragoons understood Chilton's plan. They began

to call desperately to their horses, exhorting them to give the last heartbeat of their strength.

Matt looked at the blown and lathered mounts. A mile, maybe, and the race would be ended for the jaded animals.

The sun was down. The black wave of the night was stalking noiselessly in from the east. Distant objects were losing their form. Matt began to have hopes that he could reach the darkness and the swamp before the Rangers overtook him.

His horse stumbled with exhaustion. He jerked its head up harshly with the reins. Blood and froth dripped from the beast's flaring nostrils. Chilton reached out and stroked the wet neck. Only half a mile to go, old fellow. You can do it.

A quarter of a mile. The foliage of the swamp could be made out. "Follow me close," Chilton shouted at his men.

Others cried out the orders to those behind. The dragoons plunged into the tall cane grass of the swamp.

Chilton ran his band recklessly onward for a hundred yards. The sharp cane leaves whipped at him. The ground became soft and sloppy beneath his horse's feet. He abruptly slowed to a quiet walk. Intently he stared down, scouring the surfaces of the earth for something solid. He identified a strip of grass crossing at a right angle to his course. That difference in vegetation could mean more firm footing. He swerved left and along it.

The thudding run of the Rangers ceased. They had reached the edge of the swamp. Chilton instantly halted. His ears strained, reaching out for sound. All he could hear was the wind rustling the canes.

Matt led his men on at a silent walk. He must burrow more deeply into the swamp, must somehow elude the pursuers for a few minutes longer, until full darkness fell and entirely hid the hoofprints of the horses.

He meandered left and right, following a strip of dry land that came out of the cane and cut through an area of muck and a thick growth of phreatophyte sedges and brush. The zone of dry land broadened to four or five acres and rose to stand ten feet above the surrounding marsh.

Matt led straight across to the far side and down the sloping bank. He hoped fervently for one more bit of luck, another dry avenue to take them farther into the swamp. If the dragoons could escape the Rangers, they would have all night to discover a way out.

In the thickening gray dusk Matt saw only water, mud, and scanty knee-high moisture-loving grass. It was impossible to go on. The horses, with their relatively small hooves, would become mired in the muck within the first few steps.

His men crowded forward beside him to see what was causing the delay. They started to curse in whispers.

"We're trapped," hissed Stoffer. "We'll have to fight our way out. I'd rather be shot than hung."

"Quiet," said Chilton. "Be absolutely quiet. It'll be so dark in a minute or two that no one will be able to find us."

The low thump of walking horses came from the opposite side of the meadow. Matt could tell the Rangers were fanning out, trying to find the sign of riders in the growing darkness.

A man on a horse appeared on the bank above, his form outlined against the lighter gray of the sky. The Ranger leaned on the pommel of his saddle and looked down on the swamp.

Chilton heard Stoffer's sharp intake of breath, and then the sergeant was swinging his Colt up, cocking his weapon as it rose.

Matt's arm snaked out. His hand clamped down on the gun, catching the hammer as it was tripped and began to fall. He had recognized Cavillin.

Stoffer tried to wrench the pistol free. Matt continued to hold in it a viselike grip.

The Ranger lieutenant raised his eyes and looked out across the swampland and above the heads of the dragoons. Only one short snap of his head betrayed the fact that he had spotted Chilton and his band.

Cavillin called over his shoulder to his men. "There is nobody here. Let's ride on and see if we can pick up the trail farther along."

He reined his horse sharply, as if angry. Then he was gone.

Twenty

Les Hampton watched her father, mounted on his horse, disappear along one of the aisles between the rows of six hundred army cargo wagons drawn up in the wide pasture on the outskirts of Tacubaya. She envied him the freedom to go into Mexico City and mingle with other men and women and wander the great marketplaces to buy things. She was an outcast, not of her doing and only because she was a girl. She felt lonely.

Her father had created a pleasant enough place for her. Their big wagon was drawn up under a large cypress tree just outside the fringe of the field of army vehicles. His sleeping tent was close by. He had erected a bathhouse, with a six-foot-square wooden floor and enclosed with canvas higher than a man's head. A well of cold, sweet water was a short distance toward town.

Their wagon was far removed from other people. The nearest person was a carpenter camped on the far side of the field of wagons. Tacubaya was a quarter of a mile to the south.

Both she and her father knew there was danger in this foreign land of war. Every day since the wagon train had left Vera Cruz, she had worn a pistol on her side. It was beneath her pillow at night. She had practiced many times under the expert guidance of her father. He praised her skill and said her eye was as true as most men's.

She glanced at the dirt and grease on her hands and clothing. Odd how much maintenance was required to keep all the wagons ready to roll, even though only a few were actually being used. She picked up a clean set of her usual garb, shirt and trousers, and moved toward the bathhouse. In the early morning she had filled the big wooden tub in the bathing area with water. All day it had sat warming in the sun. The daily bath was one of her few luxuries.

The caressing fingers of the water closed about her as she lowered herself into the deep tub. She bathed leisurely, then leaned back against the slanting side of the vessel. She dozed.

The sun floated below the horizon and the light grew dim. Les rose from the bath and, with the wind a cool tingle on her wet skin, dried herself.

She stared at the worn and faded clothing lying ready to be donned. Not for many days had she worn a dress. But now her father was gone. There would be no visitors, for those that had come had never been made welcome and had not returned a second time. So why not tonight, at least for an hour or so, wear the clothing a girl should?

She parted the canvas and peeked out. The sky still held light, but shadows lay thick on the meadow. Good. No one could see her. She darted the dozen steps to the wagon and scrambled inside.

Les knelt and lifted the lid of her big trunk. From the bottom, under boy's clothes, she extracted a wrapped package. Carefully she unbound it. A small packet of cachet powder was laid aside, and a blue calico dress raised and shook out. She pressed the soft cotton to her face and breathed deeply of the perfume lingering there from the cachet.

Swiftly she dropped the dress over her head and smoothed it against her hips and waist to remove some of the wrinkles. She jumped to the ground and spun around. The wind was free on her legs and thighs, so very nice after the tight fit and heavy fabric of trousers.

As the night gradually deepened, Les strolled across the meadow to the well. The fine dust on the path was soft to her bare feet, and the slow wind cooled her. She watched the first big stars come to life. In the last fleeting memories of daylight, she drank fresh water from the well and returned to the wagon.

She fingered the ruffles at the neck of the dress, which were black now, the blue having vanished with the sunlight. She felt pretty. Could a girl be pretty if no one could see her? She laughed roguishly at the thought.

The night hung silent, and the myriad of stars wheeled westerly. When the moon rose so the road could be seen, her father would return. The next time he went to Mexico City, she would also go. She would insist on it.

Silver moon glow came to life and gilded the leaves of the cypress tree. The hulking forms of the wagons in the meadow took shape. On the nearest wagon, the bent, naked wooden ribs that supported the canvas when the vehicle was in use could almost be counted.

In the east, the moon had broken loose from the horizon and rode unbridled in the vast sky. Les sighed sadly. Now she must put aside the lovely dress and once again wear the coarse clothing of a wheelwright's son.

She began to turn. She flinched back, startled. A man stood not ten paces from her.

Cavillin rode up the hill in the deep dark and stopped at the drinking trough near the horse remuda. He stepped from the saddle and waited as his mount sucked thirstily at the water. It finished and tossed its head with a jangle of bridle metal.

Tom tied the horse to the picket rope that held the mounts meant for use in the coming morning. He poured a ration of grain in one of the wooden boxes that sat within reach of the horse. It was munching contentedly as he left.

After failing to catch the outlaws, Tom had placed Sergeant

Granger in charge of the Ranger company, telling them to make camp and to go back on patrol at first light. He must continue the pretense of a diligent effort to catch the American robbers.

Tom was angered and saddened at the discovery that Chilton was the leader of the band that had stolen and killed. He would find Matt and convince him that the raids must never happen again. Then Tom would report to General Scott. What he would tell the general would not go over well.

He passed through the edge of Tacubaya and walked onward. The field of wagons was almost invisible in the deep gloom. Tom's unerring course led him directly to the camp of Carl Hampton. Not once had he lost track of the wheelwright and his daughter.

Cavillin arrived as the moon shoved one thin arc of its yellow disk above the mountains. Quietly he surveyed the dark wagon. Where were Hampton and Les?

The moon became full-faced. The night retreated, almost like dusk returning. A slight figure in a dress stood at the rear of the wagon. Tom's spirits, depressed by his knowledge of Chilton's deeds, lifted in a pleasant wave. His nerve endings strummed with pleasure. He hoped the sight of her would always make him feel this way.

Tom saw Les's startled reaction as she caught sight of him. He was sorry for that. He had not meant to frighten her.

Les recognized Tom Cavillin. Her heart persisted in its rapid pounding, but now for a different reason.

"You're beautiful." Tom's voice was hardly more than a thought on the night.

"You can't tell that in the dark."

"Oh, yes, I can." He paused. "Perhaps you're correct. I should come closer to be certain."

Les watched Tom's countenance as he drew near, trying to read his thoughts.

He stopped in front of her. Gently he turned her by the

shoulders and in the full moonlight examined the planes and curves of her face. "I wasn't wrong," he said. The urge to kiss her was almost overpowering.

"Your father, where is he?"

"He went into the city. He will return soon."

"He leaves you all alone?" questioned Tom in deep concern. He felt protective of her.

"Not often. And not alone. There are American patrols guarding the wagons, and more of them on perimeter guard just over there. They would give the alarm if we were attacked, and I could hide and be safe. Besides, I have a gun. Why are you here?"

"To talk with you and your father."

"He will not be pleased. I believe he thinks you may one day come to take me away from him. He is afraid of being all alone. We have no other family, just we two."

"Yes. I may come to do that. Would you go?"

She raised her chin. "When or if you ask, then I will decide the answer to that."

Tenderly Tom drew Les toward him. He did it very slowly, allowing her time to pull back if she desired.

She resisted but a fraction of time, then came willingly, and they stood, their bodies touching.

"I must tell you something," said Tom. "Soon I will be leaving Mexico City, probably tomorrow. General Scott has given me an order I can't carry out. Once I have told him that, he will force me to leave Mexico."

"How can you not obey a general's orders?"

"My enlistment for this war ended more than two months ago. I have voluntarily stayed here to help finish the fighting. I can leave anytime and return to the States. To Texas."

He moved her away so he could see her face. "After your father's contract with the army is finished, have him come to Austin, Texas. Many people are traveling from the East to settle there. A good wheelwright would have plenty of work."

"I'll try to get him to do that. But he may not."

"Then write to me there at the general post office and I'll get your letters. Tell me where you go. I'll come and find you wherever you are. You will write, won't you?"

"Yes, I would like to do that."

"Good. Remember, Tom Cavillin, Austin, Texas. Send your letters with the army dispatch coach to Vera Cruz."

"I won't forget." Her mouth curled up in a happy smile as she stepped back from him.

Tom turned reluctantly and walked away. When the wagon was but a darker shade of the night, he halted and waited.

Les went into the wagon and, a moment later, dressed in pants and shirt, climbed back down to the ground. She lit an oil lantern and began to work on something Tom could not make out.

When the moon was half a hand width high, Hampton returned. Tom left noiselessly.

From the curtained alcove of the large sitting room, Wade Ussing spied upon the blond women and the half score army officers. The women talked with their male companions, laughing and bantering with them. Ussing appreciated the skill of the women. With their soft white skin and willing, pliable bodies they were like rich deposits of gold, waiting to be mined and converted to gold coins.

Wade motioned to Jungling, seated at the rear of the alcove. The big man came to stand beside him.

"You stay here and make certain every man pays for his whiskey and for the pleasure of the women," Ussing said.

"Sure, Wade," replied Jungling. He dragged up a chair and dropped down on it.

The whoremaster left by a rear door and walked to the nearby stables. He saddled without making a light. The horse carried him at a gallop, traversing the stone-paved surface of the central city streets and causeways, and then the dirt road onward to Tacubaya.

In the border of the woods on the hillside below Chilton's quarters, Ussing stopped and whistled. An answering whistle immediately sounded nearby. The Spaniard, Gonzalez, came out of the murky shadows.

"Has he returned?" questioned Ussing.

"There has been no light in the room, and nobody has entered," said Gonzalez. "It is strange he has been gone for so long a period. The woman must be very beautiful to keep him."

"Did you check his possessions? Are they still there?"

"Yes. He owns very little, but it was there. He was badly wounded in one of the battles. Maybe he has died."

"He's not dead," Ussing said. "He will return. You can go and get some rest."

"I am ready for that." The Spaniard moved back into the woods. A moment later he left astride his horse.

Ussing stepped down and led his mount into the blackness among the trees. He seated himself, shifting once to find a comfortable position. He pulled his knife from its sheath and began to strop it on the leather top of his boot.

This was the second night he had waited in ambush for Lieutenant Chilton. Wade would be there every day until the soldier appeared. The Texan would also die as soon as he returned from the campaign to the north. The Ranger and the dragoon had threatened Wade with their guns merely because he refused to give money to a whore. The action of the two men had been foolish, for women such as that had no rights.

He tested the edge of the blade with his thumb. Then he started to whet the knife again, stroke after stroke. There was something very satisfying in preparing to kill one's enemies.

Chilton's exhausted horse stumbled and almost fell on the rocky trail leading up to La Piedad. He spoke softly to Stoffer, and both men dismounted and climbed wearily ahead. The ragged breathing of the men and animals drifted eerily in the gloom among the trees.

"At last." Matt gasped as they reached the flat ground behind the church. He leaned, half faint, against the grain bin that held their stolen wealth.

"You can soon lie down and rest," the sergeant said. He feared for the life of his lieutenant. "Let me bury the sacks. You catch your wind."

"Thanks," replied Matt. He straightened, pulling his shoulders back so his breath could come more easily. He watched Stoffer carry the bags of gold and pesos from the packhorses and hide them beneath the corncobs in the bin.

There could be no more raids upon the towns now that Cavillin knew Chilton and his dragoons were the culprits. However, that made no real difference, for there was no longer a reason to ride and rob. His troopers had accumulated a treasure trove far greater than they had ever thought possible, and much more than was required to satisfy their goal.

"All snugly buried," Stoffer said.

"That's fine, Sergeant. Take the horses and leave. I'll brush the tracks away. Tomorrow we'll meet and plan our departure from Mexico. Soon this money will be in the hands of our crippled comrades or the families of our dead."

"I'm glad for that. It's way past time. I'm certain they have need for it. But, Lieutenant, we must fully pay those men who have ridden so bravely with us to get the gold."

"I haven't forgotten them, and they'll receive a share," Matt said. "Good night, Sergeant."

"Until tomorrow, Lieutenant. Rest well and long."

Chilton broke a small branch from a tree and moved to the aged grain bin. A minute's work and all sign of men and horses would be erased. He bent to sweep the ground with the limb.

Matt did not see the shadow in the woods rise and creep

toward him. A long-bladed knife slid from its sheath. The moonlight glinted in brittle silver rays from the honed metal of the weapon as the man came out from the trees. With his footsteps masked by the scouring sound of the limb, the shadow man stole upon Matt.

The task completed, Chilton stood erect. Now to bed, he thought.

A horrible stabbing pain ripped through Matt's back. Instantly a second shaft of pain, huge beyond agony, speared him higher up. The blade drove in between his ribs, deeply into the soft lungs.

Matt jerked away, pivoting to face his attacker, feeling the knife cutting sideways as it was wrenched out at an angle. He recognized Ussing as the man's long arm reached to strike again with the sharp steel blade.

Matt could not breathe with the intensity of the pain. His lungs were locked and rigid, as if somehow they had frozen solid in the time span of one heartbeat.

His mind remained crystal clear. It screamed at his body to lash out and drive away the man with the knife that was killing him.

The only response from Matt's stricken body was a quiver of his fingers. He fell heavily upon the freshly swept ground.

The shadow man stared down at the motionless body. He laughed a short string of guttural chuckles. The knife had struck true.

He walked to the dilapidated grain bin where the church fathers had once dispensed charitable measures of food. He opened the door and dug into the cobs. One after the other, he lifted out the sacks of pesos and gold.

He hoisted the sacks of treasure and lugged them off into the woods. He piled them, a load at a time, in one mound. Then carefully it was covered with leaves and brambles from the floor of the woods.

Ussing laughed a happy laugh as he contemplated his great

luck. The land of Mexico had delivered up its wealth to him much sooner than he had ever hoped. He hastened to his horse and rode swiftly toward Mexico City.

Twenty-one

Slinking low and slow against the ground, the animal moved in the night beneath the trees on the slope of the hill. It stopped and, lying prone, was very still. After a time the dark form rose, seeming to tremble as it did so, and again advanced at a sluggish, halting pace.

Cavillin sat waiting on Chilton's doorstep. He watched the creeping figure in the woods. One of the dogs of the town stalking something in the weeds, he thought.

A shuddering human moan escaped from the crawling thing. Tom leaped to his feet at the sound. He sprang across the space separating them and knelt beside the man.

"Easy, fellow, let me help you." The man's shirt was wet and sticky under Tom's hands. He smelled the cloying odor of blood.

Tom scooped the figure up in his arms. He was surprised at the slight weight.

Thinking there was something familiar about the man, Cavillin stepped hurriedly out into the full fall of the moon's rays. He looked down into the gaunt, bony face of Chilton.

"Matt? What has happened to you?"

"Tom, is that you?" Chilton asked, bubbles of blood bursting on his lips. "I can't see too good. Is it dark?"

"Yes, Tom, it's dark, but the moon is bright. I'll get you to Dr. Campbell. He'll fix you up."

Matt quivered with a terrible spasm of pain. He was weakening swiftly from his dreadful wounds. "It's too late for the surgeon this time, Tom. Ussing has killed me."

"Ussing did this to you? That damn whoremaster!" Cavillin was angry beyond imagination, his breath scalding in his lungs. His throat tightened so that he could not speak.

As Matt fought to hold off death he saw the ghosts of his men. They were lying on the ground of the many battlefields where they had fought and fallen. Some had their legs shot off by cannonballs; arms were missing and some bodies were mere masses of crumpled human flesh. Matt saw their eyes dimming to cold, blank stares. His laboring heart felt lonesome and squeezed, and his mind drew back from the awful remembrance.

Tom leaned very close to Matt. "Let me take you to Campbell."

"No. Just set me up a little so I can breathe and talk with me for a moment."

"Sure, Matt." Tom gently propped Chilton against his leg.

"I want you to know why I've done all this robbing." Matt's voice was barely a whisper. "Please understand and do not judge me too badly. I have no family, only my troop of dragoons. They were everything to me. And I helped kill many of them by the orders I gave. I wanted only to try in some way to partially make up for what I did." Matt was quiet. Oh, what he would give for a family and longtime friends.

"Yes, Matt, go on," Tom said, hoping that in keeping him talking, he would somehow prolong his life.

"Tom, are we still friends?"

"Always."

"Good. It is not a good thing to die in the dark without a friend."

"You can live. You have been hurt bad before."

"Not like this. I am dying. Man was never meant to last forever, or even for very long."

Matt coughed blood. He sucked in a shallow breath of air. "Ussing took the gold and Mexican paper money we had. It was a fortune. He must have been hiding and saw where I hid it. Will you get it back from him and give it to my men?"

"I'll surely do that." Tom could promise nothing less to his dying friend, even knowing all the money was stolen and men had died protecting it.

"Will you kill Ussing for me?"

"I'll find him and do that."

"I'll be waiting in hell for him. Send him to me soon."

"Right. Very soon."

Matt pulled a trembling draft of the black night air. "In my things is a list of my men that are to receive part of the money. If they are dead, the names of their families are written down. See that it is divided that way."

"How about you? Is there anyone in the States you want me to go and see or give part of the money to?"

"No, there is nobody in the States. Perhaps you would tell Sophia and Stoffer what has happened. . . ." Time flew around Matt like a hurricane. He heard Tom calling to him from a great distance. He felt the Ranger's hands gripping him. It was not so bad dying in the dark when a friend held you.

"The bastard has left us stranded in this damn country." Emily was screaming and crying at the same time. She moved across the room nearer Cavillin. "He took every dollar he was holding for us."

Cavillin swung his view over Ussing's three harlots with their rouged faces and silk dresses. The whoremaster and the guards and all the customers were gone now. Beneath the rouge, the women's faces were strained and no longer pretty in their fear at being abandoned. Cavillin was sorry for them.

"How long has he been gone?" Cavillin asked.

"About an hour," answered Helen.

"He took Jungling and Gonzalez with him," Emily added. "They loaded their belongings on a wagon and had extra riding horses. Wade seemed in damn high spirits."

"Where did Ussing go?"

"He said something about picking up something valuable at a church, then straight away to Vera Cruz," Emily replied.

Cavillin believed the women told the truth. "Then I must leave immediately," he said.

"You're going to try to catch Ussing and kill him," Helen said.

Tom did not reply. The answer was in his face, tight and masklike in his anger.

"Would you wait until we pack our belongings and then help us to travel to the coast?" asked Emily.

"No, I can't do that. Ussing would reach the coast before us and leave aboard a ship. Then I could never overtake him. However, several companies of volunteer soldiers are being released. They will be going home. Ask them, and they will be glad to see you safely to Vera Cruz. Go see Sophia. Help her get back to New Orleans." He turned quickly to the door.

Emily cried out behind him. "Don't give the son of a bitch a chance. Shoot him in the back. Watch the Spaniard more than Jungling."

Cavillin ran his horse in the blackness of the Mexican night, lying densely on the ancient El Camino Real. The stalwart beast carried him past a string of six large cinder cone hills, then through the sleeping village of San Marcos Huixtaco, and began the long climb to the high pass between Ixtacihuatl and Cerro Telapon.

After leaving Ussing's brothel, Tom had gone to General Scott's headquarters in the Governor's Palace. He left a message with the lieutenant on duty, telling the general that Ussing had killed Chilton and that he was going in pursuit.

Tom stopped at Sophia's quarters in Tacubaya. She had cried when told of Matt's death. In her grief, her frail body seemed to collapse in upon itself. Tom could not convince her that she was not at fault for what Ussing had done. He left after a time and found Sergeant Stoffer.

"He was not just my lieutenant but also my friend," Stoffer said. His eyes were filled with his misery. "Do you want me to ride with you after Ussing?"

"No. Take your wounded men and go home. I'll do what I can to complete Matt's plan."

Tom departed Tacubaya with his few belongings and a small supply of food rolled in his sleeping blankets and tied behind his saddle. At the border of the town he lit a lucifer, and in the light of its flame examined the many tracks in the deep dust on the road. The recent passage of Ussing's wagon of gold drawn by trotting horses with two flanking riders was easy to detect among the other tracks.

Tom touched his horse with spurs and held the brute to a grueling pace, mile after mile. A man on horseback could run down a loaded wagon if he pressed hard. Soon he would have the whoremaster in the sight of his pistol.

In the small hours of the night, the sky became very black and half obscured by the mountains that crowded in to tower over Cavillin. A cold wind came tumbling and moaning down from the huge ice fields on the crown of Ixtacihuatl. Tom hunched his shoulders against the stiff, chilling breeze and hurried onward.

The walls of the mountains started to retreat. The moon became visible, pallid and hazy behind high thin clouds. The stars were nothing but weakly shimmering halos far away.

The El Camino Real angled down. Soon it entered a zone of large trees interspersed with small open parks.

The icy wind from the peaks of Ixtacihuatl was left to the rear, giving way to a warmer breeze blowing in from the direction of the sea, which lay more than two hundred miles to the east.

Tom let the tired horse slow and finally stop on its own volition. He felt his own weariness, his head light and woozy from the long ride after Chilton, and now the race across the night in pursuit of Ussing. Before they day arrived, he would rest a couple of hours.

He guided his mount from the road and into deep woods. In a small hidden meadow, the horse was staked out on the end of a long Mexican lariat. Tom spread his blankets beneath a giant tree.

For several minutes he lay recalling, distinct and sharp, the pleasant comrade Chilton had been. "God damn you, Ussing," Tom cursed. "You killed a man a hundred times better than you." He reached out and rubbed the butt of one of his Colt revolvers in its holster.

Cavillin went to sleep with his hand on his weapon.

Tom awoke to the first weakening of the night. In the east, a drop of dawn had made a hole in the darkness. He saddled his horse and left the meadow. He struck the El Camino Real and kicked his horse to a fast gallop.

The road soon came out of the woods and ran straight across a land of knee-high grass. The night dew lay thick on everything, bending the reeds down in a million fragile arches. In the day's first sunlight, the chill was lifting off the earth in little gray lines of vapor.

In mid-morning, thick clouds, heralding a storm, appeared on the eastern horizon. The long gray line grew rapidly as Tom and the storm raced at each other.

For an hour the storm and the sun battled for possession of the sky. The clouds won and hung threateningly over the darkened land. Rain began to leak from their swollen bellies. Stiff, blustery winds thrust out ahead of the storm.

Cavillin pulled on his slicker and jammed his hat down hard. He turtled his head down between his shoulders and ran his steed into the maw of the storm.

A gale-force wind tore at him and knocked him around. He turned his head to the side to breathe, and he gasped to ease the aching emptiness in his lungs.

The rain became frigid. An instant later, hail as large as the rocks that boys throw was pummeling Cavillin. The ice balls beat the crown of his hat down tight against his skull with hammer blows.

The horse whinnied in pain. Tom halted the suffering beast, and it whirled to put its rump to the driving hail.

Cavillin jumped to the ground and crouched beneath the horse's drooping head. He pushed backward between the animal's front legs for as much shelter as he could find and shouted to the stalwart beast to stand against the hail and wind.

Man and horse humped their backs as the slashing hail fell cold upon their aching bodies.

Cavillin sat his horse at the crossroads in the center of the town of Texmelucan. He cautiously swept a look over the few townsfolk watching him from doorways and windows. One gringo would be a tempting target to an angry Mexican with a gun.

He removed his slicker as he impatiently scanned the rain-washed road. Not one track of man or horse marred the mud.

Due east, the three-mile-high round dome of Sierra La Malinche loomed over the town. A road ran off to the south, skirting the base of the mountain. That way led through Perote and onward to Vera Cruz. A short, but rougher route to the sea by way of Huamantla curled north around the giant volcanic mountain.

Cavillin stared searchingly along first one road and then the other. The storm had cleaned and cooled the air and sharpened his eyesight to a greater distance; still, he saw no men or horses moving on either road.

Tom pointed his finger at the nearest man and called out in Spanish, "Two Americans and a Spaniard and a wagon passed her in the last few hours. Which way did they go?"

"*El Camino Real a Huamantla,*" replied the man.

"*Gracias,*" Tom said. He reined his horse to the northern route. Throwing mud, the mount sped along the street. On the border of Texmelucan, the road dipped down to the Rio Atoyac. The horse took the shallow ford of the river in long, wet splashes.

In the afternoon, Cavillin found fresh tracks imbedded in the muddy surface of the road. He could tell by the sign that Ussing was running his horses. That explained why Tom was gaining but slowly. He spurred his mount to a faster pace.

Cavillin stopped to change horses at the army outpost in Huamantla. As he shifted his gear to the new mount, he spoke to the corporal in charge of the remuda. "Have you seen three men with a wagon? Two were riding horseback."

"Yes, sir," answered the corporal. He had fought with Cavillin in the battle for Huamantla and remembered the Ranger lieutenant. "They tried to talk me into giving them fresh horses. But, hell, they were civilians, so I told them nothing doing. I thought the tall, dark fellow was going to shoot me. Damnation, but he was mad. Are you after them, Lieutenant?"

"They killed a cavalry officer in Mexico City."

"Then that explains why their horses were sweating and blowing hard, for they had been pushing them plenty fast."

"How long ago did they pass by?"

"Two, maybe three hours. You've picked a good mount. You can catch them, Lieutenant. Do you want to see the captain? He'd most likely send a patrol to help you."

"I can take care of this by myself," replied Cavillin. "My food has run out. Where can I get something to eat?"

"There's a cantina two blocks up the street that way." He pointed. "I've eaten there. They dish out only Mexican food, but it's good."

Two miles east of Huamantla, Cavillin found two Mexican men and a boy dead on the El Camino Real. Close by, three exhausted horses stood with drooping heads. Ussing had killed to obtain a rested team for the wagon and a replacement for one of the riding mounts.

Tom hurried faster, passing over land populated with herds of sheep and cattle. On the level creek bottoms, there were small farms protected with stone fences. In the afternoon, Tom traveled in the bottom of an intermontane basin, a sunken area into which streams flowed but could not escape. He passed Laguna Totolcingo on his left. Six miles later he reach Laguna Salado.

When night swarmed across the sky, the tracks of Ussing and the others still lay on the El Camino Real. Cavillin continued on into the dark for an hour. On a rise of land he made a damp bed among the rustling blades of grass and fretfully waited the gloomy hours away.

Dawn light crept in slowly as Tom pounded through Perote. In the morning's drowsy first hours, only the wood peddlers were stirring. With long, limber switches, they whipped the donkeys out of Cavillin's path as he charged past.

The King's Highway began to climb, twisting and curving as it crawled up the flank of the coastal mountains. Cavillin crossed over the summit at the cluster of eight wooden houses that marked the villages of Acajete. Two hours later he arrived at the city of Jalapa.

Certain that Ussing would acquire fresh mounts in the city, Tom turned aside to the army garrison and traded horses. He stopped briefly at a *mercado,* a marketplace, and purchased cheese, hard bread, and apples. His canteen was filled at a public well. He ate as the rested horse settled into a ground-devouring gallop, running directly upon the new sign of a wagon and two riders.

Tom sped down the slanting stretch of The King's Highway leading to Vera Cruz and the sea. He looked out over the wooded sweep of the mountain, straining to pierce the great distance to the coastal city. All he could see were the hills stepping down and away and gradually fading to a blue-gray haze.

The vegetation became more dense as the route descended. On this wetter side of the mountain, the road was badly eroded and cut with gullies, and all the depressions stood full of water. The hot breath of the tropical lowlands near the coast thrust sweaty fingers up the mountainside.

When the night flung a thick, dark curtain over the land, the horse slowed to a walk. Tom rode on as the moon rose and lit the road. Lulled by the soft, quiet step of the horse on the moist ground and feeling safe in the blackness, Cavillin half slept.

He stopped at Cerro Gordo, where the arching stone bridge crossed the Rio del Plan. The horse was unsaddled and staked out to graze.

Sensing the presence of the warm-blooded animals, mosquitoes flushed up off the river and out of the groves of trees in a dense, seething swarm. They swooped upon Tom with a hungry, hostile buzzing. He batted once at them and took a tin of grease from his pack and smeared a thin coating on his face and hands. It was poor protection from the pests, but the

best the Americans had devised during their months in this
alien land.

Cavillin crossed the bridge on foot and halted. Beneath the
moon, the terrain lay gently rolling with meadows and pockets
of trees. The big hill, El Telegrafo, lying a mile northeast, was
a dark mound blanking out the lower stars of the sky. An innocent land. However, one of the toughest battles of the American march inland had been fought over El Telegrafo and the
bridge that spanned the fast-flowing Rio del Plan. The inno-
cence of the place had been destroyed by the deaths of hundreds of men.

Tom peered into the gloom of the night. On the killing
ground one cannon-blasted tree looked like a skinny, stump-
armed man. Craters made by exploding bombs were everywhere. The stone sides of the bridge were pockmarked with
bullet strikes too numerous to count.

On a rise of land above the river, Tom had shot seven Mexicans making a stand against the invading Americans. In his
mind, as if it were happening all over again, he heard the
moans and screams of the dying men and horses, and smelled
the stench of burned gunpowder.

He moved a short distance up from the river and onto a
meadow. The Americans killed in the fighting had been gathered and buried near where they fell. Scores and scores of
those graves were spread in front of Tom. The graves gaped
empty and partially full of foul, dank water.

The graveyard patrols had been here, and now mounds of
excavated dirt were ridged beside each hole. The corpses had
been removed, crated in wooden boxes, and hauled to the coast
and homeward-bound ships.

Tom turned away, greatly saddened by the cost of the war
in dead and crippled men. By the time he had passed back
over the bridge, he fully understood Chilton, and the final
dredges of his anger at his friend for his deeds had been
washed away.

* * *

The voice floated across the empty graves, ghostly and complaining. Cavillin yanked his horse to a fast halt with a tight rein. A prickle ran along his back.

The night was at its blackest, that time of morning when the moon is lost behind the horizon and the sun has not yet risen above the curve of the earth. Tom had awakened early, determined to overtake Ussing before he could reach the coast and escape on a swift ship.

Tom waited for the voice to come again. However, nothing broke the eerie silence lying on the deserted cemetery.

He guided his mount down from the road and tied it at the abutment of the bridge. He climbed back up the bank and carefully started to feel his way among the water-filled holes of the temporary graveyard. He had heard a man's voice—of that he was certain. He did not think the defeated Mexicans would spend the night there until the graves were closed. The victorious Americans would.

He shadowed his way to the opposite side of the meadow and to a patch of trees. He hunkered down, listening.

An owl glided past, close overhead, to check him out. A few moments later a red glow came to life on the far side of the woods. Men's voice began to grumble. A camp was stirring.

Cavillin stole through the woods. The fire grew larger, casting a red bubble in the darkness. A group of men sat within the flickering zone of light.

To Cavillin's surprise, five American soldiers sat eating breakfast with Ussing and his men. The whoremaster had joined with an army patrol. Tom made out the outlines of a wagon and stagecoach in the murk beyond the reach of the fire. The soldiers were escorting one of General Scott's dispatch coaches.

Tom wormed backward. He veered around the camp and

came to the wagon. Shoving his hand under the tarp covering the bed, he felt the small, heavy sacks underneath. Here was the fortune Chilton had stolen. If the women had told him the truth, here also was Ussing's own accumulation of wealth.

Cavillin's vengeful eyes glittered as hotly as the coals of the fire. He could not shoot Ussing and his cohorts from ambush. Neither could he walk out into the firelight and ask the patrol officer to help him arrest the murderer. Either way, Chilton's money would be found by the army and surely kept.

Ussing, you are safe for tonight, Tom thought. *But still I will kill you. If not now, then tomorrow or the next day.*

Twenty-two

The beggar sidled toward the redheaded gringo standing on the corner of the street. The man was partially facing away, looking intently to the north where the El Camino Real cut across the flat coastal plain. A stage and wagon and six riders were speeding along the road to Vera Cruz.

The beggar shuffled closer to the American. If he had not been so hungry, never would he have shown such bravery. He was tensed, ready to dodge back. Sometimes the hateful gringos would knock a man down merely for coming too near them.

"Deme un centavo, por favor," said the beggar in a wheedling voice. He cautiously extended a dirty hand.

The gringo turned, and his eyes were riveted on the little brown man. The beggar flinched as if he had been slapped. He stood locked in place by the angry gray orbs of the American. How could a man have so much evident hate, such a deadly intent to kill him? He had done nothing except ask for a mere penny.

With an effort the beggar gathered himself and pivoted around. He would run very fast, and maybe the gringo could not catch him or shoot him before he could turn the corner.

"Un momento," Cavillin called, *"Por favor,"* he added.

The beggar warily looked over his shoulder. The gringo's

face had softened. The fierce gray eyes held a tinge of blue, a sad blue, thought the beggar.

Tom put his hand into a pocket and brought out a handful of silver and copper coins. He sorted through the money.

"Aqui es tres centavos." He continued in Spanish. "They are owed to a candy peddler in Mexico City but never paid to him. I want you to have them."

"I do not understand," said the beggar. "I know no candy peddler in La Capital."

"That doesn't matter. He is dead now and can't use the money. Please take it."

"If you insist." The beggar watched for a trick from the strange American. *"Gracias."* He grasped the large copper coins and hurried away.

He looked back once. The big gringo had mounted his horse and was riding down the street toward the stage, wagon, and riders entering the town.

Cavillin had changed tactics from one of chasing Ussing to that of leading him. He had arrived in Vera Cruz and waited. Now, as he trailed behind again, he saw the army patrol angle away from Ussing and gallop in the direction of the army commander's headquarters on a high point of land a few blocks off the north end of the waterfront.

Ussing and his men made their way to the stone-paved quay, passing the first two rows of warehouses and stopping just off the end of one of the piers. The gang leader spoke to his men, and they continued to the last warehouse. There they halted and climbed down to lean against the wall of the building. Ussing walked toward the nearest ship.

Tom stopped his mount in the evening shadows, growing long and filling the street west of the quay. The harbor was nearly deserted. The mighty fleet of ships that had crowded Campeche Bay when he had been here before was gone. Only three clipper ships were at anchor. Two other clippers and three steamships were tied up at berths beside the piers.

The dockworkers had ceased their labors and left. A few sailors moved about on the decks of the berthed ships. A cabin boy fished off the pier. Ussing passed the boy and climbed the gangway of the ship.

As Cavillin planned his strategy, a wave of evening dusk chased the last of the sunlight from the town, scattering it far out over the sea. Beside the warehouse, a match flared as the Spaniard lit a cigarette.

Ussing left the first ship and proceeded to the next one along the pier. He hailed the deck and was invited aboard by a crewman.

When Ussing disappeared within one of the cabins of the ship, Cavillin pulled his Colts. He checked to insure that the lead balls were tightly seated upon the powder and the caps were in place on the nipples. He must act now while Ussing was separated from Jungling and the Spaniard. Tom spoke to his horse, and it moved out from the street onto the waterfront.

Tom let his left-hand gun hang beside his leg. The second rested across the saddle in front of him. It pointed left, the side Jungling and the Spaniard would be on. He lowered his head so that the brim of his hat hid most of his face.

Ussing's men ceased talking and studied the horseman approaching along the quay. Gonzalez noted the mud and dried sweat on the army horse. His gunman's wariness felt a tingle. He tried to see the rider's hands. One appeared to be beside the man's leg, the other on the pommel of his saddle. The rider's lowered head bobbed as if he were dozing. Still, the slouched figure somehow seemed menacing.

Gonzalez shoved away from the wall. He knew what bothered him. It was the unmatched clothing and the way the man so easily sat on his horse. If he had been in uniform, Gonzalez would have figured him for a cavalryman.

"Watch it, Jungling!" hissed the Spaniard. "It's a Texas Ranger."

Jungling stepped to the Spaniard's side. "What's he doing here? Aren't they all supposed to be clearing guerrillas off the road to Matamoros?"

The rider gave no sign he'd observed the two men. The horse walked on, even paced, the dull clank of the metal of its hooves reverberating on the warehouse sides. The rider would pass within a few body lengths of the two men.

Gonzalez peered hard through the deepening shadows. Though he could not see the man's face, there was something familiar about the cut and size of his body. He considered drawing a pistol to be ready for action. Then his honed sense of survival thought of a better plan.

"Jungling, pull your gun. The fellow means trouble."

The blond man's hand quickly reached for a weapon.

Cavillin surveyed his opponents from under the brim of his hat as he allowed his body to move loosely and sleepily to the step of the horse. He was within long-range shooting distance. But he wanted to be much nearer. The killing time must be short, finished before Ussing could come to the aid of his men.

The distance decreased to seventy-five feet, then to sixty. He heard the Spaniard call out. Jungling swung up his pistol.

Damnation, thought Cavillin as he lifted his right-hand gun. He had wanted to shoot the Spaniard first, for the smaller man would most likely be the faster of the two men. But that plan was ruined by the wily Spaniard.

Cavillin's revolver bucked in his hand, and a lance of flame stabbed toward Jungling's chest. At the same time Tom jammed sharp spurs into his horse and threw himself forward on the animal's neck.

The Spaniard drew his weapon with a sure, smooth deftness. The bright red wink of the pistol was almost instantaneous with Cavillin's shot.

Tom heard the whizzing passage of the round ball tearing the air. Then the lunging horse had carried him past the Spaniard. Tom twisted to look behind and raised his left-hand Colt.

The Spaniard was cocking his pistol for a second shot when Cavillin's bullet slammed him backward into the warehouse. The small man caught himself from falling and propped his body against the wall. He struggled to hold his pistol steady, to bring the sights in alignment on the Ranger.

Cavillin yanked his steed back on its haunches and spun it around. His right-hand gun swept its arc and roared. The hurtling sphere of lead stopped the frantic beating of the Spaniard's heart.

Tom sped up to the two dead men and sprang down. He hoisted Jungling's body up with a powerful heave and flung it into the bed of the wagon on top of the tarp-covered gold. Gonzalez's slack corpse followed.

The men on the decks of the ships started to shout out to each other, questioning what had happened. The cabin boy dropped his fishing pole and turned to look down the pier toward the quay.

Tom tied his horse to the wagon and vaulted up into the seat. He slapped the team with the reins, and they moved out at a brisk step. The mounts of the two dead men, not wanting to be left, followed behind.

A minute later Cavillin heard a savage cry and the pounding of running feet. A grim smile stretched his lips. *Ussing, I knew you would never let the gold be taken without a fight.* He pulled the team to a halt and stepped down. Now he was going to kill the murdering whoremaster. Or die in the attempt.

Ussing slowed to a measured walk, his spurs jangling icily. He lifted his pistol from its shoulder holster and cocked it.

Cavillin slid his right-hand Colt free. His thumb pried back the hammer, and the trigger touched his finger. Someone was going to die in a few seconds.

"Cavillin, give me the wagon and I'll let you go," Ussing called. He continued to advance with his smooth, feline step.

Tom grinned his mirthless grin. "Let me go, will you? I'll consider that. But first there's something else I want from you."

"What's that?" asked Ussing. He stopped, primed for swift action.

"Your rotten life."

"Then take it if you can," snarled Ussing. He snapped his gun up and fired. He knew the shot had gone directly at the center of the Ranger.

But somehow, swift beyond imagination, Cavillin had moved aside. Ussing saw the flaming explosion of his foe's pistol. The lead projectile broke Ussing's sternum, bore inward to the very core of him. The stone pavement was rushing up at him. It crashed into his dead face.

Cavillin lifted Ussing's loose-limbed body and dumped it on top of his two dead cohorts. He drove off into the darkness. Before pursuit could be organized, he would have disposed of the bodies of his enemies and be far away.

The waterfront, piers, and ships were left to the rear, and Cavillin drove along the sandy shoreline. A mile later he came to a high, wave-cut cliff. He sat for a time listening to the wet sounds of the sea and smelling its tangy saltiness on the air. He gazed out at the signal light on the Isle of Sacrifice, the place where the Americans had staged part of their forces for the invasion of Mexico those long months ago.

He climbed down to the ground and, one after the other, lugged the bodies of Jungling and the Spaniard to the cliff and hurled them down into the surf. Then last, as he raised Ussing's corpse above his head, Tom shouted out, "Matthew Chilton, I've sent your murderer to you. Do as you wish with him—for eternity."

Tom flung the dead body from him. It vanished into the blackness below the lip of the cliff.

There was no sound of the corpse hitting. Only the endless pounding of the waves on the shore of the far battleground.

Epilogue

Blood Debt is fiction; however, it is based upon real events, events of a foreign war little remembered in the United States.

By the end of the war, 12,876 American soldiers had died, 1,721 by battle action and 11,155 by disease and exposure. They kept on dying after the war by the lingering effects of disease contracted during the campaign.

The Texas Rangers continued, notorious for their vengeful and violent ways against the Mexican population. General Scott kept them on constant patrol after the capture of Mexico City, thus hoping to keep them out of trouble in the capital city. Yet the Rangers found time to abuse the citizens. In one episode, a Ranger shot and killed a lad for grabbing a bandana from his pocket. Finally exasperated beyond endurance, General Scott ordered the Rangers out of Mexico, even before a peace treaty could be ratified.

The general had great trouble in finding a Mexican government with which to make peace. There was no coherent national leadership; rather, there was chaos with many competing power centers hoping to emerge in control after the terrible, devastating war. After many months, influential Mexicans shaped a tentative government.

The Treaty of Guadalupe-Hidalgo was ratified May 30, 1848. Mexico surrendered claim to New Mexico and California and all the vast wilderness from the Rocky Mountains to the Pacific Ocean, an area larger than France and Germany combined.

BOOK YOUR PLACE ON OUR WEBSITE
AND MAKE THE
READING CONNECTION!

We've created a customized website just for our very special readers, where you can get the inside scoop on everything that's going on with Zebra, Pinnacle and Kensington books.

When you come online, you'll have the exciting opportunity to:

- View covers of upcoming books
- Read sample chapters
- Learn about our future publishing schedule (listed by publication month *and author*)
- Find out when your favorite authors will be visiting a city near you
- Search for and order backlist books from our online catalog
- Check out author bios and background information
- Send e-mail to your favorite authors
- Meet the Kensington staff online
- Join us in weekly chats with authors, readers and other guests
- Get writing guidelines
- AND MUCH MORE!

Visit our website at
http://www.pinnaclebooks.com

The Wingman Series
By Mack Maloney